PRAISE FOR ELEANOR & SAM

"Rachel Del Grosso is a gifted and natural storyteller whose debut is sure to please readers who enjoy layered novels about writing and women's relationships."

CAMILLE PAGÁN, BESTSELLING AUTHOR OF *GOOD FOR YOU.*

"I absolutely flew through this book. Compulsively readable and wholly satisfying, *Eleanor & Sam* is a love letter to authors, to books, to the creative process, to friendship—especially the unique, often tricky, bond that forms between artists. I loved every minute of it."

SUZY KRAUSE, BESTSELLING AUTHOR OF *SORRY I MISSED YOU* AND *I THINK WE'VE BEEN HERE BEFORE*

"A powerful story of two women and the choices they make that affect their lives forever. Two very different women bond over their love of story and how difficult it can be for women to find their way as writers in a world that still doesn't make it easy for creatives. A riveting page-turner you don't want to miss!"

JANUARY BAIN, AUTHOR OF THE *ANNA HALE P.I.* SERIES

FINE, BUT NOT FINISHED

TITLES BY RACHEL DEL GROSSO

Eleanor & Sam
Fine, But Not Finished

FINE, BUT NOT FINISHED

RACHEL DEL GROSSO

Fine, But Not Finished
Paperback Edition
Copyright © 2025 by Rachel Del Grosso

Love N. Books Press
An Imprint of Wolfpack Publishing
1707 E. Diana Street
Tampa, FL 33610

www.lovenbookspress.com

Edited by My Brother's Editor

Paperback ISBN 979-8-89567-990-6
Ebook ISBN 979-8-89567-989-0
LCCN 2025933467

To all the incredible women's fiction writers before me who made me fall in love with the genre, specifically Taylor Jenkins Reid and Camille Pagán.

FINE, BUT NOT FINISHED

PART ONE
FALLING

CHAPTER
ONE

The air is mild for February, and though it feels wrong, I tilt my head up toward the sky, savoring the warmth of the sun on my face before stepping through the ornate church doors. I'm wearing a black dress that's too tight across my middle, and the stockings make my legs itch. The bobby pins holding my low bun in place dig sharply into my scalp, adding to my discomfort.

The church is hot and musty, smelling faintly of hairspray and stale air. I see a few familiar faces, but there are far more strangers than I expected. I had anticipated a much smaller crowd.

Beside me, Daisy sits silently, her presence grounding me. At one point, she reaches out and squeezes my hand, a silent gesture of support. I feel her warmth but can't bring myself to return it. I remain still, as though any movement might crack the fragile composure I'm clinging to.

The service is short. I keep my eyes fixed on the floor ahead of me, listening but not fully absorbing the words. A dull, sharp pain blooms between my eyes—a headache building, one I know will linger long after this day is over.

I follow the casket down the aisle, avoiding the pitying glances scattered among the pews. Outside, the sunlight feels too bright, too harsh against the grief hanging in the air. I watch as the casket slides into the back of the hearse. Jack's hand grazes mine, his touch tentative, as if he's asking, pleading for something.

I pull my hand away.

"Hazel." His voice is quiet, pleading.

"Just get the car."

Later, Jack will tell me he finds it worrisome I didn't cry, that I haven't yet cried.

I'll remind him there is always more to the story.

I'll remind him I am no longer someone he has to worry about.

CHAPTER
TWO

TWENTY YEARS AGO

A t eighteen, I trade one lonely city for another, dragging along an old, graying suitcase stuffed to bursting with every piece of clothing I own—unfolded, unwashed, and doomed to never find its way back to my mother. (I will, predictably, lose it entirely within a year.) My books and CDs crammed into plastic sleeves, and all the sentimental junk of my childhood—journals, photo albums, bad poetry, and worse, love letters—get packed into boxes destined to gather dust in Daisy's basement for the next three years. Leaving them at home would have been a gamble, putting too much faith in a mother who showed me, time and time again, just what she is capable of.

When I leave, my room is spotless, almost sterile, like I've already been erased. My brother, Andy, wastes no time reclaiming it, and transforming it into a makeshift weight room where he grunts and groans himself into the kind of muscles that look downright suspicious on a man his age.

My big escape doesn't take me far, geographically—just to UNLV—but emotionally, it feels like the moon. Las Vegas isn't the neon wonderland I'd hoped for. Instead, it's baffling. Some students show up dressed like they're auditioning for Wall Street, others like they're training to be the city's next headliner, and I can't tell which I dislike more. Making friends is harder than I imagined; I've always been the kind of quiet that reads as aloof, the kind of shy that passes for unfriendly. I preferred spending most of my time with my best friend, Daisy, or in my bedroom reading or listening to music.

Andy, forever the optimist, calls constantly to remind me that Anaheim is just a freeway away, as if I might suddenly miss our mother's passive-aggressive commentary or his protein-shake fumes. I don't. Instead, I bury myself in textbooks, eat meals hunched over a desk or in the farthest corner of the dining commons, and fill journal pages with furious determination. I stay on campus for Thanksgiving, Christmas, and New Year's, earning the dubious honor of being one of the last ghosts haunting the dorms. When a small package arrives two days into January, I recognize Andy's handwriting immediately. Inside: a ring with an oval black onyx stone—thoughtful and weirdly on-brand for him—and a fifty-cent used paperback copy of *The Summerhouse* by Jude Deveraux from my mother, price sticker still attached.

Andy starts campaigning for my return by February, offering up my birthday weekend like it's a shiny prize, and when that doesn't work, he pins his hopes on spring break. But by then, his efforts are wasted. I've already met Jack.

———

The first time I see him, he's in the dining commons, piling his plate high with a second helping of pasta whose sauce is an alarming shade of orange. It looks like something you'd use to patch a road, not eat, but he shovels it down like he's in a race. I decide he must come from a big family, the kind where every meal is a survival of the fittest. Why else would someone eat like that?

He doesn't notice me that day, or if he does, I never know about it, but it's only a few days later we exchange our first words. They are, rather unfortunately, "I like your buns." This line, destined for infamy, will later become a cornerstone of our "how we met" story.

For the record, the "buns" are croissants. Not technically buns, but I'm too busy turning red to correct him. I'm clutching a small pile of them, intending to smuggle them back to my dorm where my roommate will undoubtedly give me her signature disapproving stare. She's one of those tall, impossibly thin people who treats my snack choices as a personal affront. Still, I can't resist the pull of those buttery crescents. Mom used to make the kind from a tube—Andy and I experimented with fillings like Nutella, jam, hot dogs, and once, disastrously, whole garlic cloves. For days afterward, we reeked like cursed vampires.

His pale green eyes contrast sharply with his black hair, and his mouth—full, soft, maddeningly perfect—is the kind of mouth that belongs on a perfume ad. I stare long enough for him to laugh, a low, rumbling sound that feels entirely unfair.

"I—I'm hungry," I finally say, which only makes him laugh harder.

"Those are all for you?"

In an unprecedented act of confidence, I drop my head to the side, settle my gaze on him, and say, "I was hoping you'd join me."

The second the words leave my mouth, I become excruciatingly aware of how I must look: messy ponytail, third-day jeans, and a face that screams *sleep-deprived student*. Meanwhile, Jack looks like he's just stepped out of a rain-kissed montage in a rom-com. He's cute. Too cute. But when he smiles, I know I've hit the mark.

"I'm Jack. Greenwood," he says. He glances at my occupied hands, and I swear he might've gone for a handshake if I wasn't balancing my croissant hoard.

"Hazel Danler."

Jack doesn't know the weight of my name, the baggage of being tied to a father who walked out before my first birthday. He left nothing behind but a monthly check and the vague memory of a man who was better at running away than staying. Daisy once told me it's a miracle I turned out so well. I don't remind her she had a full-blown crush on Andy during his awkward braces-and-buzz-cut phase, so her judgment is questionable at best.

"Well, Hazel Danler. Where are we headed?"

My name on his lips is like catnip. It makes me buzz with emotion. I hadn't seriously expected him to take me up on my invitation. In fact, I really did want to eat all the croissants myself while I finished my essay.

I figure honesty is the best route and admit my big plans for the night. He looks crestfallen.

"I thought we were going to hang out tonight."

I wet my lips. "How about tomorrow night?"

He smiles. "Let's get some real food prepared solely for us instead of this..." He waves his hand around vaguely.

"How's five?" I ask.

Jack's face screws up. "You want to eat at five?"

I shrug, opting for honesty. "I'm not much of a night owl. Early dinners work for me."

"For you, Hazel Danler, I'll eat at 5:00 p.m."

I'm still holding the plate with both hands. "Should we just meet here then?"

"I'll find you," he says, already walking away.

I stand there, grinning like an idiot, watching until he's gone. By the time I sit down to finish my croissants, my cheeks ache from smiling.

––––––––––

At 4:40 p.m. the following night, I close the door behind me and stand motionless, unsure of where to go. Jack's plan to find me had been sexy yesterday but now fills me with unease. Schedules, due dates, and appointments are what keep me sane in a household that is anything but organized. Because I can't count on my mother to be where she says she will be, I come to rely on myself. Trust in myself. I can control only what I do.

My feet carry me back to the dining commons. I wait for ten minutes, my back to the door so as not to appear too eager. At 4:56 p.m., I turn to the door with the intention of leaving, only to walk straight into Jack.

His hands grasp my upper arms for purchase. "Whoa," he says. "You aren't leaving, are you? I'm four minutes early."

My face flushes. I've blown it. I've shown my neurotic, damaged cards too soon.

I really do want to leave then. That is until Jack takes my hand in his and says, "Come on."

He pulls me outside into the student lot where we approach a late model Honda Accord. He holds open the door for me, and when I sink into the seat, I'm hit with the fruity smell from the air freshener attached to the air vent. I've never been in a car smelling this nice or—as a quick look around confirms—this clean. It matches what little I know about Jack so far.

He waits until we arrive outside of a Metro Pizza to ask how I feel about pizza. We've already gone over our majors—me: English with a creative writing concentration, him: architecture—and a brief overview of our families, which is when I find out he has no siblings to fight for food against. I guess he just eats as though he does.

"I feel great about pizza," I say, trying to sound cute. I move my weight from one leg to the other.

On the way in, we're greeted by a middle-aged host with a complexion that suggests he's been deep-frying his skincare routine. Jack slides in next to me with a smile. "I hope you don't mind," he says, but my heart is beating too loudly to register his words.

Jack wants to know what it's like having a sibling. His family is small: just him and his parents and an aunt, uncle, and much older cousin who live across the country in New Hampshire and rarely leaves his hometown.

I try to find a way to tell him he has more family than I do, but no matter how I practice it in my head, it only comes out sounding terribly sad. I could tell him the truth: that Andy and I are more survivors than siblings, forged in the fires of our chaotic childhood. But no matter how I phrase it in my head, it sounds too tragic, and I've had enough pity to last a lifetime. Here in Las Vegas, no one knows me or my story. It's like an empty notebook—I can fill it however I want.

"I couldn't have asked for a better brother," I tell him. "We were really close growing up. I wouldn't be the person I am today without him."

Under the table, Jack's leg brushes mine, sending an electric jolt up my spine. "Remind me to thank him one day."

Oh, okay, I'm obsessed with you already. "I will."

The pizza arrives, hot and unapologetically greasy. We eat like kids at a sleepover, unbothered by cheese strings or sauce smears. The Coke—something Mom rarely let us have growing up—feels like liquid rebellion. When the server asks about dessert, I decline, too full of carbs and butterflies to even consider it.

On the drive back to campus, Jack keeps glancing at me, and finally, I can't take it. "What?" I ask. "Do I have sauce on my face or something?"

Jack laughs, looking embarrassed. "No, it's just...you're so beautiful, I can't believe you're here with me right now."

"Oh," I touch my neck. "Thank you."

We pull up to a red light, and suddenly, I know exactly what's going to happen. The second the car stops, Jack turns, leans in, and kisses me, his mouth warm and tasting faintly of basil.

I smile against his mouth, and he pulls away, grinning. The car behind us honks. As he drives, I can't stop staring at his mouth, replaying the kiss in my head like my favorite song on repeat.

Oh.

CHAPTER
THREE

A LITTLE LESS THAN TWENTY YEARS AGO

Andy and I don't have the kind of relationship where we can talk about sex without spiraling into mutual humiliation. We tried it once, back in high school when Andy started seeing this girl one year above us. She drove a red Civic with a vanity plate that screamed **PRNCSS**, and Andy was completely smitten—like, writing-her-name-on-his-shoes level of obsessed. One afternoon, he came to me for advice, claiming he needed "a girl's perspective." The second the words left his mouth, we both burst into a fit of awkward, nervous laughter so intense it ended with Andy wheezing and me in tears. After that, the topic of sex was banished from sibling discussions, unspoken but universally understood.

So, when things with Jack begin heading in a decidedly *adult* direction, I skip Andy and email Daisy for advice. She's my best friend and therefore the designated keeper of my secrets, including the fact that my knowledge of sex is roughly equivalent to that of an Amish teenager on rumspringa. I've never watched porn, and the sum total of my sexual experience is the vague memory of a boy flashing me his penis on the kindergarten playground.

Instead of returning my email, Daisy calls me.

"Hazel, just do it. There's no wrong way to have sex. You're wet, he's hard, you stick it in."

I nearly choke on the Diet Coke I'm drinking.

She continues: "For real though…Jack will be grateful just to see you naked."

I know she's right. Jack and I have a rare connection, and the sex will surely reflect it.

When it does finally happen, we are alone in his room, his suite mate having gone home for the weekend. I thought I would be more nervous, especially since Jack has been with other girls before me, but I know right away he's never been with anyone like this before. It simply isn't possible he knows his way around their bodies like he does with mine. He knows exactly what I want before even I know. For the first time ever, I'm out of my head and fully in my body.

Afterward, we lay naked beside each other as the sun goes down. I can't stop touching the skin below my lips. Around him, I am beginning to feel a kind of safe I've failed to experience in my life before now. I am falling in love.

———

It's an Olympic-level challenge not to think about Jack every waking moment. His arms, his mouth, the way I seem to slot perfectly against him like the final piece in a very attractive puzzle—it's all-consuming. In Philosophy 101, a class led by a professor whose enthusiasm is only rivaled by her spring-loaded curls, I start off clinging to her every word about the meaning of existence. But then, halfway through her passionate monologue about Descartes, my mind drifts to the texture of Jack's hair between my fingers. Suddenly, the only question I'm contemplating is, *How soon can I see him again?*

It's during this class one Thursday morning that the professor asks us to partner up and complete the critical thinking workbook questions up on the screen. We're weeks into the class by then, so most people find their partner quickly and without trouble. I stare down at my laptop, hoping no one will notice I'm alone. Eventually, I see a flash of red hair and feel someone sit down next to me.

"Do you have a partner?" she says. I shake my head. "Cool. I'm Emily, by the way."

I can tell immediately she has no idea what she's doing, so I take the lead. We finish the assignment with time to spare. I think Emily will run for the hills, but to my surprise, she stays put. She's a freshman too, who chose UNLV because she wanted to get away from the Reno winters but couldn't afford to go to school out of state. She's happy to have gotten a spot in the Tonopah Resident Complex because it's close to the dining commons. "I like to eat," she says with a shrug, and I think back to my plateful of food the night Jack and I met.

Emily continues to sit next to me during our next three classes, but it's during the fourth class I think, *Wait, are we friends?* The idea fills me with equal parts excitement and nervousness. I've been in Las Vegas for months by then, and the only person I've connected with is Jack. Even my roommate, in what minuscule space we share, has perfected the art of indifference. I spend most of my free time at Jack's place anyway, as he's scored a deluxe single in the Upper Class Complex.

I want so badly to invite Emily out for coffee, or even to study, but there's no way to be certain she won't turn me down. It's entirely plausible she's just being friendly and has zero interest in taking our banter outside the classroom.

One day after class, I finally have an excuse to ask for her number. She has me recite mine first, and then sends a text.

hey. it's emily.

I save her as a new contact in my phone and spent the next week staring at her name like it's a rare artifact, feeling like I've unlocked a whole new version of myself. For the first time since Daisy, I'm someone who can actually make friends.

Emily told me to text her anytime, but it feels like the first text has to *matter*. Like it should be engraved on some metaphorical stone tablet of friendship-worthy communication. I can't waste it on something mundane, like the guy in the dining commons sporting a mullet so bad it looked like roadkill glued to his head—even if Emily once admitted the hottest guy she ever dated had a mullet.

And God forbid my first message to her is school-related. "Hey, did you get the Philosophy 101 homework?" is not the vibe I want to establish. I'm aiming for *cool*—whatever that means.

The opportunity presents itself some two weeks after I've added her to my phone. I'm crossing campus, headed toward my next class when a small flyer whacks the side of my face. I hold the flyer tightly in my fist, embarrassed. It isn't until twenty minutes later I unfold it to see it's an ad for a local band I'm fairly certain Emily mentioned. I pull out my phone, tucking it discreetly between my knees, and type out a text. I hit send before I can change my mind.

Her reply comes instantaneously.

Oh yeah I love them! When's the show?

Next month. The 12th.

I know you've never heard of them but would you want to go with me?

I feel my smile down to the tips of my toes. First Jack and now a new friend. It took a beat, but I'm starting to come around to Las Vegas.

I wait until the night before the concert to tell Jack. At the very beginning of our relationship, he introduced me to some of his friends, and we often spend time with them eating, playing video games, or drinking cheap vodka someone's older brother bought us. But as time goes on, we see less and less of his friends until one day, it seems like I can't recall the last time we've been with anyone other than each other.

When I bring this up, Jack shrugs as though it isn't a big deal, like, *Oh, there's plenty of time for that later.* I'm enjoying my time with him too much to make it into something it isn't. When I finally tell him about Emily, he looks up from his textbook with a look on his face that, years later, I will come to recognize as insecurity but in the moment looks only like he's about to say something profound.

"We have each other, and that's all we'll ever need," he says.

The next day I text Emily, telling her I'm not feeling well and can't make the concert. I offer her my ticket so she can find someone else to go with her. She's disappointed but understanding about the whole thing, which makes me feel worse about never texting her again. I have Jack, I don't need anyone else.

CHAPTER
FOUR

NINETEEN AND A HALF YEARS AGO

I spend less than one month back home in Anaheim the summer after my freshman year before Jack invites me to come back to Las Vegas to visit him. He's working construction with his uncle, but because of the heat, they're up and out early, leaving his days open from mid-afternoon on. Jack pays for my flight and picks me up at the airport—and not at the passenger pickup, no, he self-parks and waits for me at baggage claim, the new suitcase I've bought just for the trip already beside him. I collapse into his arms, feeling as though we've been apart for years. He kisses me until our lips are chapped, and an elderly man coughs pointedly in our direction.

On the drive to his parents' home, we talk about how difficult it is to be apart for the last twenty-two days. By the time he parks in front of a large brown two-story house, we're desperate to be alone, but his parents are at the door to greet us.

Jack is a clear younger version of his father, Michael, but has his mother's coloring. They just look like a family. They smile at one another, touch each other, listen to each other. It feels a little like I'm staring into the sun. I smile past a pang of envy that my family could never, ever feel this way.

They're wonderful people: Michael is a professor of economics at UNLV and Sue works in marketing. They're smart, funny, and incredibly warm. I like them both immediately.

"Can I keep them?" I say to Jack later when we're finally alone. There'd been no awkwardness when we slunk off to bed, no talk about where we would sleep or reiteration of house rules. I'm fairly certain there aren't any.

Jack smiles at me, and it has little to do with the fact I've just removed my shirt. "They're pretty smitten with you, too."

"Really? Did they say something to you?"

He shakes his head. "I know them. They already adore you." He kisses me. "I mean, how could they not?"

Besides Daisy's parents, Michael and Sue are the only married couple I know. My mother's parents had been married for fifty-five years but passed away when I was little. Not that it mattered much—my mother barely talked about them anyway. I get the sense their relationship wasn't exactly a fairy tale, which somehow makes it worse that she didn't try harder to rewrite the story for her own kids. I've seen photos of them smiling—cheerful, posed snapshots—but a photograph is just a second frozen in time. You can't see what happens before or after the flash.

I don't know much about what it means to be married, but something in my gut tells me Sue and Michael have cracked the code. And if I pay close attention, I could learn how to truly be in love. Jack and I haven't said the words yet, but I know it's coming. I've felt them rise to my lips plenty of times, but I always swallow them back down. I don't want to be the one to go first. Jack has been amazing to me, but trust? That's still a work in progress. Not to be one of *those* people blaming their problems on their childhood, but it's hard to ignore the fact that my dad bailed before I could even string two words together. That kind of thing doesn't exactly build a solid foundation for believing in "forever."

I awake my first morning in Jack's house to an empty bed. It's ten a.m. and Jack has been at work for over four hours. His parents aren't home, but there's a note on the fridge written in Sue's immaculate handwriting: *Make yourself at home, there's plenty of food in the fridge. Michael and I will be home for dinner—Sue.* I take the note back upstairs to Jack's bedroom where I carefully slip it between the pages of *Extremely Loud & Incredibly Close* and return the book to the bottom of my suitcase. I study myself in the small mirror on the wall opposite the bed, considering an alternative history, one where I have a mother who writes notes like this. I wouldn't have been so consumed with trying to be perfect in the hopes she might pay me some real attention. Without so much time spent trying to be the perfect student I'd have had more time for friends, and instead of just having Daisy, I'd have had a whole gaggle of close girlfriends, maybe even a boyfriend or two. I'd have come to college with the proper tools to make new friends instead of hunkering down with the first person to have paid me any attention. But in this alternative reality, I may not have met Jack, and that was simply unfathomable.

Jack—and his parents, everything his family stood for—they are a missing puzzle piece clicking into place.

Over dinner, after Jack's unofficial tour of his greatest hits—his old middle school and high school, the house he was born in, and the park where he earned eight stitches by headbutting a set of monkey bars—I feel a warmth I've never known before. Sitting here with Jack and his parents, I'm struck by a thought so scandalous I barely recognize it as my own: *What if I just stayed here forever and never went back to Anaheim?*.

I'm so lost in the fantasy that I don't notice Sue asking me a question until she waves a hand in front of my face. "Earth to Hazel," she teases, smiling. "Jack used to do the same thing as a kid. I'd say, 'Where'd you go, buddy?'"

The ring on her left hand catches my eye. "Oh, your ring is beautiful."

Sue lights up, extending her hand so I can admire it up close. Her fingers are long and slender, like mine, and the delicate emerald ring is framed by tiny pave diamonds, the kind of heirloom you'd expect to find in a fairy tale. "It was my mother's," she says. "She gave it to Michael when he asked for her permission to marry me."

"That's so lovely," I say, trying not to sound like I'm auditioning for a Hallmark movie.

The look Sue gives Michael makes my stomach do a flip-flop. She leans in closer, her voice dropping to a whisper. "Maybe it will be yours one day."

I'm nineteen.

CHAPTER
FIVE

EIGHTEEN AND A HALF YEARS AGO

On the last day of my sophomore year, I can barely open my eyes because of all the crying. Jack hovers nearby, completely at a loss. I've convinced myself that explaining why I'm so upset will somehow make him stop loving me. (It's a gift, really—this ability to catastrophize.) In desperation, he calls Daisy, who promptly talks me off the ledge. Leave it to her to cut through my melodrama with a single, *"What the hell is wrong with you?"*

The truth is, I can't stand the thought of another summer apart. The two weeks we've spent together has barely scratched the surface. Going back to Anaheim feels like going back in time: working every waking hour to save money, clinging to Daisy whenever she's free, and keeping up a relentless back-and-forth email chain with Jack that only makes the distance worse.

My room is already packed up, boxes stacked against the walls. Tomorrow, Daisy and I are supposed to load up her mom's ancient SUV and make the drive back to California. But tonight, Jack looks at me, eyes steady and serious.

"Don't go back to Anaheim," he says. "Stay here with me."

And just like that, I do.

CHAPTER SIX

A LITTLE OVER SIXTEEN YEARS AGO

On the day I graduate, Jack and his parents are in the crowd, cheering me on. Next to them, Andy sits looking hot and uncomfortable in a suit that's too tight for him. When my name is called, I walk up on stage and receive my diploma feeling euphoric. When I look out into the crowd, I can just make out Andy and Jack sitting next to one another, watching me, their faces alight with pride. My two favorite men together.

After the ceremony, Michael and Sue treat us to dinner at some Italian place I forget the name of the second we're through with our meal. Jack is elated after the ceremony, hugging me and kissing me and telling me our real life together is finally beginning, but at dinner, he becomes quiet and nervous. Even Andy notices.

He nudges me for the third time. "What is *up* with him?"

We're finishing up dessert and Jack, across the round table between his parents, keeps playing with his hands as though they're new and he doesn't know what to do with them.

I cock my head toward my brother. "I really have no idea." My heart feels like it's trying to escape my chest, settling instead in the pit of my stomach.

Andy is staying in the guest room at our place, so we all drive back together, crowded into Jack's Accord. He always wants to be the driver; being a passenger bores him. I always think it's because he likes the sense of control, but I never admit it to him. Andy disappears upstairs the second we get home, and Michael and Sue settle into the living room couch to catch up on the latest episode of *Breaking Bad*. I find it hilarious that two people who have openly admitted to never having even touched a cigarette, let alone anything worse, are so addicted to a show about a broke chemistry teacher who finds out he has cancer and in an attempt to not leave his family in piles of debt after his death, turns an old RV into a meth lab. I've tried to get Jack to watch the show, but he has little interest.

In our bedroom, Jack still hasn't shaken out of his stupor. In fact, he seems even worse now that we're alone.

"What is up with you today? You're all fidgety and weird."

"I'm fine," he says, a clear brush-off.

I go into the bathroom to clean my face, and when I return to change for bed, the sound of my favorite artist fills the bedroom. I hum along, smiling to myself. I spin on my heels, ready to tease Jack for playing a song I know he hates, and there he is, down on one knee, holding out his mother's ring to me.

"What are you doing?" I bite back a smile.

"I had planned to quote some lines back to you, but I don't want anyone to come after me for copyright infringement or something."

I drop my head backward, smiling up at the ceiling. "Is this supposed to be a proposal?"

He bites his bottom lip. In this moment, he is glowing. Vibrating with excitement.

My hands cup his face, and I sink down to the floor. I press my lips to his, tasting the beer he had at dinner. "You have to say the words."

He pulls away, but just barely. His nose is nearly touching mine. "Hazel Danler, will you marry me?"

I kiss him again, whisper "Yes" against his mouth. There's no hesitation, no second to consider any other option other than *Yes, Yes.*

I begin to cry, and Jack laughs, pulling me into his arms. We fall against the edge of the queen bed, where we remain until my tears have run dry. I have never, ever felt so happy as I do in that moment, and by the way Jack looks at me, I know he feels the same.

We sit there for hours, talking about our plans. As much as we want to be married, we don't want to rush into the wedding. We want to do it right and enjoy being engaged. We want time to think everything through: the wedding, a house, starting a family. "There's no pressure," Jack says. "If we have kids, great. If we don't, that's okay too."

I kiss him then, with everything I have, feeling safe and loved and seen.

CHAPTER SEVEN

SIXTEEN YEARS AGO

On the day I finally take Jack back to Anaheim to meet my mother, it's abnormally hot. The sun is high, the sky a blinding, endless blue, and sweat trickles down my back despite the air conditioning blasting in the car. I've had my sunglasses on for so long they feel like a permanent part of my face, and when I finally take them off, there are deep red marks on the sides of my nose. The drive from Vegas has been slow, the hours stretched by my nerves, and the closer we get to Anaheim, the more tightly wound I become.

I'm fiddling with my engagement ring, spinning it in anxious circles around my finger. Jack keeps glancing at me, his calm, steady presence only making me more irritable. I've snapped at him more times than I care to admit—over the speed he's driving, the music on the radio—but the truth is, I'm terrified. I haven't seen my mother in over three years.

I feel like I have a lot of explaining to do, but at the same time, I don't want to explain a thing. Living with Jack and his family for the past three years has cemented a harsh reality in my mind: My mother was never cut out for the job. Sure, she kept a roof over our heads and food in the fridge, but she was woefully unprepared for the emotional labor motherhood demanded.

I wonder, for the first time, if I could be a *motherly* mother—someone who could actually do it right.

I can't stop fiddling with my ring, which, two months in, still feels like a stranger on my hand. I try to push my mother from my thoughts, but the effort only makes her loom larger in my mind. I try not to dwell on what this ring really means, or what comes after the wedding...after everything settles and the dust clears.

Instead of sharing these anxieties with my fiancé, I bury them in pages and pages of journal entries, each week adding to the pile of unresolved thoughts. I'm engaged to be married, and yet, I'm absolutely terrified of what comes next.

Just outside of Rancho del Sol, Jack reaches over and takes my hand in his. I feel the stone on my ring dig into his palm. "We can turn around if you want," Jack says gently. "We don't have to do this today."

"No," I say quickly, shaking my head. "I have to."

My throat is dry, and my chest feels tight, like I can't get enough air. My thoughts race ahead of me, spinning out scenarios of how this reunion with my mother will go. What if she's angry? What if she doesn't care at all? I haven't even told Jack how bad things were between us the last time we spoke, how much baggage I'm dragging with me into this visit. He just knows I haven't been home in years, that my mother and I aren't close.

We pull up in front of the house, and my stomach twists. My palms are sweaty, and I rub them against my jeans, trying to steady my breathing. Jack turns off the engine, and I sit there, frozen, staring at the front door. My hands tremble as I reach for the door handle, and for a second, I think about staying in the car, letting Jack go in without me.

"At least Andy will be there."

I don't have the nerve to tell him something has been feeling off with Andy these past few months. That he's been ignoring my emails and then my calls. It's become something, along with my fear of starting a family with Jack one day, I keep to myself. *There's no pressure,* he'd said. *If we have kids, great. If we don't, that's okay too.*

"You ready?" Jack asks, giving me a soft, encouraging smile.

"I guess," I mutter, my voice barely above a whisper. My heart pounds in my chest, and I swallow hard, trying to force down the nausea rising in my throat. My legs feel weak as I step out of the car, and I have to consciously keep my breathing steady. I hate Jack seeing me like this, unraveling before we even make it to the front door.

The second we step out, the door swings open, and there she is—my mother, Sarah Danler, standing in the doorway with a bright, rehearsed smile on her face. Her appearance is jarring—thinner than I remember, her hair darker, her clothes too loose—but I barely have time to process it before she's moving toward us.

"Hazel, baby!" she exclaims, her arms open wide.

My body tenses, and I force myself to move toward her, every step feeling heavier than the last. My mind is screaming at me to turn around, to get back in the car, but I'm trapped, caught in the momentum of this moment. She wraps her arms around me in a hug that feels too tight, too staged, and I stand there stiffly, my arms barely moving to return the gesture.

"Oh, baby, it's been too long!" she says, pulling back to look at me. Her eyes flick to Jack, and her smile widens. "And this must be Jack!"

Jack steps forward to shake her hand, and I step back, trying to steady myself. My breath comes shallow, my chest tightening again. I watch the two of them, my heart still racing, my mind spinning. My mother is putting on a show, as if we're some kind of happy family reunion, and it makes my skin crawl.

Jack's voice sounds far away as he introduces himself, and I'm barely aware of my surroundings as we walk into the house. Everything feels smaller—too close, too suffocating. I tug at the collar of my shirt, trying to loosen the fabric from my damp skin. The walls seem to close in on me, the air too thick, and I feel like I'm back in my teenage bedroom, trapped all over again.

At the dining table, I sit rigid, my hands clenched in my lap. I can't eat. My stomach is in knots, my appetite long gone. My mother chats away, her words washing over me as I sit there, numb. I can barely focus on what she's saying, every part of me consumed with the effort of keeping it together.

I glance over at Andy, hoping for some kind of reprieve, but his face is unreadable. He hasn't said much since we arrived, and when he does speak, his words are clipped, his tone distant. I feel the weight of his silence, like something is festering between us I can't see.

Apologies form on my lips as Jack and I sit at the table with my family, but all I can do is squeeze his hand under the table: when my mother makes a backhanded comment about the length of Jack's hair, when she points out that "at least one of her children stayed close by," when Andy fails to defend my choice to have our wedding in Vegas instead of Anaheim.

I narrow my eyes at him. Something is definitely off.

"It's just an awfully long drive for a *party*," she says. Under the table, Jack tightens his grip around my hand. I meet his eye. *See.*

After lunch, I follow Andy into the hallway. My heart pounds harder now, and my hands shake as I grab his arm. "What's going on with you? Why have you been ignoring me?" My voice is higher than I'd intended, raw with desperation.

He pulls his arm away, not looking at me. "Don't do that, Hazel. Don't act like you don't know."

"What are you talking about?" My throat feels tight, and my hands twitch with nervous energy. I can feel something slipping away, something I can't quite grasp. "Please, Andy, just talk to me."

His eyes finally meet mine, but they're cold, guarded. "You've been gone for three years. What do you think is going on?"

I blink, taken aback. "I don't know what you're talking about."

"Of course you don't." He lets out a sharp, bitter laugh. "Go back to Vegas, Hazel. You've made it pretty clear it's where you belong."

His words hit me like a punch to the gut, and I stand there, frozen in place as he brushes past me. My heart pounds in my ears, the hallway spinning around me. I don't understand what's happening, and the not knowing gnaws at me, filling me with dread.

The finality in his voice leaves me hollow, like something important has just slipped through my fingers.

I find Jack in the living room, perched on the edge of the

couch as my mother drones on about my childhood. He startles when he sees me, but I'm too exhausted to ask what story she's telling.

"We should go," I say, my voice sharper than I intend.

"You've barely been here two hours." My mother's tone is indignant, but the look on her face reveals she expects nothing less of me.

"It's my fault, I have an early start tomorrow." After all this time, it's still so easy to lie to her. What was born out of necessity has quickly become natural.

My mother stands as we head for the door, all false warmth as she pulls Jack into a hug. "You come back anytime, Jack. We'd love to have you."

She doesn't even look at me as she leads us outside.

In the car, Jack lets out a long breath. "That was...something."

"Yeah," I say, staring out the window. My engagement ring catches the light, and I twist it absently on my finger. "Soon you'll be my family."

"I already am," he says softly.

I look over at him, forcing a smile. "Promise you'll still love me when I'm forty and squishy."

He laughs, pulling me closer. "I don't understand this obsession you have with turning forty, but okay, I promise. I promise to love you even when you're forty and squishy, and when you're fifty and sixty and even when you're seventy and most certainly squishy all over. I'm not going anywhere."

"At least by then you'll be squishy, too."

But as we drive away, I can't shake the feeling that something is breaking, and I don't know how to fix it.

CHAPTER
EIGHT

FOURTEEN YEARS AGO

In a turn of events that surprised absolutely no one, including us, we end up having a January wedding. It's one of the wettest days in recent years, dumping 0.89 inches of rain on the valley. But, as it turns out, wet feet and frizzy hair can't put a damper on the smiles plastered across our faces as we walk down the aisle under a last-minute white tent. I'm wearing an off-white lace gown with a faux fur shawl, while Jack rocks a dark blue suit that's seen better days—thanks to the weather. Daisy, in a deep blue dress, stands beside us, and Jack's father watches on, pride written all over his face.

Despite the soaked fabrics and my dress clinging to every inch of my body, we don't care. The red flower in my hair matches his tie, and everything about us feels exactly as it should. Except for the awkward weight in the corner of my eye, where my mother sits. I try not to look, but it's like a magnetic pull. Her gaze is downcast, while Andy's fingers are wrapped around hers, squeezing her hand sympathetically. They both look detached, as though they're witnessing someone else's wedding, not the one we're all actually attending. My stomach tightens in response, and for a second, I'm not floating—I'm sinking, caught between joy and something I can't quite name. Jack and I stand under a floral arch, surrounded by thirty of our closest friends and family, promising to support each other, share our dreams, and never go to bed angry. Then, when we're pronounced husband and wife, I throw myself at him for a kiss that's both the first and the last of its kind—trying to drown out the confusion bubbling up inside.

As we walk back down the aisle hand-in-hand, I steal another glance at my mother. Her hair is a lighter shade of brown now, and she wears a deep purple dress that almost makes her blend into the background. I wish I could tell her how beautiful she looks.

Her lips quiver into a half-smile that doesn't quite reach her eyes. Andy avoids my gaze altogether, as though the wedding is more of a burden they're carrying than something they're meant to share in. It's a sight that unexpectedly twists my heart.

Michael and Sue graciously foot the bill for the wedding, but we draw the line at them paying for our honeymoon too. We head to Reno and then drive to Lake Tahoe, where we spend four peaceful days in a quiet cabin surrounded by snow. On the plane, we hold hands, steal kisses, and bask in the newness of being husband and wife. It still doesn't quite feel real, but the rings on our fingers are proof that it is. We're more than ready to leave the wedding stress behind and start this new chapter together.

"First things first." We are standing in line at the Reno airport waiting for our car rental. "Before we unpack, before we do anything, I'm getting you into bed, Mrs. Greenwood."

"Then we better get some food on the way. I need my energy."

As we drive, we stop at a Jack in the Box—destiny, he jokes. The humor settles my nerves, and for a while, it feels like everything is falling into place. We go through the drive-thru, ordering two burgers which we eat in the car, trying not to get grease on the seats of the rental car.

We tumble into bed, making love with a frantic intensity, as if our connection can erase the strange hollowness that remains. Afterward, I find myself staring at the ceiling, my mind drifting back to my mother's face, to Andy's silence. Jack turns to me, palm resting against my stomach, murmuring about the future, about the family he dreams of.

"One day," he murmurs, smiling at my skin. His voice is tender, full of hope.

But my stomach churns. I slip out of bed, the nausea overwhelming me, and lock myself in the bathroom. My reflection in the mirror is a mix of emotions I can't quite place. My skin is blotchy, my heart races, and the tears prick at my eyes. I lean over the sink, splashing cool water on my face. *Keep it together. It's your honeymoon.*

When I return to the bedroom, Jack is propped up in bed, completely at ease, flipping through a book on midcentury architecture. He talks about his dreams of the Eames house, of the life he wants to give me, but I'm still caught between worlds—the warmth of his words and the coldness that lingers from my family's detachment.

I move closer to him, let my head rest on his shoulder. "We are going to have a wonderful life, Jack Greenwood."

I believe it, but a part of me wonders why the people who should be happiest for me—Andy, Mom—are the ones who seem the farthest away.

———

I awake sometime in the middle of the night with excruciating stomach pains, barely making it to the bathroom before I lunge over the toilet, coughing and choking. When Jack wakes, hours later, long after the sun has comes up, I am still in the bathroom, balled up on the floor, shaking.

"Hazel, are you okay?" His eyes are as wide as saucers as he sinks down next to me. He tries to lift me, but I murmur my discontent.

"I-I think it's food poisoning."

He rubs my back, first in a circular motion and then from side to side. "Why don't I track down some ginger ale? Maybe make you some toast? You need to eat something."

Just the thought of food makes my stomach roil, but I suddenly know I want him gone.

"Ginger ale would be good," I say. I don't lift my head from the floor until I hear the cabin door lock and the car start up. I climb slowly to my feet and turn on the shower. The bar of soap smells of eucalyptus and glides effortlessly across my arms and legs. I let the scent engulf me.

I spend the day in bed, alternating between sleeping, reading, and eating small meals of lightly buttered toast, ginger ale, and applesauce. By dinnertime, I am feeling better, stronger. I ask Jack to make a fire there in the bedroom as the temperature seems to have suddenly dipped. Jack gathers the wood and goes about meticulously organizing it in the fireplace, but when it comes time to light it, the flame remains low and weak.

"You need more kindling in the middle," I tell him.

He waves me off. "Give it a minute."

We wait, but nothing changes.

"Add more in the middle," I say again.

"I know, OK? I'm trying."

I sit back on the bed with a sigh.

"You sighing isn't helping anything."

I close my mouth. For a moment, I say nothing. I even try to breathe as quietly as possible. Eventually, I stand from the bed. "Can I help you?"

Jack throws the log in his hand to the ground. "Jesus, Hazel! Just let me do it!"

I get back into bed and try to focus on my book, but I keep having to read the same sentence over and over again.

Eventually, the fire is lit and the room warms. Jack goes into the kitchen, returning with two cups of chamomile tea. He sips his, wincing.

"I wanted to see what all the fuss was."

I take his mug and mine. "I'll drink them both."

He smiles, but it is strained. "I'm sorry about snapping at you. I wanted this trip to be perfect and, well…"

"I'm feeling better now, and the fire looks great. It's all up from here."

———

It snows overnight, dumping an alarming eleven feet of snow over the cabin. Jack and I packed warmly but are surprisingly unprepared for so much snow. We spend the second day of our honeymoon inside, trying to stay warm, eating the bread and applesauce he picked up the day before. Our car is buried under the snow continuing to fall that day and for the next twenty-four hours.

By the end of day three in Lake Tahoe, having exhausted the one book I've brought with me, there is little to do but rest and talk. Tomorrow we will return to Las Vegas, to our jobs and to our two-bedroom apartment, but for one final day, nothing can touch us. There is nothing in the world except the two of us.

We make love as often as we can, searching for warmth from each other's bodies.

———

Jack holds my hand tightly the entire short flight home from Reno, as though he doesn't want to break the honeymoon spell. I look down at the rings on my finger, almost surprised to see them there. I am someone's wife.

I rest my head on Jack's shoulder. "I'm so sorry for ruining the honeymoon." But even as the words come from my mouth I know how ridiculous they sound. I haven't chosen to get food poisoning. I haven't chosen to spend that first night wrapped around the toilet instead of in bed with my new husband.

Jack kisses the top of my head. "You don't ruin anything. Yeah, things started out a little rocky, but we did okay in the end."

We won't speak of the food poisoning or the cold, or of the failed attempts at lighting a fire before getting it right. When we look back on this day we will remember the feeling of our bodies entwined, the copious amounts of ginger ale consumed, the beautiful, untouched snow outside our cabin door, the privilege of suddenly belonging to someone else.

CHAPTER
NINE

THIRTEEN YEARS AGO

Shortly after our first anniversary, after throwing up for days but hiding it from Jack, I take a pregnancy test. My hands are shaking as I unwrap the box, and I feel an overwhelming need to not do this alone.

So, I call Daisy.

"Hey, can you stay on the line with me for a bit?" I ask, trying to keep my voice steady.

"What's going on?" Daisy's voice immediately shifts from lighthearted to concerned. "You okay?"

I let out a shaky breath. "I, um…I'm taking a pregnancy test."

There's a pause, then a slight gasp. "Oh my god, you're kidding! Wait, are you excited? Nervous? What do you feel right now?"

"Mostly terrified," I admit, sitting on the bathroom floor with the test in my hand. "I don't even know if I want kids."

Daisy hums softly, letting me talk. "It's okay to feel that way, you know. You don't have to have it all figured out."

"I just…I don't know if I'm ready, and what if I'm never ready? What if I don't want to be a mom at all?" I say, biting my lip.

"Hazel, listen to me," Daisy says firmly, but with kindness. "You don't have to decide anything today. Take it one step at a time. And if it's positive, we'll figure it out. You'll figure it out. You're not alone in this."

Her words calm me, but the uncertainty still hangs in the air. "What if it's negative? Should I feel relieved? I don't even know what I want."

Daisy chuckles softly. "You don't have to have the perfect reaction. Whatever you feel is valid. Seriously, Hazel, you've got time to figure out the whole kid thing, whether it's now or later or never."

Her voice is so steady, so sure, it grounds me. I glance at the test, my pulse quickening. "It's time," I whisper.

"I'm right here. What does it say?"

The test is negative. My reaction is not. I burst into tears, surprising even myself.

"Hazel? What's going on? Talk to me."

"It's negative."

"And how do you feel?" she asks softly.

"I don't know," I say. "I should be relieved, right?"

"Not necessarily. You're allowed to feel however you feel," Daisy says gently. "And it's okay if you don't have an answer right now."

I sit on the floor for a few minutes, listening to Daisy's calm breathing on the other end of the line. "I don't know what's wrong with me."

"There's nothing wrong with you," she says firmly. "You're just processing. Take your time."

I nod again, feeling grateful for her steady presence. "Thank you for staying with me."

"Anytime," she replies. "We'll talk more when you're ready. And remember, no pressure, okay? You're amazing, with or without a kid. Jack knows that too."

Her words are like a lifeline, pulling me out of my spiraling thoughts. "I seriously don't know what I'd do without you."

"Right back at you," she says softly.

———

I wait a week before telling Jack. He's just walked in the door from work, and I'm in the kitchen preparing dinner. He kisses me and, the second he breaks away, the words are out of my mouth. He stands stock-still for a moment before taking a step back.

"Wow," he breathes. I can't tell if he's relieved or disappointed. "I wish you'd told me you thought you might be pregnant."

"I mean, it doesn't matter, right? I'm not."

I stir the orzo gently. Jack leans over to see what I'm cooking. He makes a hum of approval before touching the small of my back.

"I should've been there when you took the test." He looks me square in the eye as he says it, and—of course, it makes sense now. He feels left out.

He waits until I've plated dinner and we've settled at the table before he speaks again. "What do you think about maybe trying soon?"

I've known it would come to this. "We've only been married fourteen months, Jack." I suddenly feel as though I might cry. I'm never ready for this conversation, not when he first asked me how I felt about kids six months into our relationship, after he proposed, or shortly after I brought him back to Anaheim. And though I'm not ready now, I have the distinct understanding it can no longer be avoided.

Jack doesn't answer right away. I imagine him smiling, saying: "But just imagine a little Hazel running around. Or a boy Hazel." It's the same thing he said two days after he slid the ring on my finger. I laughed then, but it isn't as clever the second time. I fork a mouthful of chicken into my mouth and chew intensely. Under normal circumstances, I'd have moaned my delight with the meal, its rich creaminess and tart lemon finish. It's a new recipe and I've nailed it.

"When then?" Jack asks.

"I don't know."

"After two years?"

"I don't know."

"Five?"

"Jack," I say. "I told you I don't know."

"In five years you'll be thirty, you're not going to want to wait too long after that."

I shovel more food into my mouth as Jack watches me. I chew, swallow, feel the food drop into my stomach. "I'm still not sure I want kids." I look at the food on my plate, notice the way the sauce is separating from the orzo, pooling in the corner of the gray stoneware plates we picked out together. "You know that."

Jack answers with his mouth full. "So you say. But I know you'd make a great mother." He waves me off when I try to interrupt him. "I know what you're going to say about your mom, but you're not her, Hazel. Sarah got a lot wrong so that you could know how to do it right." His plate now empty, he rises from the table. I feel him standing behind me. "You're fucking phenomenal, Hazel Greenwood. I wish you could see yourself the way I see you."

"I don't want to end up like her," I say eventually.

"You won't. You're already more motherly than she ever was."

I swallow, tasting nothing.

CHAPTER
TEN

ELEVEN YEARS AGO

Maxwell Michael Greenwood is born on a sticky summer afternoon in mid-July. Nine pounds, eight ounces, with a full head of dark hair.

The moment I found out I was pregnant, shock rippled through me, sharp and undeniable. I wasn't ready for this—how could I be? I wasn't sure I even wanted children. But Jack, steady as ever, was there every day, reminding me in his calm way that I wasn't my past, that our son would have the kind of childhood I never did. Slowly, hesitantly, I began to believe him.

Jack gained twenty pounds while I was pregnant. He claimed it was sympathy weight, but it stuck around long after. I loved his soft center, and not only because it matched my own.

Nothing could have prepared me for the moment they placed Max in my arms. His tiny body was warm, his cries loud and piercing, and yet, all I could think was he was perfect. It wasn't the promise Jack had made, or the idea of fixing my own broken past, that struck me then. It was this: I had created something beautiful. Something I didn't know I needed until he was here, breathing against my skin.

In that moment, everything else fell away. Whatever doubts

or fears I had melted, replaced with a fierce, overwhelming love I didn't expect. I wasn't just warming to the idea of motherhood—I was already all in, and I would do anything to give Max the world.

CHAPTER
ELEVEN

JUST OVER EIGHT YEARS AGO

'm sitting up in bed with a book when Jack walks into the room after putting Max to sleep. It's been one of those rare, perfect days where everything falls into place—no messes, no tantrums, no raised voices. I'm absorbed in a twisty domestic thriller, but I set it aside as soon as Jack appears.

I readjust my pillows, turning on my side to face him.

"We've got to get Max some new books. If I have to read *Room on the Broom* one more time..." He trails off. His pale green eyes meet mine, and I feel a familiar flutter in my chest.

Even after all these years, his gaze still manages to catch me off guard. He's always been handsome, but now, at thirty-three, he's aging like fine wine—thinner face, a few streaks of gray at his temples, and the faint lines that deepen when he smiles. It makes him look distinguished, while I'm still fighting the lingering softness around my middle from three years ago.

I swallow and glance away, trying to shake the creeping feeling I'm being left behind.

"I can see them, you know," I murmur, not quite meeting his eyes. "The lines, the gray hairs. All the reminders we're getting older."

Jack's voice is soft, as though he's trying to draw me back from my thoughts. "You're still beautiful."

I wish I could let his words wash over me and make the fear disappear, but the anxiety clings to me, a knot I can't untangle. I want to believe him, but the doubt, the fear of time slipping away, is always there. "Sometimes it feels like I'm just watching my time run out," I say quietly. "Like everything is slipping away too fast."

He sighs, pulling me into his arms. "Hazel, you're thirty-two. We have plenty of time. Gray hair and wrinkles are just part of life."

I rest my head against his chest, listening to the steady rhythm of his heart. His words are meant to reassure me, but I can't shake the feeling that time is racing ahead, dragging me with it. Still, I let myself sink into his embrace, trying to forget about the ticking clock.

I run my hand along his arm, feeling the strength beneath my fingers. When his head turns toward me, I take the chance to lean in, kissing him softly, lingering for a moment. Just as I'm about to shift closer, he pulls away, turning to grab the remote. The soft glow of the TV fills the room as the nightly news begins.

I try to focus on the headlines—an unidentified man has fired a few shots in front of the White House before turning the gun on himself, and a helicopter has crashed in New York City's East River—but the only truth that really sinks in is Jack and I aren't going to have sex tonight. Again.

I wait until the news is halfway through before I say quietly, "Do you still find me attractive?"

He glances at me, confused. "Didn't I just tell you you're beautiful?"

"Well, we haven't had sex in a while," I say, the words coming out sharper than I intended.

Jack's eyes remain on the TV. "We have a young kid at home."

"He's three, Jack. We can't keep using that as an excuse."

This gets his attention. He turns to me, a flicker of irritation crossing his face. "I wasn't aware I needed an excuse. I don't push you for one when you're not in the mood."

"Why are you getting angry?" I ask, my voice soft but defensive.

"I'm not angry," he snaps, then takes a breath. "I'm not."

"Okay."

"Don't say 'okay' like that." His irritation flares again, but this time I decide not to engage. I'm too tired to fight, and I don't want this to spiral further.

We sit in silence as the news continues. I can feel the tension between us, thick and unresolved. When the program ends, I wait, wondering what he'll do next.

He surprises me by speaking first, his tone more relaxed. "Isn't it supposed to be me complaining about the lack of sex?"

I can't tell if he's joking or not. His voice sounds light, but I'm wary. I don't answer.

He sighs. "We haven't had as much sex as we used to, sure. But we have a kid now, Hazel. A mortgage. A lot more responsibility."

"But don't you miss it?" I ask, my voice tinged with nostalgia. "What about the time you took me up against the car on the dark road by your office? Or when you lifted my skirt in the front hallway? I had a bruise on my ass from the table for a week. Or the time I woke you at four a.m. in New York?"

He smiles at the memories, but his response isn't what I expect. "That was all before Max."

I frown. "We're still the same people, Jack."

"You don't initiate anymore."

"Not true," I protest. "I try all the time, but you brush me off. Like tonight—"

"Tonight?" His tone is incredulous. "You're telling me I turned you down tonight?"

"Well... yeah."

"Bullshit."

I exhale, feeling the frustration rising again. "You turned on the TV as soon as I kissed you."

"You know I watch the news when Max goes down."

"Okay," I say.

But it's far from okay. It's *so* far from okay.

CHAPTER
TWELVE

THREE YEARS AGO

Jack and I have never been much for going out, but there's something about this particular invite from his work colleague that makes us feel like we have no choice. It's a Saturday night in late March, one of those beautiful nights where the warmth of the day sticks around, so I dress for the occasion in a tight black dress and heels.

The invite comes from Milo, one of the fellow architects at the firm Jack has been working at since graduation. There have been rumblings of promotion opportunities, of a shake-up in management, and Milo wants to pick Jack's brain. Why he has to do this over a fancy dinner with wives in tow is beyond me but, when it comes down to it, a night out is probably a good thing for Jack and me. Things have been so tense at home lately.

Jack and Milo come straight from the office, so I arrive at the restaurant after them. As a hostess leads me to the table, I see Jack and Milo notice me at the same time. Where Milo's eyes linger, taking me in in my entirety, looking pleased, Jack's gaze almost immediately returns to the menu in front of him. My good mood plummets and I can feel the sting of tears; how easily he can hurt me now.

Milo stands and introduces himself, shakes my hand. His

wife, Amie, a petite, frail-looking thing, arrives soon after. She stops a passing waiter and asks for a glass of white wine. I look at Jack but he refuses to meet my eye.

Once everyone has ordered and drinks are in hand, Milo adjusts his position in his seat to better face Jack. "I heard William might be pushed out."

And so begins an hour of shop talk while I try to pull any string of words out of Amie, who seems put out by the whole evening—or perhaps just by having been forced to converse with me instead of being a part of the greater conversation.

By the time dinner is over and Milo has signed the bill, I know only three things about Amie: One, her name; two, she is a fifth grade math teacher; and three, I will do everything in my power to never have to spend a second more of my time in her company.

———

Jack beats me home and is waiting in the kitchen when I walk in. He's already sent the babysitter home and has poured himself something strong and dark. There was a time he would have had something waiting for me, a glass of wine or maybe a vodka tonic. But the way he forces the liquid down his throat tells me he isn't in the mood for niceties.

"What's…" I trail off.

"Dinner was a disaster."

"What do you want me to say, Jack? I tried. Milo did literally nothing to try and involve me in the conversation and Amie, bless her heart, has the personality of a wet sponge."

"Well, you should have tried harder, it was obvious you didn't want to be there. It was embarrassing."

"I'm sure they didn't even notice anything was amiss."

Jack's fist hits the kitchen island. "I noticed."

"Finally."

His eyes narrow, his jaw working back and forth. Eventually, he says, "Would it kill you to be friendly and make some friends?"

"So now you *want* me to make friends? Okay, got it."

Jack makes a face. "I don't even know what that's supposed to mean."

"It means you had no problem keeping me from making friends when we were dating, or when we were first married. I believe your exact words were 'We have each other and that's all we'll ever need.'"

"Well, things change."

My head bobs up and down. "No kidding."

I glance at the clock over Jack's shoulder. It's past ten thirty p.m. When I turn my attention back to him he's looking me over, wearing a strange expression.

"What's with the get-up, by the way? Who exactly were you dressing up for?"

I drop my head back and close my eyes. I feel the muscles in my neck extend in an altogether not unpleasant manner. "You are unbelievable! I did it for you—and maybe a little for me, just to prove I still had it in me somewhere—but you barely even noticed." I bite my lip. "Milo noticed."

"Milo's a pig."

We stand in the middle of the kitchen staring at each other but not seeing one another. How has it taken me so long to realize it's happening? It feels...permanent.

I turn my back to him. "I'm tired and going to bed."

"I'm not done talking to you."

"Well, I'm done talking to you."

I feel his hand on my arm and turn slowly to face him. "Get your hand off me."

He releases me and takes a step back, putting distance between us we desperately need. "I'm sorry, I just..."

Have had too much to drink. I study his face, the face I have loved more than anything else in this world. But he doesn't look like that man anymore. He doesn't feel like him either.

"I think you're unhappy." I attempt to keep my tone polite, though we're beyond that.

His eyes flash. "And why do you think that?"

"Because you're sitting here judging and evaluating me and all my failings instead of evaluating and improving yourself."

Jack clicks his tongue. "So let me get this straight. You think just because I'm not out there every day obsessing over my life and what I've done wrong or what I can improve, that I'm unhappy? Not everyone is you, Hazel. Some of us don't need to think everything to death, we can just *be*."

I bite my bottom lip, my head bobbing up and down slowly. A chuckle escapes my lips. "You know you used to love that about me—my desire to grow and change and adapt."

"I'm pretty sure it's called growing up. Everyone does it."

I smile, though unkindly. "If that's the case, then you're doing it all wrong."

"Oh, screw you."

I meet his eyes. "Right back at you."

CHAPTER
THIRTEEN

ONE YEAR AGO

Max requests only one thing for his ninth birthday: an ice cream cake from Dairy Queen. I put in the order the week before and Jack agrees to pick up the cake on his way home from the office. I text him a reminder at four p.m. that goes unanswered and follow up just before five. I order pizza for us all from Hungry Howie's, one of Max's favorites, but we want to wait for Jack's arrival to dig in.

I call his phone at six p.m. but it goes straight to voicemail. The same happens at six-thirty-nine. When he isn't home by seven, Max and I reheat the pizza and eat it on the couch while watching Fuller House. Amid Max's barks and laughter, I try not to look at my phone.

At nine, I tuck him into bed and then take a copy of *Sweetbitter* with me to the couch.

———

I awake to the sound of Jack stumbling around the kitchen, opening and closing the refrigerator, slamming a cup onto the counter, and filling it with water. I had intended to confront him as soon as he came home, but now he's back and I don't have the energy. I creep up the stairs, hearing him not far behind.

In the bedroom, Jack begins to undress me. I am wearing the lace bra he likes and he moans approvingly. I push him away, reaching for my shirt and holding it against my chest as though to shield myself. I can smell the alcohol on his breath.

"You aren't seriously trying to sleep with me after what you pulled tonight."

"Oh, come on. I just had a few drinks with Milo." He grasps my hips and tugs me against him.

I pull away. His hands fall to his side limply. "You're drunk. Go to bed."

He clicks his tongue. "You know, you used to be so fun. You used to be so carefree and—"

"I've never been carefree a day in my life, Jack. I'm too anxious. You must be thinking of someone else."

He rolls his eyes, sitting on the edge of the bed.

"Why would you even come home like this? Why bother?"

"Would you have preferred I didn't? To wake up in the morning and find the other side of the bed empty? I thought I was doing the right thing."

"It's your son's birthday." My lip curls.

He waves his hand about in the air. "Exactly."

"Which you missed."

"Oh calm down, I made him pancakes this morning and said happy birthday to him then."

"Don't you dare tell me to calm down!"

I retreat to the bathroom where I wash my face and brush my teeth. Once changed, I get into the left side of the bed—always the left, because Jack likes to be closest to the door because, or at least he's said, he wants to be the first person a burglar comes across. I have so many stories just like this one: Jack, the protector; Jack, the hero.

"This isn't working," I say eventually.

"No shit."

I stare at him, burning a hole in his back. "I have to know you're going to take this family seriously. This marriage."

He laughs unkindly. "I'm here, aren't I?"

"Are you though?"

He waves his hands in a circular motion. "Do you not see me sitting here having this conversation with you?"

"I know you'd rather not be here, so just go. Just go then."

Jack growls. "Don't do that. Don't put words into my mouth. I never said I didn't want to be here."

"Actions speak loudly, Jack. And your actions lately…"

"Oh, yes, is this where you overthink the situation and analyze me to death?" He claps his hands together. "Oh, I can't wait!"

There's a voice in my head repeating the same phrase over and over again but I banish it. Instead, I lay down on the bed, turning my back to him. "Take a walk, Jack, before you say something you'll really regret."

A minute later, I hear the front door slam shut.

CHAPTER
FOURTEEN

FOUR MONTHS AGO

We can't even decide where to go for dinner.

It's painfully obvious neither of us wants to go out, but we've had this date marked on the calendar for months—a weak attempt to rekindle the closeness that feels more and more out of reach.

I settle onto the couch across from Jack. "What do you feel like? Thai? Chinese?"

He doesn't look up from his phone. "Ugh, no."

"Pizza? Italian? We haven't tried the new place by the grocery store."

"I don't know if I feel like going out."

I bite back the frustration building inside me. "Okay," I say slowly. "We'll order in. Any ideas?"

"I don't know, Hazel."

The way he says it, so flat, so dismissive, grates on my last nerve. "Well, think then. Instead of just shooting down everything I suggest."

"Just get whatever you want," he says, voice sharp, as if he's the one who should be irritated instead of me.

I throw my hands up. "You know what? I'm good. You decide. I'll just find something in the fridge."

His phone hits the cushion with a thud as he snaps his head toward me, eyes blazing. "Just say what you want to say, Hazel. All this passive-aggressive bullshit is getting old."

"Funny coming from the guy who's just as angry and frustrated as I am." My words sting, but it's the truth. The tension between us is suffocating, and neither of us seems willing to address it.

Jack leans back, running a hand through his hair. "Okay, so we're both mad. Now what? What do we do about it?"

"I don't want to talk about this now."

"Well, I do." His gaze sharpens, daring me to back down. "Let's stop dancing around it and get to the point."

I cross my arms, trying to shield myself from the inevitable blow. "Fine. You want to have this conversation so badly, go ahead. You start."

"You've changed," he says without hesitation, his words cutting through the air like a blade.

I let out a bitter laugh. "*I've* changed? What about you?"

He makes a sound in the back of his throat—the one he always does when he's fed up. "This is going nowhere fast."

"What, I can't ask a question?"

Jack sighs deeply, as if he's exhausted by the very sight of me. "Okay, let's try something different. Tell me one thing you can't stand about me right now."

His challenge catches me off guard, and for a second, I'm speechless. "How is that going to help anything?"

"Just humor me."

It kills me how quickly it comes to me. "You've become super judgmental."

He nods, slowly, as though weighing my words. "And you're a slob."

The accusation bounces around inside me, landing like a punch to the gut.

"You never want to have sex."

"*You* never want to have sex," he fires back. He's right. I used to care we weren't intimate anymore; now I'm almost relieved.

"You care more about what people like Milo and his idiot wife think of you than what I think."

He falters, just for a moment, and I see a flicker of the Jack I used to know. But it vanishes just as quickly.

"You're too emotional. You take everything personally."

I feel something snap inside me. "You bullied me into having a baby."

The second the words leave my mouth, I regret them. I love our son. I've never regretted him, but the way we got here... that's something I can't deny.

Jack recoils, his face twisting with anger. "Oh, bullshit."

There it is—the temper, the defensiveness. The Jack who always manages to twist things until I'm the one who feels guilty, who's in the wrong. We could keep going like this, trading barbs all night, but it won't change anything.

"Jack... are you even attracted to me anymore?"

The silence that follows is unbearable. I count every agonizing second before he finally speaks.

"I don't know."

And there it is.

"This is..." I stand, unable to sit under the weight of his words any longer. "I need a break."

Jack doesn't move, doesn't argue. He just watches me, his eyes darting around the room like he's searching for an escape. His mouth opens slightly, but nothing comes out.

"A break could be good," he says quietly.

I walk toward the kitchen, feeling the distance between us grow with each step. "I think I'm going to make some tea."

He follows me with his eyes, his voice a low murmur. "Maybe what we need is time apart. To think."

I freeze, my hand hovering over the kettle. "What are you saying?"

"I'm saying maybe a break is the answer."

"To what question?"

"I think you know the answer." His eyes meet mine.

I feel a knot tighten in my stomach as I turn back to the counter, my hands trembling as I measure out the tea leaves. I can't believe we've come to this. I wanted him to be honest, but now that he is, I'm not sure I'm ready to hear it.

"If you want out of this marriage, just say it," I whisper. "Call it what it is."

"I don't want out," he says, but his voice is weak. "I just...this doesn't feel like it used to. Does it?"

No, it doesn't. But it wasn't me who gave up.

"Of course it doesn't feel like it used to. We're not the same people anymore. It's normal."

"I don't accept that," he says.

The kettle whistles loudly and I pull it off the burner. I feel Jack before I hear him, wrapping his arms around my middle, tucking my head under his chin. His touch feels familiar but has little effect otherwise. I pinch my eyes shut, trying to drum up some of the old feelings we had for one another.

I think about our first date, the hot, greasy pizza washed down with ice-cold Coke, of the first time we made love in his college dorm, and the way he knew his way around my body from the beginning. I think of how I knew then I was falling in love with him. I think of our wedding, the honeymoon, and of coming home every day knowing he was there made me feel the kind of safe I'd never had before him.

I think of the way he looked down at Max in my arms in the hospital on the day he was born. How I'd never seen a smile so genuine. I think of his pale eyes, how they were the first thing I noticed about him and the one thing that still takes my breath away after all these years.

I think of him brushing me off when I try to initiate sex, of the arguments we've had in the following weeks. Of every big or little argument we've ever had. Of him spending the night drinking with his work buddies when he should have been home celebrating his son's birthday.

I think about the possibility of coming home day after day to a house without him in it, to a house absent of his things: his toothbrush on the counter, his beard trimmings in the sink, the lingering scent of his cologne.

But all I feel now is tired.

I leave my cup of tea in the kitchen and go upstairs to bed where I cry and cry and cry.

CHAPTER
FIFTEEN

TEN WEEKS AGO

'm alone in my office when my phone starts ringing. Andy's name flashes on the screen, and for a moment, all I can do is stare. The last time we spoke feels like a distant memory. His name, in bold letters on the screen, feels oddly significant—like he knows I need him, like there's something only he can tell me.

I pick up, my voice shaky with surprise. "Andy! Hi!"

"Hey," he says, his voice flat.

There's a beat of awkward silence. I'm suddenly filled with hope. Maybe he's calling with good news, a promotion, or even a trip to Vegas to meet Max. "It's so good to hear from you," I babble. "How are you?"

"I have to tell you something," he says. His next words come out like a punch I didn't see coming. "It's Mom. She died this morning."

I freeze, breath caught in my throat. "I...What happened? How?"

"It was the cancer. It came back."

For a moment, all I hear is the blood rushing in my ears. "What *cancer*?"

His sharp intake of breath echoes through the phone. "Don't do this," he says, voice hardening.

I blink, confused. "Do what?"

"You're unbelievable. The woman is dead, Hazel. Our mother is dead. She's gone, and you're playing dumb?"

"Andy," I whisper, my heart racing, "I swear, I don't know what you're talking about. What cancer?"

The silence following is unbearable, stretching thin across the miles between us. When Andy speaks again, his voice is hoarse, almost broken. "She had breast cancer, Hazel. She was diagnosed years ago, went into remission, but it came back. Last year, it spread."

My mind whirls, fragments of the past coming at me like shards of glass: the calls I missed, the voicemails from Mom—vague, unreturned; Andy's standoffish behavior at my wedding; the months of cold silence. All the little signs I'd ignored.

"I didn't know," I finally whisper, my voice sounding smaller than I've ever heard it.

"She tried to tell you," Andy says, his anger simmering beneath the surface.

I snap back, "Well, she obviously didn't try hard enough, did she?"

Andy lets out a harsh, bitter laugh. "You never came home, Hazel. You never answered her calls. What else was she supposed to do? You made it clear...you were done with us."

I shake my head, though he can't see me. "That's not fair. You can't blame me for trying to move on from everything we went through growing up. You knew we both wanted to get out of there."

"She was sick, Hazel! What was I supposed to do? Walk away while she was dying?"

"I didn't know." My voice cracks. "I would have done something if I knew. I would've helped."

There's a pause, and when he speaks again, his voice is colder, like a door closing between us. "It doesn't matter now. It's too late."

"Why are you so angry with me?" I ask, my voice trembling. "Why did you think I'd ignore something like this?"

"Because that's what it looked like," he says, voice tight with restrained emotion. "It looked like you didn't care."

"You could have called me! You could have made me listen!"

His voice is gruff as he says, "She told me you knew...That she told you."

I feel the tears welling up, but I force them back. How could he think this of me? "Andy, I would never have ignored her if I knew. I didn't know. You have to believe me."

He doesn't respond. His silence speaks louder than anything else, as if he's weighed my words and found them lacking.

"I'm sorry," I say finally, the weight of everything pressing on my chest. "I'm so, so sorry."

There's nothing left to say. I thank him for telling me, for being there for her when I wasn't, and offer my support, though I know it's too late for that, too.

"I love you," I whisper. He doesn't say it back.

I stare at my phone long after the call ends, the room closing in around me.

Later, when I tell Jack, the words barely make it out. His face twists in confusion and helplessness, his hands hovering like he doesn't know what to do. He pulls me into a loose embrace, but I can tell he's waiting for something—for me to break down, to cry, to scream.

But I don't. I can't.

When he finally leaves me alone, I lie in the dark, staring at the ceiling, trying to make sense of it all. The phone call replays in my mind, the way Andy's voice cracked, the accusation in his words.

How could he have thought I would just...not care? All these years, he believed I was capable of abandoning her in her sickness.

Somehow, this feels like the deepest cut of all.

CHAPTER
SIXTEEN

LAST WEEK

I load the dishwasher wrong—again. Though we both know it isn't really about how I stack the bowls on the bottom instead of the top like Jack does. My husband of fourteen years has decided he needs a break from our marriage, and though we don't yet know what it means, it's a sentiment he can't take back. We've been existing around each other for weeks, speaking but not really speaking, there but not really there.

I slam the dishwasher door shut, ignoring the cry from the glassware inside and the look on Jack's face because enough is enough. "Do it yourself then."

My hands shake as I walk out the front door, closing it quietly behind me so as not to alert Max to my departure.

CHAPTER
SEVENTEEN

NOW

I strip off the dress I wore to my mother's funeral the second I'm through the bedroom door, feeling immediate relief from the tight elastic digging into my midsection. The fabric pools at my feet in a heap of black, like the weight of the day shed from my skin. Jack follows me into the room in silence, his usual meticulousness on display as he begins undressing. He moves with practiced efficiency—unbuttoning his shirt, folding it carefully, hanging his suit and tie with precision. Each movement is slow and deliberate, as if keeping things in order will somehow hold everything else together.

He tosses his charcoal gray dress suit into the dry cleaning bin, the sound a soft thud that echoes louder in my head than it should. I stare at him for a moment. He'll have to take care of his own dry cleaning, I suppose. There will be a lot of things he'll have to do for himself.

And then I realize I'm already thinking of what life will be like without him.

I don't feel guilty, just sad.

I come out of the closet dressed in old jeans and a UNLV hoodie frayed at the sleeves and faded from years of washing. I should throw it away, but it's one of the few things I feel comfortable in, like it's wrapped around all the versions of me that existed before life got this hard.

Jack's voice breaks the quiet. "I think we need to talk."

I stiffen, the words slicing through the calm I've tried to pull around myself like a shield. But I don't want to talk. Not now. Not after burying my mother—God, my mother—and the whirlwind of emotions clawing at me since we saw Andy for the first time in years. Everything feels too raw, too jagged.

"I'm in pain, Jack." I don't say it out loud, but the words pulse beneath my skin, burning for release. In two days, I'll turn thirty-nine. My mother is gone. My marriage is disintegrating. Forty is around the corner, and I feel like I'm standing in the rubble of all the things I thought would make sense by now.

But Jack takes my silence as permission to push forward. He always does.

"What are we going to do, Hazel?" His voice cracks a little, but I barely register it. "We've both said some things...things that can't be taken back."

I turn to him, the words coming out before I can stop them. "I'm not doing this right now."

The drive back from Anaheim was long and stifling, the silence in the car unbearable, but necessary. Now, being back in our house, with our things—*my* things—I feel a flicker of relief. This is my space, my sanctuary.

But Jack...he doesn't let up.

"I know the timing isn't ideal, but—"

I whirl around, cutting him off. "'The timing isn't ideal?' Jesus, Jack! We literally just came from my mother's funeral. Do you hear yourself?"

But he's undeterred. "Every time I try to bring it up, you brush me off. I just want to know what you're thinking. I used to know, Hazel. I used to know everything you were feeling, but now...you're a closed book."

I laugh, a harsh, bitter sound that surprises even me. "A closed book? You think I'm a closed book? Fine. You want to know what I'm thinking?" I step closer, feeling the anger bubbling up, surging past the numbness I've been trying to hold onto. "I'm frustrated, Jack. I'm angry. I feel overlooked and unappreciated.

I'm exhausted from all the eye rolls, the sighs, the disappointed glances. I'm tired of being tired."

He doesn't flinch. "Tired of what, Hazel? Say it."

I don't want to. I shouldn't.

But I do. "You. I'm tired of you."

Jack's face tightens, his jaw clenching as if the words physically hit him. "Real nice. Thank you."

"You asked." My voice is flat and emotionless, but inside, I feel the weight of it—the truth in what I've just said.

"What am I supposed to do with that?" He looks at me, eyes wide and pleading, as if waiting for me to pull back, to say something to make it all better.

But I don't. I can't.

"You've wanted to leave for a long time. You just won't admit it." I pause, watching him as the words sink in. "It's like you're waiting for permission. So here it is. Consider this my blessing."

For a moment, Jack just stands there, his mouth opening and closing like he's searching for the right thing to say. He looks lost, and maybe I should feel something—guilt, regret—but I don't. Instead, I feel numb.

When he finally speaks, his voice is low, shaky. "The break... it's not just for me. It's for both of us."

I look at him and nod slowly, knowing this was inevitable. After everything that's happened—the funeral, the silence, the years of missed connections—we are both already living in the space between the life we once shared and the future that no longer feels like ours.

CHAPTER
EIGHTEEN

I wake up the morning before my thirty-ninth birthday with a searing headache and eyes swollen from crying myself to sleep. As I lie there, chastened, I can't discern what I'm most upset about, my mother dying or my mess of a marriage. Both fractures happened slowly and without my foreseeing it. A string of poor decisions.

Overnight, guilt has settled in. *You. I'm tired of you.* I had not been gentle with my words and would now have to deal with the consequences of my brutal honesty.

The familiar sounds of my family shuffling around downstairs drift toward me. I dress quickly and head down the stairs, arranging a smile on my face as I turn the corner into the kitchen. Max sees me first, his ten-year-old face lighting up over his plate of chocolate chip waffles covered with sickly sweet syrup. They are the kind I'd never buy him, but Jack did the groceries last, probably in an attempt to be more helpful. Or maybe just to get out of the house and away from me, something he's been doing a lot lately.

"Morning, bud." Max's sweet face, moving further and further away from a child each day, makes my heart ache. I come to the distinct, immediate conclusion I want to shield him from my grief as much as possible. *Let him be a kid.*

Jack sits to Max's left, his hands wrapped around a steaming cup of coffee. His laptop is open in front of him, a news site open. He didn't look up when I first entered the room but does so now.

"How'd you sleep?" he asks after a beat.

I kiss the top of Max's head and then turn in search of my own cup of coffee. "Not great." It's a vast understatement, but I'm not looking to get into it. "You?"

We are so polite. So cordial. At this point, we don't know how else to act.

"Not well."

"Mommy," Max says, wiping his mouth with the back of his hand. I'm grateful it isn't his uniform shirt sleeve. "What do you want to do for your birthday tomorrow?"

I sip my coffee. "Absolutely nothing, bud. Hanging here at home with you sounds perfect to me."

"And Dad?"

I swallow past a lump in my throat. "And Dad."

"What about cake?" Max asks.

"No cake." No balloons, no birthday candles, no mention of age whatsoever. I don't need a reminder that I'm growing older. "It's just a day like any other."

I figure if I say it out loud enough, I might will it to be fact. But the truth is I'm only one year away from forty, and to me, there's always something about turning forty that feels so final, as though it can no longer be denied I'm officially aging.

Too young to be old, too old to be young.

The small silver lining is that Jack, a year older than me, is having his own issues with growing older. Aging is different for men than women. For one, Jack's worth in society will not diminish with every passing year the way mine will, and his graying hair is considered sexy while mine is something to be dyed and hidden away like a bad secret. What I really need is to stop caring about things like my hair. Yes, at fifty I will stop caring. I'll let the gray take over completely if it wants to.

Max's face falls.

"We could make something together," I offer. "Cupcakes?" I'll make him take them into school the next day so I'm not tempted to eat them all.

"With sprinkles?" Max's eyes are wide like saucers.

"Whatever you want."

Jack seems to finally take real notice of me. "You look nice."

He's lying, trying to make me feel better, trying to make up for the shitty things we've said to one another over the past couple years. The shitty things we said just yesterday.

"Oh...um, thanks." I turn my attention to Max. "You done eating, bud?"

I shoo him toward the bathroom to brush his teeth and do something with his hair. In the kitchen, Jack and I descend into silence. I sip my coffee and try not to wonder what he's thinking at the moment. It doesn't need to be said anyway. We've been moving around each other like walking on eggshells, looking but not quite looking at each other for months. Yesterday was a breaking point, a clear and distinct tear in the fabric of our marriage I'm not sure we can come back from.

The water turns off in the bathroom and Max appears fully dressed. Lunch in backpack, jacket and shoes on, and we're out the door. In the car, I back out of the garage and then reach back to hand Max my phone. "You're the emcee this morning."

The car quickly fills with the sounds of Taylor Swift. Jack groans whenever she comes on the radio, but I'm more accepting. Most of the time my thoughts drown out whatever is playing anyway. Max often becomes quiet in the car, which he gets from me, and so our morning carpool is often spent listening to whatever is playing through Car Play. He has a lot more to say after school: relaying a joke his Social Science teacher made or rehashing a silly argument he'd heard at recess. He's a good kid, smart and respectful, with a sensitive side that makes my heart ache. I know, firsthand, what can happen to kids like him. If only I could keep him in a bubble to protect him from the world and the people ready to tear him down.

Pulling into the school parking lot, I find the last spot available and back in. Through the windshield, I can already spot the gaggle of fifth grade mothers gathered by the gate. I know from experience they arrive at the same time each morning, a solid five minutes before the first of three bells, where they can talk to one another for the next fifteen minutes. At least half of them are dressed in athletic wear, another third clutching to-go cups in their hands. One of them, a blond with perfectly styled hair, is always dressed in a stylish suit, ready to dash off to whatever meeting is on her morning schedule. I always imagine that's what I'd look like had I worked in an office as opposed to working from home. These days I only dress up for Zoom calls with clients or for literary conferences which I mostly avoid. I know other agents who attend every conference they can, swearing by the connections made during the week-long events, but they have never been my thing and I've done just fine without them.

A few of the mothers' heads turn to look at me as Max and I approach the gate. I am certain they know I have just lost my mother. They must, otherwise why are they looking at me this way?

In the past they've tried to engage me in conversation, perhaps taking pity on us as new to the school this year, but I shrugged them off, feeling too nervous and self-conscious.

The bell goes off as soon as we reach the gate, and I bend down to kiss Max quickly on the cheek before he can run off. "Have a good day, bud!" I yell after him. From the corner of my eye, I can see one of the mothers watching me, her gaze searing into my back as I walk back to my car. She knows.

Eventually, I reach for my phone and pull up my brother's name, engaging the call. His voicemail picks up after four rings. "Hey Andy, it's Hazel—again. Call me back, okay? Please?"

I glance again at the group of women by the gate and, with a sigh, put the car in drive and head home. I hope Jack is not still there.

CHAPTER
NINETEEN

On the morning of my thirty-ninth birthday, it's not the alarm that wakes me as usual, but the shock of seeing my mother's face. I've dreamed of her before, but she is always in the periphery, untouchable and silent. Normally I can't see her face but know it is her. I can feel it is her. This time, we stand in her kitchen, the same one in which I watched her stir pasta on the stove—one of few meals she knew how to cook. She is standing over the stove but turns to face me, a spatula in her raised hand. I watch as her mouth opens, awaiting her first words to me in the twelve weeks since her death. I look my mother in the eye and then—

I awaken with a start. As the room calibrates around me, I feel the sting of tears behind my eyes. I've woken up every morning for the past three weeks in the same way.

The bed next to me is empty, untouched. I don't know where Jack has been sleeping and I don't really care. It's my birthday and I don't want to have to think about him or any of *that* today.

It's hard to get out of bed but I do so, knowing there is breakfast to be prepared and a child to take to school.

After I drop Max off, the day slips into routine. I make myself a cup of coffee, sit at my desk, and open my laptop. Manuscripts fill my inbox, waiting for feedback, and I sift through them one by one. The process is familiar, calming in its predictability—

reading, assessing, making notes for the authors. I catch glimpses of potential, flashes of brilliance, but most of the work feels ordinary. Still, I focus, letting the steady rhythm of work carry me through the day.

I try not to think about the fact I am another year older.

———

After dinner, there are cupcakes drowning in rainbow sprinkles. Max looks so damn proud of his work as he shovels a second one into his mouth. There's icing everywhere, but he doesn't care. I love that he doesn't care.

I reach for my phone and snap a photo, smiling at the result.

"Now one of you and Dad!" Max says, his face glowing with excitement.

Jack's stiffness mirrors mine as he comes around the table to stand next to me. We force smiles for the camera, a hollow gesture that doesn't reach our eyes. The moment Max lowers the phone, we break apart, retreating back to our separate corners, as though the brief connection through the lens was too much to hold onto.

I eat my cupcake slowly, the sugar coating my teeth, almost gritty against the tension in the room. Across the table, Jack picks at his, his eyes cast downward, saying nothing. The silence feels familiar now—comfortable in its discomfort. We've run out of words.

Max reaches for a third cupcake, and I stop him. "Two's enough, bud. You're going to give yourself an upset stomach."

He puts it on his plate anyway. "It's not for me," he says, his voice softening with an almost innocent earnestness. "We forgot you need to make a birthday wish. Do we have candles?"

I find some in the kitchen drawer, press a single candle into the center of the cupcake, and light it. The flicker of the flame feels strangely solemn.

It's hard to know what to wish for. It feels too late for so many things—the words Jack and I can't take back, my mother's absence, the soft lines etched between my brows. If I had been more honest with myself, maybe my life could have turned out differently.

I lean over the candle, pulling in a deep breath. My eyes meet Jack's across the table. The corner of his eyes are downturned and heavy with resignation. It's a look I recognize too well. It's the look of someone who's given up, who has made peace with what is, instead of fighting for what could be. I'm sure my eyes reflect the same.

I wish I had all the answers. And then I blow out the candle.

CHAPTER
TWENTY

My mother's face lingers in the haze between sleep and waking, tugging me into the harsh light of day. Jack is next to me. I feel the warmth of his body before I see him, and for a brief moment, I don't question it. But then reality floods in. I can't remember when he got into bed, or how we ended up pressed together in the night. Somehow, under the cover of darkness, we found our way back to one another. But now, in the unforgiving daylight, it's painfully obvious—we're lost.

One of us shifts first, and the space between us grows again. My neck aches from resting on his shoulder, and from the way he flexes his arm, I know he must be sore, too. I want to say something gentle, something that will keep this fragile peace alive a little longer, but my mouth betrays me.

"What are you doing in here?" I blurt out, startling both of us. The words spill out unchecked, jagged and sharp.

Jack meets my gaze, his expression unreadable. He seems to weigh his response, searching for the right way to say what he's been holding inside. "I wanted—" he pauses, then exhales like he's bracing for impact. "I needed to. Before…"

He doesn't finish, but I understand.

He needed to spend this last night together, even if neither of us will admit it's the last.

I inch closer to him, an ache of tenderness swelling inside me. His arms circle around me, pulling me to his chest, and for a moment, it feels familiar—safe, even. He rests his chin on my head like he always used to, and I close my eyes, letting the tears slip free. I feel his body tense, and I know he's holding back his own tears.

We eventually untangle, sitting up in bed like strangers trying to remember what comes next. The words we're avoiding hang heavy in the air, and I can't stand the silence any longer.

"How are we going to do this?" I ask, my voice barely above a whisper. It's the only question that matters now, but I'm terrified of the answer.

Jack shakes his head. "I don't know."

"You're not attracted to me anymore," I say, my voice cracking with the weight of it. The thought barely formed in my mind, but it tumbled out anyway, unstoppable.

He flinches, but he doesn't deny it. Instead, he says, "When you look at me, you're not really seeing me."

I nod slowly, the truth settling between us. "I know."

The silence stretches, thick and suffocating. He runs a hand through his hair, his brow furrowed with the weight of indecision. "Maybe I should be the one to go."

But that doesn't feel right either. Neither of us leaving feels right, yet one of us has to. We both know it.

He leans in and presses a soft kiss to my forehead. I hear the quiet hitch in his breath as he swallows hard. "I'll miss you."

I look into his pale eyes, so light they almost seem to disappear. I know the response I should give, but the words stick in my throat. I'm too exhausted, too hollowed out by all the unsaid things between us.

Because deep down, I'm not sure I'll miss him at all.

———

Two days after my birthday, I reach out to Daisy, and I'm surprised to find out she's still in town. She stayed after the funeral, just in case I needed her.

I always do. I always will.

We meet at Foxtail, and over the familiar comfort of coffee, I fill her in on everything that's transpired since we last saw each other. Daisy listens intently, her gaze soft and open, as if ready to catch all the pieces of my scattered heart.

When I finish, she leans back in her chair, a thoughtful smile playing on her lips. "So, what now? What do *you* want to do?"

I shake my head, feeling the weight of all the uncertainty. "It's always been him, Daisy. I've literally never been with anyone else."

Her smile grows warmer, not judgmental in the slightest. "Maybe this is why it feels so hard."

I blink, caught off guard. "What do you mean?"

Her laugh is gentle. "I think...maybe you've been so wrapped up in Jack and Max that you've forgotten about *you*. And it's okay to admit it. It doesn't make you a bad wife or mother."

I look down at my coffee, swirling the liquid in my cup. "I just...I never thought it would come to this. We've said such horrible things to each other. I don't know if we can come back from it."

Daisy reaches across the table, taking my hand in hers. "You don't have to know that right now. Maybe you guys just need some time. Some space to breathe and figure things out."

"For how long?" My voice trembles. "And...what if we don't come back from this?"

Her thumb rubs soothing circles over my hand. "Then you'll face it when it comes. But for now, don't think of it as the end. Think of it as a pause. A way to clear your heads, to really think about what you both need."

I nod, though uncertainty still gnaws at me. "I don't want this to hurt Max. He needs stability."

"Of course." Daisy nods, her voice softening with understanding. "Maybe you and Jack can take turns being home with him. That way, he's not dealing with too much change all at once."

"Maybe." I press my fingertips to my lips. "But what about Jack and me? Do we just...not talk?"

She hesitates for a moment, considering. "Maybe at first, some distance would help. Give you both time to think without all the emotion getting in the way. But you set the rules. You decide what feels right for you."

My eyes sting with unshed tears. "I just don't know how to do this, Daisy. I don't know what I want."

Her gaze softens further, and she gives my hand a gentle squeeze. "You don't have to have all the answers today. Take this time to focus on you for a change. You deserve that."

I let out a shaky breath. "I just...I don't want to be alone."

Daisy's smile brightens, the kind that makes you feel like everything will be okay. "You're not alone, Hazel. Not ever. You've got me. And I'll be here whenever you need, even if it's three a.m. and you just need to vent. Deal?"

I can't help but smile a little. "Deal."

"Good." She leans back, taking a sip of her coffee. "But I think it wouldn't hurt to make some new friends too. People you can lean on when I'm not around. As much as I wish I could stay here with you for as long as you need, Finn and the kids need me back home."

I reach across the table and clasp her hand tightly. "Thank you for being here." Then I sit back with a sigh. "As for making friends, I don't even know where to begin. My marriage is falling apart, I just lost my mother...what do I even have to offer anyone right now?"

Daisy meets my eyes, her expression so full of warmth and belief it makes me pause. "You, Hazel. You have *you* to offer. And that's more than enough."

CHAPTER
TWENTY-ONE

I t takes us ten days to come to an agreement we are both content with. Jack and I will be apart for the remainder of my thirty-ninth year. More than eleven months without contact other than logistics surrounding Max and trading off the house. We won't speak about what happens during our time apart, nor are we bound to any set of rules about what we can and cannot do.

When Jack asks me if I'm okay with this, I surprise myself by saying yes.

We aren't ending our marriage—this much is clear—but there's an unspoken understanding that anything can happen.

We will move slowly, carefully, which is what he tells me Sunday morning as he begins packing. His voice sounds too calm, too collected, and it irritates me how practical he's being while everything inside me feels like it's shattering into pieces. I want him to be more upset. I want him to show me some sliver of regret or doubt.

It happens quickly: Jack showers and packs an overnight bag, makes himself a sandwich, brews a cup of coffee for the road, and then he's at the door, looking back at me. I'm sitting on the couch, an open book in my hand, but the words blur into nonsense. I don't even know what I'm pretending to read anymore. We don't know what to say, so we say nothing.

Eventually, I stand, and we hug each other awkwardly. His arms feel foreign, like they're only half-committed to the embrace. I think about telling him I love him, but the words won't come out. What would they even mean now? Right now, "I love you" feels empty—meaningless, when I don't even like him very much at the moment.

After Jack leaves, the house feels impossibly quiet, the kind of silence that presses down on your chest, making it hard to breathe. I roam from room to room, touching things just to remind myself this is still my home. But it doesn't feel like home anymore. It feels like a place waiting for something to happen, and I'm terrified of what it might be.

I make coffee in the french press just for something to do. The act of pouring hot water over the grounds feels grounding, almost meditative. I drink it standing at the kitchen island, one eye on the door as if expecting Jack to come back and tell me this is all a mistake, that we don't need to do this. But he doesn't come back, and I don't call him. As much as it hurts, I know this is what we need. *Because* it hurts.

I had the foresight to send Max to a friend's house for the evening. I wanted to spare him the pain of watching his father pack. I don't know how to explain this kind of situation to an eleven-year-old in a way that doesn't make him feel like his world is crumbling.

He knows, though. He knows he'll come home tonight and it'll just be me. And in two weeks, his father will return, and I'll pack my own bag and leave. This back-and-forth existence feels cruel, but we tell ourselves it's for him, that we're doing this to keep his life as normal as possible.

The conversation with Max had been one of the hardest I've ever had. Trying to explain to him that his parents are going to live apart for a year without making it sound like we are abandoning him was nearly impossible. His eyes, wide and innocent, had searched my face for answers I couldn't give him. I had told him it was a family matter, something between the three of us, and I hoped that would keep the burden small and contained. But I could already see the worry forming in his mind, the questions he was too afraid to ask.

The silence in the house becomes unbearable, so I leave. I don't go far, just up the street to the nail salon. It's a run-down place, the kind where the air is thick with chemical fumes, but I let them slap on a new coat of sheer pink—the only color I ever wear. It's a small, meaningless decision, but it's one thing I can control. I sit in the car afterward with the windows down, waiting for the dizziness to pass before I drive home.

When I get back, the house is still. I make myself a cup of tea, more for the warmth than the taste, and carry it into the bedroom. I light a lavender candle Daisy gave me months ago, the one I had been saving for a special occasion.

I sit on the edge of the bed, scrolling through the channels on TV until I settle on a reality show. Twenty-five women competing for one man—it used to be fun to watch, but now it just feels hollow.

The door clicks open, and I hear Max's voice calling out for me. I listen to the familiar sound of his key landing in the dish on the hallway table. When he appears in the doorway of my bedroom, his large headphones hang loosely around his neck. He scratches his arm, a nervous habit he's had since he was little.

"Dad's gone?" he asks, his voice flat.

I nod, unable to find any words to make this easier. "He is."

"Okay." His face is impassive, but I can see the hurt in his eyes, the way he's already trying to push it down. He nods curtly, like he's trying to convince himself that everything is fine, and I hate we've put him in this position.

"You want to talk about it?" I ask, though I already know the answer.

He hesitates, his eyes flicking to the floor for just a second before he shakes his head. "No."

He turns and leaves, and I'm left alone again. I can't go back to the TV. The show feels ridiculous now, so I turn it off. The room plunges into darkness, and for a moment, I feel like I'm twelve again, afraid of the dark, afraid of not knowing what's coming next.

I knock on Max's door a little while later. I know he's been crying, even though he tries to hide it. His long hair falls into his eyes, and I have to resist the urge to push it back.

I close my eyes, remembering a time when things were simpler, when Jack and I were young and in love, sitting shoulder to shoulder on the floor of his dorm room, listening to music and feeling invincible. It feels like a lifetime ago.

I hug Max tightly, feeling his small body tremble just a little.

Jack is gone, and I have no idea what's going to happen next.

But what I do know is Max will have to live through this year, just like we will. And I worry—no, I *fear*—what this will do to him. He's strong, but how much can we expect an eleven-year-old to carry? How will he handle this? How will he handle the silence that will stretch between his parents, the awkwardness of passing between two houses?

I don't know, and it terrifies me.

PART TWO
CRASHING

CHAPTER
TWENTY-TWO

MARCH

The first person I want to call isn't Daisy or Jack—it's Andy. We haven't spoken since Mom's funeral, where we argued again about her not telling me she was sick. We went in circles, tempers flaring, but we never understood each other.

I wanted him to see I wasn't selfish, but we were both too stubborn. Now we're estranged, like strangers who share a past.

So why do I want to call him? Maybe because he's the only one who knows what it's like to lose her. And despite everything, he's still my brother. I miss that version of him.

What's the point? We'd end up in the same cycle—me explaining, Andy not believing. Still, I call him. He doesn't answer, but I'm surprised by the sound of my own voice—gravelly, desperate. This is who I am now.

I hang up and sit in the silence. Max is at school, and work waits, but I can't focus. I stare at my laptop and finally say, "I don't feel like working today."

Normally, I'd dive into emails or research, but today, I want my bed. I need time to grieve, to process, to feel. Maybe more than a day. Maybe two. Or ten.

The feeling hasn't lifted by the next morning. I try to walk it off, but every step feels electric, as if my body is vibrating with tension I can't shake. I think of Jack, then immediately scold myself for doing so. He probably hasn't thought about me since he left. He's likely—

Stop.

I pick up the pace, the March wind biting at my cheeks. I'm not just trying to walk off Jack, but the weight of everything— our separation, Mom, the guilt over Max.

As I near the house, I spot my neighbor with her dog. The irritation rises. Her dog barks constantly, but I've never said a word, always avoiding confrontation.

But today, something shifts.

"Hi. Morning," I say, surprising myself.

"Morning! How are you?" she asks, friendly and unaware.

Without thinking, I blurt, "Actually, I'm not great. Your dog barks all day. I work from home, and it's really disruptive."

Her smile drops, but I keep going. "A little consideration would help." My face flushes as the words hang between us. I can't believe I've said them.

"Anyway, have a great day!" I wave, walking up the driveway, feeling both mortified and triumphant.

Back inside, I call Daisy at work, and before she speaks, I hear the clicking of her keyboard.

"I think this break from Jack has shaken something loose in me."

She laughs. "Maybe that's a good thing."

"No, I'm serious. I just told off my neighbor about her barking dog."

"Good! You've been complaining about it for months."

"She's going to hate me."

"So what? Not your problem."

I pause. "It did feel good," I admit, pacing the kitchen. The silence stretches for a moment, and I hear voices on the other end, the sound of a door closing.

"Are you busy? I can let you go."

"I can talk. How are you doing with Jack gone?"

The first word that comes to mind is *relief*. I tell her this, and it feels like another truth I've been holding back.

"I get it. You needed some distance."

"It's more though," I continue. "I feel like I can finally be myself. I can cry about Mom without Jack judging me."

"Why would he judge you?"

"He doesn't understand why I'm grieving so hard. We weren't close, but I thought we'd have more time to fix things." My voice cracks, and I start to cry.

Daisy's voice is soft. "Oh, Hazel, I'm so sorry."

I let the tears come, finally feeling like I'm allowed to.

CHAPTER
TWENTY-THREE

The following day is gloriously sunny, as though someone up there has conspired to make it so I can't find anything to complain about. It would be easier to be sad if the sky weren't the bluest of blues without a cloud in sight.

After dropping Max off at school—and less-than-gracefully dodging the fifth grade moms with their perfectly curated lives—I settle into my home office to prep for my first call of the day. A potential client. A good one, too.

I re-read her query letter and first two chapters, trying not to be distracted by the way my heart races. This could be a big get.

I sip my coffee, and then launch Zoom. The screen flashes, and a young woman with curly black hair and stunning green eyes appears. Her nervous energy almost makes me smile.

"Good morning, Soraya. How are you?"

"I'm well, Mrs. Greenwood, thank you. A little nervous, but so excited to be talking to you."

Her nerves are endearing. I remember feeling like that once. "Please, call me Hazel. And don't worry, nerves are normal." I give her my best reassuring smile, even though my own hands are trembling out of sight. "I know you have questions, so feel free to dive right in."

"I guess my first question is...what stood out to you about my query?"

"Your pitch was well-written and made me want to read more." I smile, easing into familiar territory.

Soraya grins, scribbling something down.

"And what kind of editor are you looking for?" I ask.

"A cheerleader, honestly. Someone who loves my work as much as I do and knows how to sell it."

I nod, knowing exactly what to say next, but something about her sincerity makes me pause. "I want that for you, too."

Then she asks, "And what kind of people do you like to work with?"

My usual response sits on the tip of my tongue, ready to go, but instead, the words that come out are...unexpected. "Honestly? People who are a little messy. Who don't have it all figured out yet. I like it when they're not afraid to admit they're terrified."

Soraya's eyebrows shoot up just as I frown.

What?

The conversation continues, but I can't help being unusually honest. When she asks how many authors I've brought on, I reply, "Around fifteen to twenty a year, though not all are a great fit long-term."

Soraya blinks, and I quickly try to recover. "But I'm sure we'll work great together."

She smiles politely, though I feel the crack in my confidence. When she asks why I became an acquisitions editor, I say, "I always wanted to be a writer, but I'm not very good at it."

It is...not what I meant to say.

What *the hell* is wrong with me? Why am I being so brutally honest?

"Oh, but I'm sure we'll work great together," I blurt out, trying to backtrack. "I didn't mean—"

"It's okay," Soraya says, her voice light but uncertain. She's being polite, but the crack in my confidence is starting to show.

She shifts in her seat before asking, "So, what made you want to become an acquisitions editor?"

This should be the easiest question. I've answered it a hundred times. But today, my mouth seems to have a mind of its own. "I always wanted to be a writer, but I'm not very good at it."

Her eyebrows shoot up again, and I can feel my face flush.

"I mean, I love books," I say. "If I can't write them, at least I can help others bring their books into the world."

Soraya laughs awkwardly, and I force myself to smile.

"And you like your agency?"

I should just say yes and move on. But no—my traitorous mouth speaks again. "Well, every company has its advantages and disadvantages."

Her face freezes, and I can practically see the confusion behind her eyes. I've lost control of this conversation.

"Inklings is great, though. It's run by two incredible women, Joan Hampton and Teresa Beverly, and—" I'm losing her. "—and I was persistent, which is probably why I'm still here."

Silence. Pure, mortifying silence. Soraya stares at me like I've just confessed a dark secret. I laugh, but it sounds more like a nervous cough.

I arrange my face into something resembling composure. "Anyway," I say, clapping my hands together. "Shall we talk about your manuscript? Because I've been dying to."

Soraya's smile is back, but it's thinner now, more cautious. I can tell she's not sure what to make of me anymore.

Great. Just great.

———

I press my palms into the cool granite countertop and stare at myself in the mirror, moving my head first to the left, then to the right. There's a small pimple forming near my mouth, but otherwise, I look just as I did yesterday and the day before. Yet, something about me is undeniably different.

I think back to my conversation with Soraya, and my cheeks burn as I recall my absurd, unfiltered honesty. What the hell had gotten into me? I knew what I wanted to say, what I've always said in those calls, but the words wouldn't come out. It was like they were there, lodged in my throat, but—

Then it hits me. A ridiculous, irrational thought, yet it rings clear as a bell. I freeze. It can't be…right?

My hand trembles as I pull my phone from my back pocket and FaceTime Daisy. As the ringing sounds, my heart pounds harder with each chime. When she finally picks up, I practically shout, "I can't lie!"

Daisy squints at the screen, her mouth quirking in confusion. "What are you talking about?"

"I'm serious!" I set the phone down against the mirror, my hands shaking. "I can't lie! Ask me something—anything."

"Hold on, I'm pulling over." Her brow furrows as she glances away from the screen, probably thinking I've lost my mind. She parks and looks back at me, still skeptical. "Okay, what's going on?"

"I had a call with a potential author this morning, and she asked me why I became an acquisitions editor. I had my answer ready—my *usual* answer—but when I opened my mouth, something completely different came out. And then, with Jack, I—" My voice cracks, and I bury my face in my hands. "All the things I said to him..."

Daisy peers closer at the screen, her concern deepening.

From beside her I hear a deep voice say, "How much coffee have you had today? You're not making any sense."

I press my face into my hands. "You could have told me Finn was there with you."

"Hi, Hazel. How are you?"

"I think it's clear she's losing her mind," Daisy says.

"I'm serious!" I lift my head and stare at her through the phone, willing her to understand. "Ask me something. Anything."

Daisy lets out a long, exaggerated sigh, clearly humoring me. "Fine. What's your brother's name?"

"Andy." My brother's name is Andy. True.

But what if I try to lie?

I pause for a beat, mentally substituting the name Vaughan. "My brother's name is Va—" I stutter, choking on the word before it can fully escape my lips. I try again. "My brother's name is Va—" It catches again, like my mouth is physically incapable of forming the lie.

Daisy's brow furrows deeper. "Hazel...what is happening right now?"

I grip the countertop for support. "I told you; I can't lie!"

There's a little shuffling before Finn's face fills the screen. He rubs his hands together like he's just been handed the greatest opportunity of his life. "All right, Hazel. Tell me—you prefer pineapple on pizza, don't you?"

I stare at him, wide-eyed. Of all the ridiculous things!

I can't help but picture the sickly sweet fruit sitting atop perfectly good pizza, ruining it.

My mouth opens, and I want to say yes—just to prove him wrong, just to win—but the words refuse to come out. Instead, what slips through my lips is, "It's an abomination."

Daisy barks out a laugh. Finn looks delighted. "Oh, this is going to be fun," he says, winking at me.

I sigh, defeated. "Glad my misery is so entertaining."

Daisy, still processing, gripping the steering wheel tightly. "How is this even possible?"

"I don't know!" I moan, pressing my forehead into the cold surface. My mind is spinning, every potential explanation sounding crazier than the last.

"Did you rub any magic lamps recently? Or throw a penny into some enchanted fountain?" Her voice softens into a teasing lilt, though her lips twitch like she's fighting back a smile.

I let out a shaky laugh, even though I feel like crying. "This isn't funny! What do I do?"

Daisy falls silent, and I know she's gearing up to say something I won't like. "Maybe this is a good thing, Hazel. Maybe it's time for you to be brutally honest—with yourself and everyone else."

"I don't think I have any other choice," I mutter.

My phone buzzes with an incoming call, and I glance down to see Andy's name flashing on the screen. Normally, I'd pick up right away, but I'm too frazzled. I send him to voicemail, trying to focus on Daisy.

"Daisy, seriously, what do I do?"

She stares at me through the screen, her expression unreadable. "You have no idea when this started? Nothing weird happened before today?"

I rack my brain, trying to pinpoint when it all began. Was this some cosmic punishment? Is karma coming back to bite me for something? Maybe for all the times I've kept my mouth shut instead of saying what I *really* think?

"I think I'm losing my mind," I whisper, staring at my reflection as if it will offer some kind of answer.

Daisy shrugs. "Aren't we all? But seriously, when did this start?"

"This morning was the first time it felt...off," I say, rubbing my temples. "And then there was the awkward run-in with my neighbor. I felt weird then too."

"What about before?"

I squint, trying to remember. "The day we had coffee..."

"Yeah?"

"I don't know. Maybe something felt strange that day too?"

Daisy leans in closer, clearly intrigued.

I frown at my reflection, the pieces slowly clicking into place. "The day before...Jack and I talked about taking time apart. I remember waking up furious he was still sleeping next to me."

Daisy tilts her head. "And the day before that?"

"It was my birthday," I say, my voice trailing off as a memory surfaces. "We had dinner and cupcakes and..."

"And?" Daisy's eyes widen. "What?"

"The candle," I whisper. "The birthday wish."

"What did you wish for?" Finn asks.

I blink, the realization crashing into me like a wave. "I wished I had all the answers."

Daisy bursts into laughter, unable to hold it in. I stare at her, unamused, as she doubles over in her seat.

"Are you *done*?" I ask, exasperated.

"Sorry, it's just—" She wipes away a tear. "Miss 'avoids conflict at all costs' and 'hates ruffling feathers' can't lie anymore? This is going to be hilarious. Keep me on speed dial, okay?"

I groan. "This is a nightmare."

CHAPTER
TWENTY-FOUR

M y mother sits on her couch, a glass of iced tea in her hand. The television is on but she's not watching it. Instead, she is talking with Andy, who sits on a chair to the left of her. She is wearing a sweater that sits loosely on her thin frame and a pink satin scarf is tied around her head. Her eyes are even darker than I remember. I call out to her but nothing comes out.

I open my eyes and find the pillow wet.

———

I spend the next few days trying to lie. I repeat the words over and over in my head—my brother's name is Vaughan. My favorite season is winter. I loathe sushi—but the words stay lodged in my throat. I avoid the mothers at drop-off even more than normal and keep my mouth shut wherever I go. I feel as though I'm losing my mind.

Max and I make cupcakes, the same ones we made for my birthday. I'm out of sprinkles so we go to the store to buy more. When he's not looking, stuffing a second cupcake into his mouth while he watches television, I push a candle through the frosting, light it, and take back my birthday wish—*I no longer wish I had all the answers*. I blow.

My brother's name is Vaughan. My favorite season is winter.
"My brother's name is Va—"

"Mom?"

"My favorite season is win—"

"Are you talking to me?" Max looks at me curiously. A lone sprinkle is stuck to the side of his mouth and I resist the urge to pick it from his face like I would when he was younger.

"No. I'm—sorry." I look down at the cupcake, scoop some frosting with my pointer finger, and slip it into my mouth. I eat the rest of the cupcake, and then I eat another.

Max notices my quiet mood, leans back in his chair, and grabs another cupcake himself. He's not a kid anymore, but he's always known how to read me. "You okay?" he asks, his voice steady but concerned.

I nod, though it feels halfhearted. "Yeah. Just...thinking."

He watches me for a moment before shrugging. "If you need someone to talk to... you know, I'm here, right?"

His words surprise me. Max isn't usually one for heart-to-hearts. He's more into hanging with his friends and watching his favorite YouTubers these days. But there's a seriousness to him now, a subtle reminder he's growing up, whether I'm ready or not.

"Thanks, buddy," I say, my voice softening. I reach out and ruffle his hair, but he dodges it with a grin, pretending to be annoyed.

"You're getting frosting everywhere," he teases, eyeing the smudge on my hand. He tosses me a napkin, and I can't help but smile.

"Guess I am," I admit, wiping my hands. "But I'm still the cupcake expert around here."

Max rolls his eyes but gives me a small, knowing smile. "Sure, Mom. Whatever you say." He grabs the frosting spoon and hands it to me. "You wanna finish this off before I do?"

I chuckle, taking the spoon from him. "I'll share...this time."

He shakes his head, but I catch the glimmer of amusement in his eyes, and for the first time in days, I feel like things might just be okay—at least for now. We sit together in comfortable silence, sharing frosting and the quiet reassurance that, even in the middle of uncertainty, we've got each other.

———

The next morning I have a terrible stomach ache rivaling the feeling of dread I feel when I realize I still cannot lie. Did I really think I could just wish *whatever this is* away? Nothing is ever truly that simple, right?

I fight my disappointment all through breakfast, and into the car ride to school. Max, perhaps matching my mood, is nearly silent, absorbed in his eleven-year-old thoughts. As he has decided he's too old for me to walk him in, I sit in the car and watch him at the gates with his friends, laughing and playing around. A distinct longing for those joyful, simple days lodges itself in my chest.

You used to be so fun; do you know that? You used to be so carefree.

I shake Jack's words from my head and focus again on Max. He's walking toward the school building, his backpack slung over one shoulder, glancing back once before the bell rings and he disappears inside. I close the book I've been pretending to read and reach for my phone.

A new voicemail blinks on the screen. I hadn't noticed it before.

"It's Andy," he says, his voice tight, formal. A cold feeling prickles at the back of my neck. "I got your messages, and I just wanted to say… I can't do this right now."

He pauses, and I feel the distance between us stretch wider, an expanse that's been growing for years.

"I think you have the wrong idea of how this is going to go. You can't just expect to walk back into my life after all this time, acting like nothing happened, like you didn't—" His breath hitches, and I clench the phone tighter. "We're not kids anymore, Hazel. We're not the same people we used to be, and I'm just not who you seem to think I am."

Each word cuts deeper than the last.

"I'm not interested in digging up old wounds. Mom is gone,

and there's nothing we can do to change it, so why rehash things? Why talk about it at all?"

His words slam into me, hard and fast. I want to yell back, to defend myself, but the voicemail keeps playing, his voice emotionless, distant.

"I just... Please stop calling and texting me. I need space."

The line goes silent. A second later, I throw my phone, watching it hit the door over the seat next to me with a thud. I stare at the spot where it landed, my pulse pounding in my ears, anger and disbelief warring inside me.

Space? He's had nothing but space for years. Years spent holding me at arm's length, years spent hating me—without so much as a real conversation.

I bite down hard, trying to hold back the scream building in my throat. How can he not see it? After everything we've been through, after losing Mom...he should at least hear me out. He should at least try to understand. But no—he believes her. Believes I'm the kind of person who could ignore our mother's cancer, who could walk away and let him deal with it all alone.

The brother I knew would never think this of me. The boy who used to spend entire afternoons digging in the dirt with me, covered head to toe in mud, laughing like we had the whole world to ourselves—that Andy is gone. The boy who listened to every story I read aloud, who looked up to me like I was the most important person in the world...replaced by someone who wants nothing to do with me. A grumpy, bitter stranger who can't even see past his own hurt to consider mine.

Tears sting my eyes, but I blink them back. I can't cry over this. I've cried enough.

He's right, in a way. We aren't the same people anymore. We're older, and maybe some parts of us are gone for good. But it doesn't mean the bond we had is completely lost. He thinks shutting me out will protect him, but it won't.

I sit back against the car seat, wrapping my arms around myself. The pain in my chest is sharp, an ache that doesn't go away no matter how much time passes. I thought maybe after everything, we could find a way back to each other. But instead, I'm met with more walls and more distance. How long can I wait for him to come around? How long before he realizes he's not the only one hurting?

I'll give him space—because it's all I can do right now. But I know, deep down, this isn't over. We need each other, whether he admits it or not. He just doesn't see it yet.

But he will. He has to.

I startle when a shadow crosses over the book in my lap. Outside my car window stands one of the fifth grade mothers, the one with jet black hair falling in perfectly symmetrical curls over her shoulders. I've never seen her wearing workout clothes, and for this I respect her. I roll down my window.

"I'm sorry, I didn't mean to scare you," she says. Her voice is deeper than expected, almost raspy. She reminds me a little of Emma Stone. "I'm Amelia, Reese's mom. You're Max's mom, right?"

"Hazel," I say. "And yes."

"He's such a great kid. He and Reese seem to get along well."

I don't know Reese, don't recognize the name. But I say, "That's nice." And I mean it.

Amelia looks down at the book in my lap. "What are you reading?"

I turn over the book in my lap, a worn, copy of *One Hundred Years of Solitude* so she can see the cover. She looks impressed and I try not to take it as an insult, even though I've been trying to read the damn thing for three years.

"You know, I'm part of a book club that meets once a month. It's nothing intense, just me and a few of the other moms." She leans forward. "You should join in."

Daisy's words echo in my head, *It wouldn't hurt to make some new friends*, and with it my same worry I couldn't possibly have anything to offer new friends right now. It seems entirely out of the realm of possibility.

"No pressure, it just seems like something you'd be into." Amelia taps her ring on my car and takes a couple of steps back as though she's trying not to spook me. After months of me avoiding their attention, I'm not at all surprised.

When I tell her I'll think about it, I know I'm telling the truth.

CHAPTER
TWENTY-FIVE

"Do you know much about Reese's mom?" I ask Max once we've pulled away from the school that afternoon. In the rearview mirror, I see him shrug.

"Not really. She's nice though," he adds unhelpfully. "Always says hi when she sees me around. Has good snacks in her purse."

I grin. Boys are all the same: driven by their stomachs.

"Why?"

It takes me a moment to even remember what I've asked him. "Oh, I was just wondering. I might...spend some time with her is all."

"*Mom*," he groans. "Just don't embarrass me in front of my friend."

I want to tell him I haven't done anything. I'm only sitting with the idea. But it won't matter to him. *I won't*. But I say, "I can't make any promises."

"*Mom*," he says again. We descend into silence, the soft whir of the car's motor filling the space between us. I try not to think about how, in a matter of days, I will be leaving the house so Jack can come home, that I don't yet know where I will go. I don't know where Jack has been or how he is spending his time—or with whom.

I remind myself it's none of my business.

I think about a conversation I had with Daisy, how I told her Jack had always been *it* for me. I'd never been with anyone else.

She'd looked at me with a knowing expression. *Maybe that's why this feels so hard.*

She was right, but it doesn't make it easier. I have to stop this spiral, this constant need to know. And I know there's only one person who can help me get a grip.

Daisy picks up on the third ring, her voice slightly out of breath. "How are you handling everything?" I can hear her kids shouting and running around in the background.

I try to explain the obsessive thoughts, the Googling. I can't quite articulate the helplessness I feel, like there's this piece of me running around out there, completely out of my control. "I don't want to care, Daisy, but I do. I just...I need to know if he's as miserable as I am."

"He probably is," she says, but I can hear the caution in her voice.

"But how would I even know? I used to love he wasn't on social media, but now I wish he was! At least then I'd have some clue—"

"You have to stop, Hazel. No good can come from this," she interrupts, her tone shifting from sympathetic to firm. And she's right—I know she's right. "I want you to do something for me, okay? Go grab a pad of paper or open up your laptop—it doesn't matter which—and make a list of everything you can do during this time apart from Jack. Big things, little things, anything that comes to mind."

I let out a long sigh, leaning back against the bathroom wall and feel the cool tiles against my spine. "And?"

"And," she continues, "I want you to make a second list. A more fun one. Write down all the things Jack does to annoy you." There's a smile in her voice now. "Every single little thing. Put it all down on paper. And whenever you feel yourself getting lost in thoughts about him, I want you to read over those lists."

I switch the call to speaker, Daisy's voice echoing softly in the tiled room. "Okay," I mutter, feeling the weight of the idea settle into my chest. "It's not a bad plan."

"It's a great plan," she says. "Because here's the thing—you can't control what Jack is doing right now. You can only control what you do. And obsessing over him is going to keep you trapped in a place you don't want to be."

I swallow the tightness in my throat, forcing myself to listen to her. She's right, again. This constant wondering about what Jack is up to isn't going to bring me peace. I know how easily I get sucked into the vortex of overthinking, and how quickly I can lose myself in questions that will never be answered.

"I just want to feel better," I say, my voice cracking slightly. "No, not true. I'd settle for fine. I just want to feel *fine.*"

"You will, Hazel," Daisy says softly. "It's just going to take time. You need to give yourself that."

Time. The word echoes painfully, reminding me of Andy's voicemail. *Please stop calling and texting me. I need space...*

I push the thought aside, but it lingers like a bruise.

Daisy's voice continues, soothing in its familiarity, reminding me I'm not alone, even though everything feels like it's unraveling.

"I'll start on those lists," I say, more to myself than to her. Because maybe that's what I need—a reminder of the things I can control, a way to focus on me instead of him.

———

The morning of the house swap, I wake up to the image of my mother's face, frowning. Until now, it has never occurred to me to wonder what she would think about what Jack and I are doing. To wonder what she would think is a silly pursuit, but I can't stop my thoughts from drifting in that direction and I bring myself to standing. *You've got it all wrong,* she'd say. In the kitchen, I prepare tea. *This can only end poorly,* she'd add. I drink my tea slowly, savoring the quiet morning. *He's going to fuck someone else, and what then?* she'd ask. Nausea washes over to me, and I make it to the sink just in time to eject my drink all over the white porcelain.

From behind me comes a small voice. "Mom? Are you okay?"

I wipe my mouth with the dish towel and turn to Max. "No, bud, I'm not." After three weeks, I'm no longer surprised by my candor, even if I wish I could turn it off like a light switch when it suits me.

"What's wrong?"

I have to look away from the eyes he shares with his father. "I'm just sad," I say. It's the only truth I can give him right now.

Max presses his body against mine, his head tucking neatly under my chin. I breathe in his scent—a mixture of shampoo and pre-teen boy.

"I miss him too," he says. I don't correct his assumption. He should go on believing what he believes.

"I'm going to miss *you*." I squeeze him tighter. "Be good for your dad."

Max releases me. "Where are you going to stay?"

"Probably at a hotel."

His face lights up. "You can order room service!"

I don't have the heart to tell him I'll probably end up at a two-star hotel without room service but offers a fairly respectable continental breakfast. It's a temporary fix for a problem I do not yet have a solution to. At some point, I'll have to come up with something more permanent.

I mutter a noncommittal *hm* and pour the remnants of my tea down the drain. "Pour yourself a bowl of cereal or something, okay? I'm going to go hop in the shower."

After stripping down, I stop in front of the slightly chipped full-length mirror and study my body, starting with my hair which doesn't grow quite as quickly as it used to. There's a little extra skin below my chin, but my chest is holding up well enough, and while there is loose skin around my middle I can grab with an entire fist, I understand with something close to pride that this belly housed a child and isn't supposed to look like it did before.

I promise to love you even when you're forty and squishy, and when you're fifty and sixty, and even when you're seventy and most certainly squishy all over.

I think about Jack's words until I make myself sick again, diving for the toilet.

Later, in my sad little hotel room, suffocating under the stench of self-pity, I sit on the scratchy bedspread and open a new document on my laptop. The dim light flickers above me, and for a moment, I think about how tired I am of overthinking everything. What's right, what's wrong—none of it matters anymore. I just need to let go and write.

Things I Can Do During Our Separation

1. *Sleep in the middle of the bed*
2. *Use the bathroom with the door open*
3. *Eat cheese and crackers in bed and not feel guilty about crumbs*
4. *Order pizza with mushrooms on it—extra mushrooms*
5. *Kiss someone new*
6. *Cook only meals I like*
7. *Read as much as I want to*
8. *Work as much as I want to*
9. *Go out as much as I want to [first, need to meet some new people to go out with]*
10. *Load the dishwasher however I see fit*
11. *Take as long as I want getting ready for bed—not feel guilty for taking the time to care for my skin every day.*
12. *Watch a movie or TV show without Jack interrupting to ask inane questions.*
13. *Wear only comfortable bras and underwear—fuck underwires!*
14. *Masturbate whenever I feel like*
15. *Not have to listen to Jack keep me up all night with his snoring only to then tell me in the morning, when I complain about it, that he doesn't snore*
16. *Listen to all the music I know Jack hates*
17. *Sleep with someone else?*
18. *Work on figuring out how we even got to the point of needing this separation*
19. *Wear whatever I want without trying to look good for anyone*

I sit back and stare at the list, feeling a flicker of relief, like a little of the weight on my chest has lifted. It's not perfect. It's not going to solve everything. But for the first time in a long while, I feel a little bit in control of something. Even if it's just my thoughts.

I get ready for bed slowly, methodically, my mind still buzzing but quieter now. The cheap bathroom light flickers, casting shadows on the walls. I look at my reflection, at the tired lines under my eyes, the faintest hint of puffiness still lingering from days of holding it all in. There's an annoyance bubbling just beneath the surface—annoyance at this crappy hotel, annoyance at Jack, but mostly, annoyance at myself for being *here* in the first place.

I know what's coming next. The quiet. The suffocating darkness that creeps in once the lights go out. Grief, sharp and relentless, will rise up and swallow me whole. I'll toss and turn, my body betraying me as it fights the sleep I so desperately need.

I slip under the covers and let out a shaky breath, already bracing myself for what's coming. This is where I am now—alone with my thoughts, with my list, with the space I didn't ask for but now have no choice but to face.

Because it's real; this thing we're doing. This silly, fucked up thing.

CHAPTER
TWENTY-SIX

I wake disoriented, my mind thick with remnants of sleep, my mother's face lingering behind my eyelids. It takes a moment to remember where I am—the strange, unfamiliar walls, the sterile, chemical smell clinging to the air. The hotel room. The temporary, sad little box that feels nothing like home. Only two nights here, and I'm already desperate to be back in my own space, surrounded by the familiar: my books, my shower, the clutter I always tell myself I should get rid of but never do. Home with Max and—

Jack.

The thought of him still sneaks in, uninvited, like a reflex I can't control. I pull myself out of bed, the stiffness in my limbs a reminder I barely slept. I wonder how long it will take for this to stop, for the "we" to dissolve into "I." How long until I stop inserting his name into every thought, every memory, still catching myself thinking, *Wait until Jack hears this.* My heart is stubborn, clinging to the idea of us, even as my mind knows better. Even as everything we were—shiny, special, beautiful—fades into the past.

The days bleed into each other, a slow blur of nothingness. I try to work, but the words on the screen swim, refuse to stay still long enough for me to make sense of them. My thoughts scatter before I can pin them down. I close the laptop more often than not, staring at the dull walls, waiting for time to pass.

I think of the list I wrote, the one meant to remind me of all the things I could do now that Jack isn't around. I've memorized it in the lonely hours since, but it feels pointless now.

I don't want to watch a movie without him asking stupid questions.

I don't have a dishwasher to load incorrectly in this barren hotel room.

I traded Jack's snoring for sleepless nights, my overactive mind refusing to quiet down. Even the promise of freedom—of doing whatever I want—rings hollow. I don't feel like kissing anyone new, and the thought of masturbating feels like a chore rather than an indulgence.

I shut down the computer, crawl back into bed, and turn off the light. The quiet wraps around me, oppressive. All I want is sleep—sleep to drown out the noise in my head.

———

I wake again, hours later. The clock reads 4:02 a.m. The silence is thick, pressing in on me from all sides. I think of Andy, of the voicemails I've left him, still unanswered. I wonder how Max is dealing with all of this, how he's processing the sight of his parents in two different places. Is he okay? Is Jack talking to him about what's happening, or are they just skating around it like I am?

My mind drifts to my mother. The day I took Jack to meet her for the first time, the way she barely touched her lunch, picking at her food like it was a task. Her thick chestnut hair was dark and glossy then, so different from her natural hair.

Should I have known then that something wasn't right?

I close my eyes again, trying to shut out the memories, but they're stubborn, clinging to the edges of my consciousness. No matter how much time has passed, she's always there, lingering.

The room feels too small, too quiet, and I roll onto my side, staring into the darkness. I know what's coming—the slow, inevitable crawl of the morning, another day of the same fog, the same aching thoughts I can't escape. And yet, all I can do is wait. Wait for sleep to come. Wait for time to pass. Wait for the day when this no longer feels like a nightmare I can't wake from.

CHAPTER
TWENTY-SEVEN

I decide it's time to take my own advice and step out on my own, even if I'm not entirely sure I'm ready. I pick a familiar spot, somewhere safe. The restaurant hums with life as I walk in, and though my heart flutters nervously, I square my shoulders and approach the hostess.

"Table for one, please."

Her bright-eyed, fresh-out-of-high-school look almost makes me second-guess myself, but I follow her to a small table in the center of the room. It's not the tucked away corner I hoped for, but I force a smile and sit down, my spine straight, trying to project a confidence I don't fully feel.

When the server arrives, I order a glass of wine. Pinot Grigio. Light, safe, but still an indulgence. After placing my order—a simple miso soup and avocado egg rolls—I pull *Pineapple Street* from my purse. The familiar weight of the book steadies me, and I dive into its pages, letting the story sweep me away.

By the time my food arrives, I've made it through a passage that makes me laugh—Sasha's childhood crush on Harrison Ford is painfully relatable—and I sip my wine, feeling a little more at ease. The egg roll is crispy and warm, and I don't even care when a bit of oil dribbles down my chin.

This solo dinner might not be as scary as I thought. It's...free-ing. There's something powerful in the quiet. Just me, the sound of soft chatter around the restaurant, and the gentle clink of silverware against plates. No expectations, no need to make conversation or perform. For the first time in what feels like forever, I'm not worried about anyone else's comfort but my own.

I sit up a little straighter, letting the feeling sink in—the calm, the stillness, the idea that maybe, just maybe, I don't need anyone here to enjoy myself.

I take another sip of wine, savoring the crisp taste, and realize the knot of anxiety I had coming in is gone. There's no judgment, no sideways glances. The world didn't stop because I walked into a restaurant alone. If anything, it feels like the world has opened up a little wider, offering me a version of myself I'd forgotten existed—someone independent, someone who can find joy without needing to share it with anyone else.

A small smile plays on my lips. *I did it.*

For the first time in a long time, I'm enjoying my own company. I'm not just enduring the quiet or distracting myself from loneliness. I'm relishing it. There's something so intimate about being alone with my thoughts, without the buffer of another person to fill the silence. And in this quiet space, I realize how rare it is to feel this—truly content, just as I am.

I feel proud, like I've broken through some invisible wall, one I didn't even know was holding me back. The wall telling me I had to be with someone to be happy. I had to be part of a couple, a pair, to be whole. But here I am, in the middle of a bustling restaurant, entirely on my own—and it's enough.

I glance around the room, watching the ebb and flow of people coming and going, and I don't feel out of place. I don't feel like I'm missing something or someone. I'm not hiding behind my book or my phone, trying to look occupied so no one notices I'm here alone. I'm just *here*. Fully present. And I like it.

Just as I'm considering a second glass of wine, a young couple walks in and is seated at the table directly across from me. At first, I glance up casually, but something about them pulls my attention like a magnet. I try to ignore it, to keep reading my book, but my eyes flick back again. And again.

They're lost in each other. The way he gazes at her, as if

every word she says is a secret he's desperate to hear. The way she leans in when he speaks, her hand casually resting on his arm like it's the most natural thing in the world. Their legs brush under the table, small gestures of intimacy that seem effortless.

It's too familiar. Too close.

A memory of Jack surfaces before I can stop it. The way we used to sit this way, our conversations laced with unspoken promises, our touches full of meaning. I remember the warmth of his gaze, the way I'd lean into him like she does now, hanging on to every word. For a moment, I feel it all over again—the joy, the comfort of being with someone who made the world feel smaller and simpler.

Then it hits me, sharp and sudden. It's gone. Jack's gone. And I'm sitting here, alone.

My throat tightens, and I wave down the server, asking for a second glass of wine after all. I down it faster than I should, but the dull warmth of the alcohol doesn't touch the ache in my chest. I can't stop watching them, can't stop seeing everything I lost reflected in their easy affection.

Before I know it, tears prick the corners of my eyes. I can't cry here. Not now. Not over this.

I pay my check quickly, fumbling for cash, and throw a too-large tip on the table. One last glance at the couple, so full of everything I had and lost, and then I rush out of the restaurant, the weight of it all pressing down until I can barely breathe.

———

I wait until I'm back at the hotel to call Daisy, pacing the room as I dial her number. The second she picks up, the words tumble out in a confused, breathless monologue, fragmented and jumbled. She has to tell me three times to slow down and start from the beginning.

"I took myself out for dinner," I start, trying to breathe between sentences. "Good!" she says, sounding relieved. I tell her about the two glasses of wine, the amazing food, and how much I'm enjoying the book I'm reading. Then I get to the couple at the next table, the way they looked at each other, how it tore me apart in ways I hadn't expected.

"Oh," she says, her voice softening. And then, silence. A silence so heavy, so full of meaning, but I'm too wrapped up in my whirlwind to recognize it. I charge ahead.

"And this hotel...It's fine, but I'm so lonely. I thought I might enjoy some time away from Max, from parenting, from the day-to-day grind, but I *hate* it, Daisy. I literally hate it."

I hear her breathing on the other end, steady and quiet, as I keep spilling. "Maybe...would you want to come out here for a few days? Or no, wait—I should come to you! You've got room, right? I'd stay out of your hair, I promise." My voice is too eager, too desperate, but I don't stop. I don't even know why I'm asking if she has room. I know she does. I've stayed with her before, in her guest room with the rich teal walls that make you want to sink in and stay forever.

And while I'm there, I could surprise Andy. He'd probably be shocked, but in a good way, right? I mean, how could he say no to me showing up at his door? He just needed a little time, but if he saw me, things would be different...

"Hazel," Daisy cuts in, her tone gentle but firm. "You're spinning out. It's your first week away. It's going to feel weird and hard, but it'll get easier. I promise."

I blink, realizing she's not entertaining my offer to visit, not engaging in my plan to show up at Andy's door unannounced. Something cold and uncomfortable stirs in my stomach. That creeping self-consciousness, the one saying I'm being too much, too needy, too...everything.

I hear papers shuffling in the background, and Daisy sighs. "Listen, I have to go, but I really hope you're doing the lists we talked about."

I hesitate, the energy draining from me all at once. "I started the one about things I can do during the separation."

"That's great! And the other one?"

I bite my lip, feeling a weight settle in my chest. "I...I'm not ready yet. Writing about all the things Jack does to annoy me feels...wrong. Like something I should do when I'm not so sad. I don't know."

"I get it," she says, but there's something in her voice that feels distant, detached. "I'm proud of you for going out to dinner tonight."

I want to believe her, to feel the sincerity behind her words, but they sound hollow, almost rehearsed. Still, I manage a quiet, "Thank you," before we end the call.

I set my phone down on the nightstand and sit on the edge of the bed, staring out at the bland hotel room. I should feel proud of myself for getting through the day, for taking the first step on my own. But instead, all I feel is this gnawing sense I'm doing everything wrong. Not just the separation, but my life. My friendships. Rather—friend*ship*, singular.

I know what I have to do. I've been avoiding it for too long, hoping things would just fix themselves. But they won't. Not unless I start making the changes I've been too scared to face.

I arrive at Max's school early Friday morning, hoping to find Amelia before the others arrive. The parking lot is nearly empty but the drop-off lanes are full of various sized SUVs that release a string of kids every ten feet or so. It isn't until I spot Jack's white sedan I realize my mistake.

I try not to look, I really do. But his window is rolled down, granting me a clear view of his perfectly tanned forearm and the profile of his face framed with black Ray-Ban glasses. He smiles at Max as he exits the car and he must shout something after him as Max turns suddenly, dazzling him with a bright smile that melts my heart. I watch Jack from my parking spot until he is out of sight, my chest burning the entire time. He looks *good*.

I'm stuck on this thought for far too long, long enough for me to finally notice the second bell has rung and Amelia and the women are returning to their cars. I jump out of the car and practically run after them.

Amelia sees me approach. "Oh, hi!"

"The book club," I say. I'm speaking out of order, suddenly nervous. "Hi, sorry—the book club...if the offer still stands, I'd like to join."

Some form of silent communication transpires then, between Amelia and the others, voiced only through eye contact. I consider changing my mind right then and there just so I never again have to witness this look. I go so far as to open my mouth before deciding against it.

When Amelia looks at me the others follow suit. She motions to the phone in my hand. "Give me your number and I'll text you the details. We meet tomorrow night if it's not too short of notice."

I haven't had Saturday night plans in months. Except—I've said it out loud.

Two of the women have the grace to look down at their feet but one looks right at me as though to reinforce the fact she heard me. It is a look of pity—the first, I'm sure, of many that will come my way should the truth of my life come out.

I ignore her.

As soon as I'm home, I text Daisy with the news.

CHAPTER
TWENTY-EIGHT

make the rookie mistake of arriving at Amelia's empty-handed. Everyone else has come prepared with bottles of wine or snacks displayed on platters and wrapped in cellophane. The mother who is always dressed like she's off to a fancy work meeting has brought both, and hands them to Amelia triumphantly. I wish I could melt into the wall behind me.

Introductions are made. I learn the woman in head-to-toe athletic wear is Jenny and the redhead is Lucy. Miss Business is Quinn, who works high up the chain at Citibank. She wears a perpetual scowl I have to think comes from the stress of dealing with people and their money daily. She appears unimpressed by my presence, as though the book club is some illustrious club with a year-long waitlist. It's clear she takes herself far too seriously.

Jenny and Lucy, on the other hand, are warm and welcoming. They pat the seat between them on Amelia's couch and ask me to sit down, which I do feeling abnormally calm for a situation that would usually fill me with unease. Small talk is not my forte.

The book they've all read this month is *The Storied Life of A.J. Fikry*, which I read a few years back, and so only had to skim the day before.

Amelia starts with a question she reads from the back of the book. "At the beginning of the story, Amelia says she is considering quitting online dating. How would you compare the act of buying books online to the act of dating online? Is it relevant to the story that Amelia meets her eventual husband in a very analog location, a bookstore?"

I have to admit, I wasn't sure what kind of book club this would be. I've heard of clubs where no one ever opens their books, only drinks and complains about their husbands and children. I'm pleased to find it's not this kind of club.

"Easy," Lucy says. "We're all judging a book by its cover." She smiles, pleased with herself. *Oh, so you're one of those people.*

"I would hate to know what people think of me at first glance," Jenny says. "I've been told I'm not exactly everyone's cup of tea."

I sit still, saying nothing. I don't yet trust myself to speak.

"Oh shut up, you're gorgeous," Amelia says, and she's right. Jenny probably wears all that tight Lycra because she has the perfect body for it—all thin and lithe with toned arms and probably very little cellulite. I just recently charged a double order of something called B-Tight I'm hoping will firm up my rear end enough it looks like I go to the gym on a semi-regular basis, which I do not.

"And that's all men will see at first."

Jenny says, "Yeah, but try getting them to stick around long enough to get past the first few chapters when things really start getting interesting."

"Men suck," Lucy says, and I hold my breath.

"Uh uh, no. We're not going down that road again," Quinn says, her voice tinged with annoyance. "Moving on. I loved the line"—Here she flips through her book until she finds what she's looking for—"'The things we respond to at twenty are not necessarily the same things we'll respond to at forty and vice versa. This is true in books and also in life.'"

"Yes! I have a question related to that." Amelia looks down at her notebook. "Have you revisited an old favorite and discovered it didn't hold your interest like it once did? Or, like A.J., have you found a new appreciation for something you didn't enjoy in your youth?"

"Skin elasticity," Jenny says dreamily, and I laugh even though her outfit has made me think a little less of her.

Amelia says, "When I was ten, I thought there would never be a book better than *Deenie* by Judy Blume, so I wouldn't pay much attention to my opinions on literature. I depend on you guys to expand my horizons."

Lucy takes a moment to think through her response. She smiles as she speaks. "Great sex. You think you're living it up, enjoying it while you can, but one day you wake up and realize you've shackled yourself to one penis for the rest of your life."

We're all still laughing when Quinn adds, "I never appreciated my thick hair," which confuses me because her hair looks plenty thick to me. I try not to stare at her.

Eventually, I realize they're waiting for an answer from me. "Oh. Um—" I scramble to think of something. "When you're young, adults are always telling you to look at a particular view, but I honestly think it's something you can't appreciate until you're older. Now a sunset over The Strip or snow covering the tips of Mount Charleston is enough to stop me in my tracks." My answer evokes a few murmurs of understanding.

Amelia consults her notebook once again. "The author chooses to end the novel with a new sales rep coming to an Island Books no longer owned by A.J. Did you like this ending?"

"I thought it was sweet," Lucy says. "Like maybe now it's his turn to fall in love."

"Same," I add, though it's entirely unhelpful. I look up to see Quinn suddenly avert her eyes, as though the family portrait hanging behind my head is much more interesting than whatever it was about me she was just studying so intently. I am certain she doesn't like me, and equally certain I don't care if she does or not.

"He better make sure whoever he ends up with is good in bed!" Lucy says, cackling.

"You're awfully obsessed with sex," I say before I can stop myself. I look anywhere but at Quinn, not wanting to know how she has reacted to my outburst.

Not again...

Lucy's smile is brilliant. "Shouldn't we all be? We're gorgeous women in the prime of our lives!"

"Speak for yourself," Jenny says, but she is smiling. "I don't feel like I'm in the prime of anything."

"Oh, I see. You're not having the great sex," Lucy says in a mock whisper.

Jenny makes a noncommittal face. I can't blame her, it's best to stay quiet at a time like this.

"What about you, Hazel? I hope you know what I'm talking about!"

Oh.

I don't want anyone to know about my marriage. In an ideal world, no one besides Jack, Daisy, and me would know, but I certainly don't want these women to know. Don't want their pitying glances and turned-down mouths, drooping shoulders, and cocked heads. The problem, of course, is I can't control myself. If one of them asks, I have no choice but to tell them the truth, which is that we're…separated, I guess. Temporarily.

"Lucy, for god's sake, you've just met the woman. At least let her get through one meeting before you're asking about her sex life." Amelia catches my eye and shakes her head, a smile tugging at her lips. She continues to watch me.

"Fine," Lucy says. She throws herself back against the couch so roughly it sloshes the water in my glass onto my pant leg. She waves her hand at Amelia, urging her to continue.

"I don't have this written down, but I was just thinking about how this book brings to life the importance of human connection. Any thoughts?"

"Is it really such a surprise? That human connection and social contact is important?" Quinn asks. "I don't think we need to be reminded in the books we read, do you?"

I snort, and all eyes fall on me.

Quinn's brows jump revealing thin lines across her forehead. I'd clock her at somewhere about my age, but you never can tell with anyone these days. "You disagree?"

"No, not at all. I think you're exactly right. I just don't see the problem with it being reinforced in literature."

She waves her hand dismissively. "To each his own, I suppose."

The conversation moves on but I can't seem to follow it. I'm too caught up in Quinn's response. Her entire attitude, really. The fact that no one has called her out only seems to reinforce the idea in my mind this is just who she is. If she's the type of "friend" I can look forward to making, I'd rather just stay home.

The skin on the back of my neck prickles as though someone is watching me, and indeed, when I slowly lift my gaze, I find Amelia watching me quietly and curiously.

As for making friends...what do I even have to offer anyone right now? Daisy makes sure to look me right in the eye when she says, You have you to offer. And that's more than enough."

I feel entirely unsure these are women I could be friends with. Then again, making new friends as an adult is often more a matter of proximity than anything else.

I shoot Amelia an uncertain smile which she only half-heartedly returns and think about the motel room waiting for me. If I don't want to spend all my time in my room, alone, I've got to make this book club work.

CHAPTER
TWENTY-NINE

I spend my final night and day at the hotel shuttling between the purple-walled isolation of my room and the sterile emptiness of the business center, trying to convince myself that at least here, in this dull corner of the world, I'm not hiding from everyone. The first book club meeting was a disaster, and I've spent every hour since agonizing over all the ways the others could implode too. But I know that hiding—especially during this separation from Jack—isn't going to fix anything. It's just more avoidance.

By Sunday night, as I pack my things to go home, I'm completely drained—drained by the games I've been forced to play all week, games I'm no longer any good at. I can't even dodge direct questions about the string of disheartening editorial letters without my face betraying me. When my colleagues show me their latest projects, I've lost the ability to feign even polite interest. I've spent the week giving tight-lipped responses, half-truths that aren't even half believable, and postponing meetings to dodge conversations I know I can't have.

Nine weeks ago, I could've breezed through a meeting with the Managing Editor of Fiction. I would've reassured her with confidence that I was in close contact with Atlas, the tech-nothriller author I've been wrangling for two years. I'd have said, yes, he's taking longer than we anticipated but I have faith. Now, every time I try to speak, the words tangle in my throat. I can't lie, can't even stretch the truth. And I don't want to admit how, despite my constant efforts, Atlas hasn't written a word in six months.

I'm trapped in this unbearable honesty. I have to postpone the meeting again, knowing full well it's just a temporary solution—a flimsy bandage on a wound that's gaping wider every day. If only I could reverse this bizarre curse, this birthday wish gone horribly wrong. But no. I'm stuck with this relentless truth, and it's exhausting.

———

As soon as I step through the door, I'm hit with the full weight of the reality I've been avoiding. It's the absence that strikes me first, subtle but undeniable. The house looks pristine, almost as though Jack has never set foot inside. No dishes piled in the sink, no trace of him in the bathroom, not even a pillow out of place in the guest bedroom where I assume he slept. And yet, I feel him here—his presence and his absence, both woven into every room.

His clothes are still neatly hung in the closet, organized by season, his dress shoes perfectly lined up beneath them. I pull open his sock drawer and rummage through until I find the matte black box that held his wedding ring. It's empty. The fact he's still wearing it soothes something inside me.

I glance down at my hand, at the emerald engagement ring nestled against my wedding band. I've never taken them off, not even once, except for the day I had my appendix removed. And now, looking at them, I wonder what I'm supposed to feel. Commitment? Guilt? Anger? I'm not sure anymore. All I know is that everything feels suspended in this limbo—neither here nor there, just waiting.

I put the box back, leave the closet, and sit on the edge of the bed, staring off into space. It's quiet, too quiet, and the peace I thought I'd feel being home is instead replaced with a growing sense of unease. I've barely settled into my thoughts when the front door opens.

Max bursts into the room, and I hold him tight, grateful to

have him in my arms again. He humors me with a brief hug before pulling away, the loss of his warmth immediate. "I'm going to play Roblox with Reese."

I nod, but before he can leave, I ask, "How was your time with your dad?"

He shifts on his feet, avoiding my eyes. "It was fine."

"Fine? Could you maybe give me a little more?" I ask, desperate for a glimpse into the week I missed, for some clue as to what Jack's been doing, how he's been acting, or where we even stand.

Max shrugs again, more sheepish this time. "It was nice having more time with him. But...it was weird not having you there." He pauses, as if unsure whether to say more. "He's not a very good cook, though."

A laugh escapes me despite myself. Jack's cooking skills have always been laughable. Beyond grilling chicken or throwing together a salad, he's never really bothered. Summer was our best season, when I could nudge him into cooking more on the barbecue, and we'd feast on grilled pork chops, asparagus, corn, and the occasional smash burger.

"Are you hungry?" I ask, eager for something to do, for a way to feel needed after a week of being on my own.

Max grins, a little too wide, echoing his father's usual expression. "Yeah, I could eat."

In the kitchen, I'm surprised to find the fridge fully stocked. Cherry tomatoes, spinach, apples, even a dozen free-range eggs—things Jack never buys on his own. He's gone out of his way to fill the fridge with my favorite things. My stomach flutters. This small, thoughtful gesture feels like the Jack I used to know, the Jack I miss.

But what does it mean? Is this his way of trying, or just another act of avoidance? I don't know, and the uncertainty gnaws at me as I prepare quiche for Max, cracking eggs and shredding spinach while my mind whirls.

The house is spotless. Jack's cleaned everything, even changed the sheets on our bed. He's trying, I tell myself, trying to hold on to whatever is left between us. But as I sit at the table with Max, listening to him excitedly chatter about a girl at school, I realize something I've been avoiding. I can't keep going like this—not for eleven months. Not with this silence hanging between us. Hiding away in a hotel, pretending everything is fine, isn't the answer.

When Max finishes his story, I smile and kiss his head, but inside, I know. I have to face Jack. I have to ask the questions I've been too afraid to ask.

Because I'm not sure how much longer I can pretend we're still wearing these rings for the right reasons.

CHAPTER
THIRTY

MAY

My mother is humming as she dresses. It's a familiar song but I can't think of the name. I watch her through the crack in her door as she pulls on pantyhose, and a gray skirt, a blouse she then tucks into the skirt. She fiddles with her hair and then slips a necklace over her head, the black pendant settling between her breasts. I try to sing along but nothing comes out.

———

I open my eyes to the empty bedroom, the cool, untouched sheets beside me a stark reminder of the decision Jack and I made. The bed, once a place of comfort, now feels vast and foreign. I sit up slowly, the half-eaten toast beside me long since hardened, and Soraya's manuscript lying abandoned on the pillow. I feel hungover, though I haven't touched alcohol in weeks.

For a moment, I just sit there, letting the remnants of a dream slip through my fingers, the details already fading. I stretch my legs over the edge of the bed and pad to the bathroom, the cold floor sending a shiver up my spine. As I splash water on my face, I catch my reflection in the mirror—my eyes dull, my expression heavy with uncertainty. *She's only been gone six months*, I remind myself. *One step at a time.*

I stare at my reflection longer than usual, studying the lines deepening around my eyes and mouth. My chestnut hair, streaked with gray, frames a face that looks both familiar and foreign. There's still a trace of the youthful energy I once had, but it's been swallowed by years of regret.

"Thirty-nine," I whisper, my breath fogging the mirror. "Not too late. There's still time."

I lean closer, locking eyes with my reflection. These eyes, once bright with hope, are clouded now—weighted with memories, mistakes, and so many unsaid things. But beneath it all, there's still a flicker of something, a stubborn glimmer of determination.

"It's not too late," I say again, more firmly this time. "I can still fix things."

My thoughts drift to Andy, as they so often do. We were inseparable once, bound by secrets and laughter. Now, the silence between us feels like a chasm I don't know how to cross. I think about calling him, hearing his voice—wondering if he's forgiven me yet. Would he even answer?

I picture him tonight, somewhere, maybe with someone, living his life apart from me. He probably thinks I failed him. Maybe I did. Maybe I failed us both without even knowing I was being tested. But I can't let this silence stretch on. Not like it did with Mom.

I close my eyes, inhaling deeply. The answer is obvious, though I've been trying to avoid it. I have to reach out. I have to try.

When I open my eyes again, I see the resolution written across my face. My phone is within reach, and I grab it, my fingers hesitating for only a second before typing.

I dreamed about Mom again. She was humming that song, the one stuck in her head when she cooked. Something about a dusty road. Do you remember?

I hit send before I can second-guess myself. It feels like stepping off a ledge, not knowing if there will be anything to catch me.

Downstairs, I make breakfast on autopilot, the familiar motions offering no comfort. I pour myself tea, staring into the mug as if it holds the answers I'm looking for. I know Andy likely won't respond. But for the first time in a long time, I let myself hope that maybe—just maybe—he will.

I sit at the kitchen island, Soraya's manuscript open before me, but my mind drifts, circling back to the message I sent. I imagine him reading it, maybe even smiling at the memory. And for the briefest of moments, I allow myself to believe in the possibility of forgiveness.

———

Lucy has put together quite an impressive spread of cheese, crackers, dips, olives, tapenades, and slivers of vegetables. Amelia stands pouring herself a glass of white wine as I approach. When she sees me she offers it to me but I decline. Best to keep my wits about me when I lack full control of what comes out of my mouth.

Amelia shrugs as though to say *more for me* and gulps down half the glass in one go. "Tough day," she says.

Quinn clears her throat from across the room. "Now that Hazel's finally here should we get started?"

I casually check my watch. It's two minutes to seven p.m. I was early.

We take our seats, spreading across Lucy's white living room, our books in our laps.

Lucy starts. "What are everyone's overall thoughts this time around?"

"It was delicious!" Jenny says, biting down on her bottom lip. "Talk about couples behaving badly."

I'd been surprised when I heard Quinn had picked *Bad Summer People* to read next. She didn't seem to be the type to want to read about extramarital affairs. I had her pegged as the prim and proper type who meal planned religiously and scheduled sex with her husband—Tuesdays and Saturdays.

"I just couldn't get over how catty they all were," Lucy says.

Across from her, Jenny nods vigorously. "Right? I mean, I expected some drama, but it was like a soap opera."

"Why do you think we're so interested in bad people doing bad things?" Amelia asks.

Quinn speaks up. "Fiction is meant to be an escape, right? I don't know about the rest of you but the lives of these women are nothing like my own. So, to me, it was pure entertainment. I read the entire thing in two sittings."

Lucy and Jenny nod. Amelia gets up to refill her glass.

"It felt as though everyone was bored with their lives back home and came to Fire Island to stir up some shit," I say. "Typical rich person bullshit."

Damn. I'd wondered when I'd slip up tonight and how.

With the words out of my mouth, I sit very still, and wait for someone to speak. To tell me I'm being classist or rude or something. The longer the silence extends the more uncomfortable I become. But then—

Quinn laughs. Then the others follow.

"I think what struck me most was how everyone had secrets," Amelia says finally, pulling them back into focus. "It's like, no one is ever as they seem, even to their closest friends."

I nod. "Yeah, and how those secrets can just unravel everything. It's a good reminder of how fragile trust can be."

We all fall into a comfortable silence for a moment, reflecting.

My relationship with Andy and Jack may be fractured and imperfect, but this new circle of friends fills me with hope, reminding me that even amid broken bonds, there is always the potential for fresh, meaningful connections.

CHAPTER
THIRTY-ONE

It's unseasonably warm for May, and as I stand at the school gates with the other moms, I tug at my shirt, trying to catch a breeze. The familiar chatter of our book club swirls around me, still buzzing about *Bad Summer People*. The book seems to have a hold on us that we can't quite shake.

For a brief moment, I allow myself to relax into their laughter and easy camaraderie. Maybe, just maybe, I could belong here, too.

Lucy is in her element, retelling one of the juicier lines from the book. "'Rachel reminded herself that for all of Lauren's beauty and style, her husband was having sex with another woman. That made her feel somewhat better,'" she quotes, her face glowing with amusement. I chuckle with the others, a lightness bubbling up inside me, a feeling I haven't known in what feels like forever.

So this is what having friends as an adult feels like? Nice. Normal. Safe.

The conversation shifts, as it always does, to our kids and the morning chaos. Amelia talks about Reese, and how he's old enough to make his own lunch but stubbornly refuses. We all nod in agreement. I'm about to share a similar struggle when Jenny's voice cuts through the air.

"Dealing with my kids every day feels like dying a slow death," she jokes.

Oh.

The group erupts into laughter, but the words hit me like a slap.

Slow death. Grief. Loss.

My heart stumbles, the air around me thickening. The sounds of their laughter begin to muffle, swallowed by the roar in my ears. I can't do this. Not here. Not now.

"I—I just remembered something. I need to go," I stammer, my voice barely steady. Before anyone can respond, I turn, walking as fast as I can without drawing more attention.

At the car, my hands tremble as I fumble with the keys. Once inside, I grip the steering wheel, my knuckles white as if it's the only thing holding me together. Tears sting the corners of my eyes, but I refuse to let them fall.

Not here. Not in front of them.

I steal a glance back at the gate. The women are still laughing, completely unaware of my inner storm. A pang of longing pulls at me. For a second, I consider going back. But I know I can't. Not yet. If I go back, they'll see me—really see me. And I'm not ready for that.

With a deep breath, I start the car and hit Daisy's number on speed dial.

———

At home, I work. Not because I want to, but because I have to. Time marches on, indifferent to everything crumbling in my personal life.

I slip in my earbuds as the screen flickers to life, and there he is—Atlas Delaney. His expression is a mix of frustration and apology. His manuscript is eight months late, and the Fiction Editor is breathing down my neck. I'm out of excuses.

"Hi, Atlas," I say, forcing a polite smile. "How are you?"

"Good, thank you. How are you?" He sounds hesitant, knowing what's coming.

"I'm okay." I tap my fingers on the desk. "I wanted to check in about your manuscript. As you know, we're behind schedule."

He sighs, running a hand through his hair. "I know. I'm really sorry. Some personal stuff came up, and it's been hard to focus."

"I understand, but we may have to push back the publication date."

His face freezes. "Is it that serious?"

"Yes." I can't soften the truth. "We've got marketing plans and printing schedules to work with. Delays affect everything."

His expression darkens. "It sounds like you think I'm slacking."

"I don't, but I have to consider the bigger picture. If the draft doesn't come in soon, it's not just your book that suffers—it's the entire team."

"I don't need a lecture. I need support."

"I'm not lecturing," I say, keeping my voice steady. "Just being honest. What can we do to get things back on track?"

Atlas slumps. "I need more time. I can't rush this and risk the quality."

"How about sending me what you've got? I can give feedback and maybe help pick up momentum."

He nods, though I can see the doubt in his eyes.

"We're in this together, Atlas. I want your book to be the best it can be."

"Thanks, Hazel," he mutters, frustration still in his voice. "I appreciate your honesty. Even when it's hard to hear."

"It's part of the job," I say with a faint smile. "And part of making sure your book reaches its potential."

As the call ends, I stare at the blank screen. I can't lie, even when it strains relationships. I just hope he knows I'm on his side. I hope this curse—this brutal need to always tell the truth—ends soon.

———

Now, my mother is still on my mind, which means Andy is, too. I'm trying to understand why he needs space, but I don't get it.

We should be grieving together. We did everything together until I left Anaheim for college.

Like with my mother, I thought there'd be time to fix things. Time for us to come to our senses, appreciate life and let go of old resentments. Sure, our mother had been neglectful when we were kids, but I thought there'd be time to change that—until there wasn't.

Now I worry the distance between me and Andy will only grow. Unless I do something.

I pick up my phone and start typing.

> I've been thinking about the night we were eight or nine, when Mom left us alone. I can't remember where she went, but it's not the point. I was scared when I woke up and realized she was gone. You hugged me in bed until I stopped crying and fell asleep. It's messed up that it happened, but maybe even more that we never talked about it. We never told her we knew, we just moved on. We never talked about what neglect does to a kid. I'm dealing with my own issues, Andy. I think you should too. Please call me.

Andy finally responds. My heart stutters at the sight of his name on my screen.

I glance at the clock—3:13 p.m. Max will be out of school any minute. My eyes drift toward the gate before I open Andy's message.

While I had written him a near essay, he replies with barely anything.

> We're not kids anymore. Leave the past in the past.

I stare at the words, my grip tightening on the phone. My heart sinks as a dull ache spreads through my chest. He doesn't get it. He never does.

A tap on my window startles me, yanking me from my spiraling thoughts. I look up to see Quinn, her perfectly styled hair framing a smug expression. Great. Just what I need.

I roll down the window, already irritated. I saw her this morning—what does she want now?

"Hi," Quinn chirps, her voice grating on my nerves. "Just a reminder, it's your turn to pick the next book for the club. I was going to mention it earlier, but you ran off so quickly. Anyway, if you could pick something popular but not too popular, and not too long, we—"

"Really?" The word snaps out of me, sharp and biting. Andy's message fuels my anger, and I take it out on her. "I work in publishing. I think I know how to pick a book."

Quinn's eyes widen, her smugness slipping. "I didn't mean—"

"Just go," I hiss, my temper barely in check. "I'm not in the mood for this right now."

Quinn blinks, caught off guard, but I can see the flicker of amusement in her eyes. She takes a step back, raising her eyebrows as if to say, *well, that escalated.* And right then, I know Quinn and I will never be friends.

She hesitates, then turns and walks away, her perfect hair bouncing like nothing could touch her. I push out a shaky breath, trying to steady myself, but it's too late. The dam has broken.

I drop my head against the steering wheel, the weight of Andy's rejection pressing down, guilt gnawing at me for snapping at Quinn. Tears sting my eyes, and I let them fall, feeling frustration, hurt, and anger crash over me.

I don't hear the car door open until Max's small voice pulls me from my breakdown.

CHAPTER
THIRTY-TWO

'm standing in an open field of dirt, the sun low in the sky. The air is thick with heat and summer scents. I feel both peace and dread. In the distance, I see her—my mother. She looks as she did years ago, wearing that old floral dress. She stands still, almost smiling, but her eyes are distant.

Memories flood in—the nights alone, the empty fridge, the neglect. I left it all behind for college, never looking back. "We needed you," I whisper. "But you were never there."

Her image blurs, dissolving into the golden light. I try to hold onto her, but she's slipping away.

I wake up, my cheeks wet with tears.

———

When the night of the June book club arrives, I open the door to all four women, each with snacks and drinks in their hands. Amelia told me they would take care of everything.

When we're all settled, everyone looks at me with anticipation.

"Oh, ok. I'll start," I say. I press my palm against my hardcover copy of *Funny Story*. "I absolutely loved it, which I knew I would. That's why I chose it."

There are a few nods around the room. Amelia, always the first to jump in, asks, "The perfect summer read."

"It was just so light and fun. The characters felt real, but their problems were...manageable, I guess. It was the perfect escape for me."

Quinn tilts her head, curiosity sparkling in her eyes. I think about the last time I spoke to her and want to hide. It feels highly unnatural for her to be here in my house with me. I find myself wishing she hadn't come tonight.

"Escape from what?" Quinn asks. She's baiting me, I know it.

I force a smile, trying to keep my voice steady. I don't know how to answer her question without revealing everything that's been happening in my life. If I had the power, I never would have said anything in the first place.

I speak slowly, finding my words one at a time. "Life's been... hectic lately. You know how it is. I just needed something that didn't add to the stress."

The girls nod sympathetically, and I wish I could tell them the full truth. But this book club has quickly become my sanctuary, my escape. They don't need to know everything.

Lucy jumps in. "I loved it, too. It was clever without being over-the-top. And the romance was sweet and believable which, let's be honest, is not always a given in romance books."

Jenny chimes in, "I felt the same way. It was a little pocket of sunshine. All her books are."

The conversation flows easily from there, with everyone sharing their favorite parts and how the book made them feel. I relax into the moment, grateful for this brief reprieve from my reality.

At one point, Amelia reaches over and squeezes my hand, surprising me. It's the first human touch I've felt in weeks, besides hugs from Max.

"I'm glad you picked this one, Hazel. Sometimes we all need a little break from reality."

I feel Quinn's eyes on me.

I squeeze Amelia's hand back, my heart warming at the gesture.

Quinn has said little about the book I chose. We all seem to be thinking the same thing as four pairs of eyes fall on her at once.

She shrugs. "I'm not really into romance. It's a little... simplistic in my opinion."

Oh, you're a joy!

"I know we're all entitled to our opinions, which is why I feel comfortable saying I disagree," Lucy says. I fight back a smile. "For example, think about how the story emphasized the importance of personal growth and maintaining a sense of independence within a relationship. Think about Daphne's relationship with Peter and how she lost track of herself in the relationship. If he hadn't called off the engagement, she might never have realized how important it was for her to feel independent within a relationship. I'm not sure I'd call that simplistic."

This time, I don't bother hiding my smile. Lucy has nailed it, and even Quinn can't deny it—though I wouldn't be surprised if she tries.

The conversation moves on, but I'm lost in my own thoughts.

Falling in love and committing to Jack required compromise. I know this. But sitting here, I realize just how much I've shifted —maybe too much. It's about balancing love with individuality, and I didn't do it well. I gave up too much of myself for our marriage and our family.

I see it now. I poured myself into being Jack's wife, into our life together, and somewhere along the way, I lost pieces of myself.

I glance at the book, feeling regret and determination. This break is a chance to fix this. To find those lost pieces and put myself back together. Like the characters in the book, I need to rediscover my own interests, friends, and life. It's not about pushing Jack away; it's about balance—for both of us.

My focus returns as Jenny begins speaking. We all turn to her, sensing something important.

"When I married Tom, I was over the moon. But over time, I started losing pieces of myself. At first, it was small. I stopped going to yoga because it conflicted with his schedule. I gave up my Saturday mornings at the farmers' market to do things he enjoyed."

She pauses, sipping her wine. "It wasn't just activities. I started agreeing with him on everything, even when I didn't. I'd always had strong views, but I began doubting myself, thinking his perspective must be better."

Lucy jumps in. "You? Strong views? Never!"

Jenny smiles. "It hit me when I stopped writing. Writing was my passion, and somehow, I let it slip away. One day, I sat down and realized I couldn't remember the last time I'd written for myself. It was like a part of me disappeared."

I shouldn't be surprised. Everyone has their secrets.

"I'm still finding my way back to writing," she continues. "It's slow, but I'm getting closer each day."

Jenny's story reminds me how easy it is to lose ourselves in love, but also how important it is to reclaim who we are.

After everyone leaves, I find myself whistling as I clean. The echoes of laughter from the book club still buzz in the air, and for a moment, my troubles feel lighter, shared and diminished through connection.

As I wipe down the counter, it hits me—this time apart from Jack isn't just about our marriage. It's about me. About finding myself again. If, and when, we come back together, it will be as two whole individuals—not broken halves trying to fit.

It's a scary but hopeful thought. I breathe in, letting the stillness of the house wash over me, and for the first time in a long time, I feel ready to embrace the uncertainty. Ready to embrace me.

CHAPTER
THIRTY-THREE

The studio smells of lavender and eucalyptus, a mix meant to be calming but only adds to the dull throb in my temples. I settle onto my mat, the tight leggings feeling more like a costume than actual clothing, squeezing me into a role I don't quite fit. The instructor's voice guides us through deep breaths and stretches, my muscles protesting.

This is only my second yoga class, and I'm still trying to find balance—not just in the poses, but in my life. I've always been skeptical of yoga, of the "find yourself" vibe, but here I am, hoping that stretching my body will help stretch beyond the broken parts of me.

As we move into downward dog, I notice him—the guy on the mat next to mine. He's attractive, distractingly so, with a strong jawline and messy black hair. I try to focus on my breathing, but my thoughts keep drifting to him.

"Nice form," he whispers during a tough pose, his voice low and warm. I glance at him, and he smiles, making my heart stutter. I mumble a thanks, cheeks burning. I've always been terrible at flirting.

Class ends, and I roll up my mat, trying not to trip over myself. But then he's there, standing close enough I feel his presence.

"Hey, I'm Jun," he says, smiling wider. "You're new here, right?"

"Yeah, Hazel," I reply, awkward but not wanting to brush him off. "Second class."

"You're doing great," he says, his Seoul accent giving his words a lilting charm. "Want to grab a coffee?"

For a moment, my mind freezes. Part of me wants to say no, to avoid the awkwardness. But the part that hasn't felt wanted in years speaks up. "Sure, why not?"

We walk to the café, the late afternoon sun casting long shadows. Jun's stride is relaxed, and I fall into step beside him, my nerves slowly easing. His presence feels... easy.

The café is small and cozy, with mismatched chairs and the smell of fresh coffee wafting through the door. I feel a flicker of excitement—when was the last time I'd done something like this? Just sat with someone, without history or expectations?

We order drinks, and when Jun insists on paying, I smile, warmth spreading through me. We settle at a corner table, away from the bustle. It's quiet, intimate even, the light from the windows casting a soft glow. I wrap my hands around my cup, letting the warmth seep into my skin.

"So, Hazel," Jun says, leaning back in his chair, his eyes fixed on mine. "What do you do when you're not mastering yoga poses?"

I chuckle, grateful for the casual tone. "I'm not sure I'd say I'm mastering anything," I admit, shaking my head. "But I work in publishing as an acquisitions editor."

His eyes light up with genuine curiosity. "Interesting! You must get to read a lot of great books."

"Yeah, it's a pretty big part of the job. But it's more about finding new voices and helping writers shape their stories. It's rewarding, though stressful at times."

He nods, sipping his coffee. "I can imagine. Sounds like a lot of pressure."

I meet his gaze and for a second, I wonder how much to reveal. Talking about work is safe, but there's more to why I'm sitting here. More to why I've thrown myself into yoga, into new routines, into anything that feels like it could help me rebuild something inside.

"It can be," I say, keeping my tone light. "But it's a good distraction, you know? From...other things."

Jun tilts his head, sensing the shift in my voice. "Other things?"

I hesitate, but there's something about the way he's looking at me—open, nonjudgmental—that makes it easier to be honest. "I'm separated from my husband," I finally say, the words tasting strange on my tongue. "It's been a few months now."

Jun's expression softens. "I'm sorry. That's tough."

I nod, grateful for his simple acknowledgment. No prying questions, no uncomfortable pity—just understanding.

He leans forward slightly, his elbows resting on the table. "Do you mind me asking—was yoga a part of the separation? Like, a way to cope?"

I smile, appreciating his insight. "Yeah, actually. I need something to ground me, I guess. Something that isn't tied to...everything else." I let out a small laugh. "But honestly, I'm terrible at it."

Jun grins, and his warmth is infectious. "Hey, we're all terrible in the beginning." There's no trace of smugness, just kindness.

Our conversation drifts—favorite books, bad TV shows, the best sushi spots. He talks about his job as a software developer and how much he enjoys solving puzzles and making things work. I feel more relaxed than I've been in weeks, maybe months.

At some point, I notice how close we're sitting. I don't remember leaning forward, but the space between us feels smaller, more charged. Jun's eyes linger on mine, and I wonder if he's noticed too.

"I'm glad you showed up in my regular class this morning." His eyes flicker with something—admiration, maybe.

His sincerity sends a warm flutter through my chest. He's closer now, and I catch the clean, woodsy scent of his aftershave. The pull between us is undeniable, the moment teetering on the edge of something more.

His eyes hold mine, and for a second, neither of us moves. My heart quickens as the air shifts between us. Then, almost imperceptibly, he leans in. His breath is warm against my cheek, his face just inches from mine.

And in this moment, I know. I could let this happen.

The idea is tempting—so, so tempting. But just as my body starts to respond, Jack's face flashes in my mind, pulling me back.

I turn my head slightly, breaking the moment. "I—I should go," I murmur, my voice unsteady.

Jun pulls back, his expression soft but unreadable. "Of course," he says, his smile gentle, as if he knows this was a possibility all along. He stands, offering me a hand as I gather my things. "It was really nice talking to you, Hazel."

"You too," I reply, feeling a mixture of relief and regret.

———

I wake in the middle of the night and, unable to fall back asleep, I reach for my phone, a bad habit I haven't been able to break. There is an email from Jack.

Dear Hazel,

I know we never explicitly said no contact, but I think we both understood it was what was best. So while I'm technically breaking the rules in writing this to you, you needed to know. I'm going to look for an apartment to sublet for the remainder of our time apart. I've been staying with my parents but that's not going to work long-term. They're trying to give me my space but asking too many questions I don't have the answers to. I had a long talk with Max before making this decision, and he doesn't mind moving between home and wherever I end up. I get the impression it's actually a little exciting for him—though I won't try to understand why. You know how he is with new things. So, the house will be all yours soon.

I hope you're okay with this, but knowing how much of a homebody you are, I'm thinking you'll be okay with my decision. I'll make sure to send a new address home with Max at some point. I know you'll want to know where he is staying.

I hope you are well.
Jack

I read the email again and again trying to break apart the sentences, looking for what he's saying between the lines, but there is nothing. He has given me no insight into how he is feeling or doing beyond being annoyed by staying with his parents. Eventually, I hover over the delete button, ready to purge the letter from my memory.

But I can't come to delete it.

Instead, I move it into a folder where it sits at the top of a collection of emails from Jack over the years. I wait only a couple of seconds before I click on one at random.

One thing I do know for sure is we are strongly connected, and need each other, and our bodies always seem to find a way toward one another overnight. Only a few sentences but tears prick the corner of my eyes.

I select another email.

You're my fiancée now and I'm beyond excited! The first moment I met you I was overwhelmed by how beautiful you were. And now I know you are just as beautiful on the inside. You're the person I hoped to find and the more I learn about you the more I realize how much different you are than everyone else.

And that's when I know I have gone too far.

Because all Jack's words do is remind me of how far we've fallen...and with no safety net to catch us.

CHAPTER
THIRTY-FOUR

JULY

The grocery store is much too busy for a weekday morning, and as I weave through the aisles, I wish I hadn't come. Knowing I have only a crappy hotel room to go back to doesn't help.

I'm debating between Gala apples or splurging on Honeycrisps when I hear my name. I turn and see Amelia.

"I love running into people while doing errands," she says. "We can shop together and catch up."

"Sure," I say, even though I only need a few things, and her full cart and long list tell a different story.

I slip three Honeycrisp apples into my basket so she doesn't think I'm cheap. She grabs a three-pound bag and two bags of Cuties. I reach for a prepackaged salad, destined for a hotel bed lunch. Amelia grabs Swiss chard—something I wouldn't even know how to cook.

We keep walking and talking.

It's Wednesday, and the sushi is discounted. A slim woman is handing out samples, and Amelia rushes over, popping one into her mouth with a dramatic eye-roll.

"You have to try this," she mumbles, mouth full.

"I actually can't stand grocery store sushi," I say. I can't help it.

Amelia snorts. "You're very direct. I like it."

I shrug, hoping it looks cool and not like I'm weighed down by my personal mess.

"What do you say we get real sushi sometime?" she asks, glancing past me briefly. "Maybe next week?"

Can it really be this simple to make friends as an adult? Yet as we continue walking, I feel calm, something I haven't felt in a while, and Amelia seems content too.

"I'd love to," I say.

"Great! It's a date."

I think of Max saying how nice she is, how she has the best snacks in her purse. I imagine how pleased Daisy will be to hear this.

"Now, any idea where they moved the peanut butter during the renovation?"

I don't know where it is, but I want to stay with her until we find it... and everything else on her list. The desire is so strong I swear she can sense it, and I feel my face flush.

"No matter, we'll find it," she says.

By the time we reach the dairy section, I feel confident enough to ask, "So, be honest, Quinn didn't want me to join the book club, did she?"

Amelia sets milk in her cart and looks at me. "Quinn's a pain. When we first started the club, too many people came and went. It drove her crazy. She only wanted people who'd show up every month, no excuses. We let her have her way just to avoid the complaining."

"I guess that explains why she didn't like me at first," I say, not mentioning why she might dislike me even more now.

"I'll never understand people like her," I say, tossing ice cream I don't need into my basket. "It's obvious she's miserable and takes it out on everyone."

Amelia stills beside me.

I've gone too far. She'll make an excuse to leave, and I'll never hear from her about sushi. Worse, I'll be booted from book club, giving Quinn the satisfaction she craves.

I open my mouth—unsure of what to say—when I feel Amelia's hand on my arm.

"I'm not going into detail, and I'll deny ever admitting this, but I think you're right."

I exhale with a smile, glancing up at the ceiling.

"Thank god. I thought I'd stuck my foot in my mouth. There's a fine line between being direct and being an asshole."

Amelia releases my arm, and we keep walking. I imagine what it would be like to spend more time with her. If grocery shopping can be this fun, I can't imagine what dinner will be like.

For a moment, I consider telling her everything—my mother, Andy, my marriage.

"I know a good sushi place," I say instead, wanting to show my gratitude for her olive branch.

"Great," says Amelia.

Great.

The week drags on, each day blurring into the next. At work, I fumble through tasks, my mind always elsewhere. Nights are restless, filled with fragmented dreams of my mother and the ache of unresolved emotions.

By the time my date with Amelia arrives, I'm a bundle of nerves, my chest tight with unspoken feelings. Unable to face sushi, I suggest we meet at Foxtail instead. We sit down, iced drinks in hand, but the fun, warm atmosphere does little to ease the tension building inside me.

Amelia chats casually about her day, her voice a soothing hum in the background. I nod along, but my thoughts are racing, my heart pounding.

Eventually, I realize she's stopped talking. When I don't respond, she looks at me curiously.

"Everything okay?"

I hesitate, the words stuck in my throat. "Not really."

"Do you want to talk about it?"

Max is right—she is nice.

"No," I admit, "but I think I have to before I explode. You ever feel that way?"

"I know the feeling well," she says, sipping her iced coffee.

I take a deep breath. "The talk about maintaining individuality in relationships at the book club made me realize I need to make some changes if I'm going to come out of this separation a better person."

Amelia leans in, fully focused. "What separation?"

I don't know where to start, so I begin at the beginning. I tell her about our wedding, our honeymoon, my worries about children, and how Jack and I slowly turned against each other. How we decided to spend the rest of my thirty-ninth year apart.

Amelia listens patiently, then reaches over and squeezes my hand.

"That's a lot to deal with. I'm sorry."

I look down at my hands. "I wish I could say that was it."

"You don't have to talk about it if you don't want to."

"No." I pause. "It feels good to get it all out. My best friend Daisy lets me talk, but I think she's run out of things to say."

"I can't promise I'll know what to say either," Amelia says, "but I can listen."

The coffee sits heavy in my stomach. "I lost my mother eight months ago. We had a complicated relationship. So complicated I didn't even know she had cancer until it was too late."

Amelia's eyes widen.

"And my brother thought I knew and stayed away anyway. I'm not sure he believes me. He won't talk to me."

Amelia's expression softens. "I'm so sorry, Hazel."

Her kindness cracks something open, and I start talking about my past, the neglect, and the lingering hurt.

"My mom wasn't a good person," I say, my voice catching. "She made everything about herself. Andy and I were just accessories. She'd leave us alone for days, and we'd fend for ourselves. One time, Andy got really sick, and I was terrified. We were just kids."

Amelia reaches out and takes my hand, giving me strength.

"And the men she brought home... " I pause. "Some of them were awful. I'd hear things no child should ever hear. Andy would cover his ears and hum to fall asleep. It was a nightmare."

Tears well up, but I don't stop. "She'd scream at us, call us mistakes, burdens. And when she wasn't screaming, she'd ignore us like we didn't exist."

Amelia listens intently, her grip tightening. "I can't imagine how hard that was."

I nod, wiping at my face. "It was. And it left scars. Even now, I struggle to trust, to feel like I'm enough."

Talking about it feels like a release, like I'm not carrying the weight alone anymore.

After a pause, Amelia says, "Wait. You and Jack split up *after* your mother died?" She glances past me. I turn to see Quinn at the cashier. She looks over, hesitates, then walks toward us.

"Hi, you two," Quinn says, her eyes on Amelia, not me.

Amelia glances at me before replying, but Quinn's name is called. She grabs her drink, waves, and heads out.

"That was strange," Amelia says, shaking her head. "Anyway, you were saying?"

"The timing wasn't great," I say, "but Jack made grieving harder. He thought I should be acting and feeling a certain way."

Amelia nods. "Everyone grieves differently. You can't compare experiences."

"I guess."

"And maybe Jack didn't know how to handle your grief. Has he ever lost someone close?"

"No."

"Then he couldn't understand. He was probably doing his best with something he wasn't equipped for."

Her words settle in, leaving me speechless for a moment.

Then she asks, "Do you miss her?"

I push aside my watered-down coffee. "I don't know," I admit. "Sometimes I think I miss her because I thought we'd have time to fix things."

Amelia nods.

"I need to fix things with my brother," I say, and the words spill out, feeling more like a release with each one. Amelia listens, her presence a quiet comfort.

When I finish, I feel drained but lighter, like I've finally shared the burden. Amelia squeezes my hand. "Thank you for trusting me with this, Hazel. You're not alone anymore."

At this moment, surrounded by the cool air of the café and Amelia's support, I feel a flicker of hope. Maybe healing is possible.

On my way out, I pull out my phone and compose another text to Andy.

Please. I'm all the family you have left.

I hit send.

CHAPTER
THIRTY-FIVE

I've always felt the need to keep two calendars, one electronic and one physical. There's something irreplaceable about crossing off a task on an actual paper planner, and old habits cling tight. The Google calendar is a necessity, with all the Zoom meetings with authors and the editorial team at Inklings, but I rely on my planner for everything else. And now, I can't find it.

It's not in my worn-out laptop bag or the rolling suitcase I hastily packed for the week. I check between the seats of my car, and sift through the pile of junk gathering in the backseat—nothing. There's only one place it could be.

I drive back to the house before I can talk myself out of it. It's the middle of the workday, and Jack shouldn't be home, but a knot tightens in my stomach as I pull into the driveway. I hesitate, hand on the key, before turning it in the lock.

I'm here for the planner, I remind myself. That's all.

Except the nagging voice at the back of my mind whispers a truth I don't want to admit—I'm here for more.

The house is exactly as I left it: still, quiet, too clean. It's like nothing's changed. The bed is made, the pillows fluffed, and sunlight pours through the blinds. Jack's attempt at normalcy. I glance at Max's room, his bed surprisingly made, and I wonder how much Jack had to bribe him for this small miracle.

I find my planner in the office, splayed open to last week. A chaotic jumble of notes and deadlines fills the pages. I thumb through it, absentmindedly scanning for anything I might have missed, when something stops me cold. Below the messy scribble that reads *YOGA 7AM - Tuesday,* Jack's handwriting stares back at me: *hope you had fun.*

It's a small note, nothing really, but the first contact we've had in weeks. The unexpected warmth of it sneaks up on me, and I smile—a flicker of something familiar.

I turn to leave, but as I pass through the kitchen, my gaze catches on a piece of paper, a torn scrap pinned to the fridge. My mind doesn't register it at first, but when it does, my feet stop moving. I reach out, plucking it from the magnet.

EVERLY 702-555-0135.

I stare at the number, a slow, dull ache blooming in my chest. The painfully honest truth?
This fucking hurts.

CHAPTER
THIRTY-SIX

Around the time I pick myself up off the kitchen floor I realize it's possible I'm overreacting. That name and number could mean anything: a new coworker, a headhunter who might finally pull Jack away from the company he really should have left years ago, a mother at the school wanting to get the kids together.

Except I don't think I'm overreacting. I can feel it in my gut. Something isn't quite right.

And now, I'm not sure what I'm supposed to do. Am I meant to continue with my day as though nothing has happened? Go back to work, send my silly emails and Zoom meeting requests, prepare dinner and eat dinner, get the recommended eight hours of sleep and do it all again tomorrow as Jack does who knows what with *EVERLY 702-555-0135*?

I suppose there are women about there who can do that, who can compartmentalize their life in such a way, but I'm not one of them.

It's not like I haven't thought this could happen. There was a reason Jack and I decided there would be no communication between us, no questions asked. Logically, I know him meeting someone else, even sleeping with someone else, is an option. I just didn't expect it to happen so soon. Or with someone with a name like Everly.

I can't compete with an Everly, who probably takes the time to carefully curl her long hair each morning and always has impeccable-looking nails that are neither too long nor too short. She probably wears dresses that drape over her lithe body and wedge sandals and vacations in places like St. Bart's and Aspen. Everly most certainly comes from money and has an Ivy League education: not the obvious Harvard or Yale, but something like Cornell, that makes her appear more down-to-earth like the rest of us.

I picture them together: shopping hand in hand at Downtown Summerlin, the outdoor shopping center we used to frequent, staring at each other over dinner in a dimly lit restaurant, smiling as they think about what they'll do to one another the moment they get home and into bed. She is new and shiny, and I am old, comfortable, and predictable. No wonder Jack wanted this time away from me.

I go so far as to scour the closest for his favorite black shirt, the one Jack once told me he saved for special nights, like our first night out after Max was born and the day he swore he was going to get the big promotion that ended up going to Milo.

The shirt isn't there.

And now I can see it so clearly: his lucky black shirt thrown over someone else's chair in someone else's bedroom. His hands on someone else's body.

Everly, I reason, is beautiful and simple in a way I'll never be. Which is probably why her number is displayed on our fridge in all its glory.

Where Jack and I have years of fights and menial chore division and parenting frustrations, Everly and Jack have a clean slate with which to fill with beautiful firsts: first kiss, first night spent together, first fight and the makeup sex that happens afterward. In some ways, the comfortable life Jack and I have built could never compare to the excitement of newness.

It's with this realization ringing in my ears that I finally leave the house. I never should have come here.

I call Daisy from the car, but it goes straight to voicemail.

The rest of the day is a write-off. And the next isn't much better. By the time Saturday rolls around I have convinced myself there is no possible way I can show my face at book club. Never having been one who can hide their emotions well, I reason I'm doing myself and the other women a service by canceling.

I pick up my phone intending to text Amelia to let her know but then I picture the look on Quinn's face, the lack of surprise by my absence.

This month the book is *Real Americans* by Rachel Khong, a real departure from the last three books we read. I want to ask whose choice it was but worry the question will come out sounding judgmental. I loved the book and find, despite my earlier hesitation, I'm glad I decided to come.

Amelia is hosting again. I've learned she prefers us to gather at her place, desiring the comfort of her own home over others'. This feeling I understand well.

We begin, as we do each month, with our overall thoughts on the book. Unsurprisingly, it's unanimously adored, both for its beautiful prose and its depiction of the Asian culture set against the American.

Lucy tells us she liked the short chapters and, from the corner of my eye, I see Quinn roll her eyes. Unbecoming as it is to admit this, I'm bolstered by the knowledge that Quinn's disdain may not just be aimed at me. I try, unsuccessfully, to hide a smile.

Amelia takes the lead as usual. "In what ways does Lily yearn for a greater understanding of her Chinese heritage?'" she reads from a website on her phone. I know she's reading from the publisher's discussion questions because I looked them up myself a week ago.

"I mean, there are so many little gaps in what she knows about her parent's life and she's kind of struggling to fill them in. But you saw Lily's mom's struggle to let her past come to light. It was clear she didn't want to go there. She'd rather have left the past in the past." Amelia smiles. "God, it was just such an incredible book. I wish I could erase it from my mind and read it all over again."

"That would be something, wouldn't it?" Lucy says.

"The book is essentially asking us what makes us who we are," I say, and everyone nods their heads. I've borrowed the quote from an interview I read earlier that afternoon. I continue. "Also, how we bring our preconceived notions about life and race and privilege to the way that we view and approach others."

"Like what Lily said at the party early on," Jenny says excitedly. "Something about how she was looking at Matthew and this other woman standing next to each other and thinking they looked right together because they were both well off and looked the part."

"Exactly," says Amelia. I can tell she's excited about the direction in which our literary discussion is headed.

I have the sudden thought that I don't know anything about these women other than their names and how, like me, they are mothers of a fifth grader. Lucy would gladly descend into talking about sex at any given moment, a topic that appears to make Jenny uncomfortable and Quinn downright despondent. The jury's out on where Amelia stands on the issue. Heck—I'm not even sure what I think about sex at the moment.

"My mother was born in South Africa," I say, surprising myself. "But I don't feel, in any way, South African."

Amelia looks up, her eyes connecting briefly with mine and I realize my mistake. I've opened a door to a room I have no interest in walking into.

"I did wonder about your background," says Jenny. "But I didn't want to ask."

Jenny is so obviously Irish, but I can't be sure about the others and I don't ask.

"I was out running errands the other day and I saw a Mercedes SUV painted a terrible mauve pink color and I actually thought to myself: I know exactly what type of woman is driving." Lucy looks sheepish as she says it but I can tell we are all intrigued by what she will say next. "Perfect hair, long fake nails, puffed up lips, a huge rock on her left ring finger."

Jenny nods knowingly. "See? We all do it."

Quinn is still looking at me strangely. I look back, as though daring her to say whatever it is she's thinking. Finally, she says, "You're half South African yet you don't feel half South African? Is that normal?"

I catch Amelia's eye and she winces.

"How could I when my mother never talked about it? She

didn't cook any special dishes or speak with an accent or talk about her time before she emigrated. I barely knew her parents and she married a dirtbag from Austria who took off when my brother and I were still babies."

I pull in a deep breath, certain I've said too much. But the conversation continues as though I haven't just verbally vomited all over everyone in the room.

"You know what got me?" Quinn says. "The argument that Nick and Timothy had in the hotel room in New York, where Timothy was trying to wake Nick up to his privilege he'd been handed by finding his father." She consults her book, which I see is spotted with sticky notes and writing in the margins. When she reads from the book, her voice takes on a lighter tone. It's almost mesmerizing. "'I want my *own* life. Not theirs, whatever their bullshit is. A life that belongs to me.'"

I murmur knowingly. I'd been touched by the line, too. "Every kid grows up wanting that. Especially at Nick's age."

Quinn says, "But according to Timothy, nobody gets to have it."

Amelia sips her wine.

Eventually, Lucy looks at each of us in turn before saying, "We're fortunate to look and talk the way we do. We truly have no idea how it feels to be on the outside of anything."

The room quiets, each of us seemingly lost in our thoughts.

Only later, on the drive home from Lucy's, will I realize I haven't thought of Jack and *Everly* all night.

CHAPTER
THIRTY-SEVEN

The lightness I feel after opening up to Amelia lingers for weeks, like a breath I didn't know I'd been holding finally released. After the whirlwind of the past eight months, this relief is like emerging from underwater. There's a strange liberation in having laid it all bare, speaking my truth out loud, and letting some of the regret and pain that's weighed me down drift away.

The shadows under my eyes haven't disappeared entirely—they still stare back at me when I catch my reflection in the mirror—but tonight, I feel a glimmer of something I haven't felt in a long time.

Hope. Like there's a future waiting for me beyond all this.

I stand at the kitchen sink, the soft clink of dishes accompanying the persistent drip of the faucet. I try to hold on to the fragile feeling of hope when Max barrels through the door, radiating the kind of excitement only an eleven-year-old can muster after a week at his dad's new apartment.

"So, tell me everything," I say, turning to him, grateful for the distraction.

He grins, his face flushed from the rush of being back. "It's nice enough. The furniture's kind of tacky though—it came with the place. But there's a community pool around the corner, and there's always a bunch of kids out there."

"Good job, bud. Did you have fun with your dad? Get in any quality time?"

I brace myself for what I expect to hear—stories of pizza and movie marathons, staying up way too late, and the sugary breakfasts Jack can't resist giving him. Disneyland dad at his finest.

Max shrugs. "Not really. He's still getting settled in, and he was on his phone a lot."

A wave of irritation simmers beneath my skin, but I keep my expression neutral. This is typical Jack—always distracted, always somewhere else, even when he's right in front of you. I bite back the urge to comment on his lack of boundaries, reminding myself it's not my place anymore.

Then Max says it. "He was on the phone with some woman a lot."

My heart stumbles, caught off guard by the blow. I force my voice to stay steady and casual. "What woman?"

Max looks up at me, his innocent eyes wide. "I don't know. He always takes the calls in his room. He doesn't talk where I can hear."

My mind races, grasping onto the memory of the name I'd seen scribbled on the sticky note on the fridge: *EVERLY*. A sharp pang stabs through me, the kind that spreads from your chest to your stomach in a slow, sickening churn.

I turn back to the sink, scrubbing a plate with more force than necessary. "Did you hear her name?" I ask, my voice tighter than I intended.

"Nah," Max says before scurrying off to his room, blissfully unaware of the weight his words have dropped on me.

I stand there, gripping the edge of the sink, my knuckles turning white as the drip-drip of the faucet grows louder, filling the quiet kitchen with its relentless rhythm.

Everly. Of course it's her. That torn scrap of paper on the fridge, her number staring back at me like a cruel joke. I thought we were just taking a break, giving each other space to breathe, to figure out where we went wrong. But now, it feels like I've been naive, clinging to the hope we'd come back to each other, that this wasn't the end.

But maybe, for Jack, it was. Maybe he's already started over with someone new.

The thought is like a knife twisting in my chest. I lean against the counter, trying to steady my breath as questions swirl in my mind, each one cutting deeper than the last. Has she been there all along, waiting in the wings for her moment? Or is she just some fleeting distraction, something Jack is using to forget the mess we left behind?

I pinch my eyes shut, fighting back the images of Jack laughing with her, smiling at her in the way he used to smile at me. The way he doesn't anymore. It's too much. I feel the ground shifting beneath me, the life we built together crumbling like sand slipping through my fingers.

I open my eyes, my gaze drifting around the kitchen—the place where we shared so many moments, where our lives were intertwined in laughter, in arguments, in everything. Now, it feels hollow, stripped of the meaning it once held.

Taking a deep breath, I turn off the faucet and dry my hands. I can't fall apart, not now. Not with Max here. He needs me to be strong, even if I'm breaking inside.

I glance at the clock—time to start dinner. The routine is all I have to hold on to, the one thing keeping me grounded when everything else feels like it's spiraling out of control. I gather the ingredients, my mind elsewhere, replaying every moment with Jack, every sign I might've missed. Every crack in the foundation I was too busy—or too scared—to see.

As I chop the vegetables, the questions keep gnawing at me. What happens now? How do I move forward when I feel like I'm stuck in place, like I'm the one who's been left behind?

I don't have the answers. Not yet. But I know one thing—I can't stay here, frozen in the hurt. I have to find a way to let go. For Max. For me.

———————

Later, the house quiet and nearly dark, I sit at the kitchen table, alone with my thoughts. The silence feels oppressive, pressing in on me from all sides.

I glance at the blank notepad in front of me, the pristine white pages mocking my turmoil. My thoughts keep drifting back to Max's words: *He takes the calls in his room.*

I feel a hot surge of anger rising within me, and before I know it, I grab a pen and start scribbling furiously.

Things About Jack That Drive Me Crazy:

- *He's always on his phone, even when we're supposed to be spending family time together*
- *He makes me feel bad for not being as neat and clean as he is*
- *He never listens when I talk about my day*
- *He stays at a job where he knows he is underpaid and under appreciated*
- *He rarely helps with the housework*

The words come faster, my hand almost shaking as I write. Each item on the list fuels my anger, memories of countless frustrations piling up like dry kindling.

- *He went out drinking and missed his son's ninth birthday dinner*
- *He's always late coming home*
- *He doesn't show any appreciation for what I do*
- *He always takes Everly's calls in private*

I underline the last point so hard the pen nearly tears through the paper. I can't believe he's already moved on, talking to some woman while we're supposed to be figuring things out. It feels like a betrayal, and the hurt morphs into a fierce, burning rage.

I keep writing, the list growing longer and longer.

- *He never asks how I'm feeling*
- *He stopped being okay with eating at 5:00 p.m just to be with me*
- *He said he would love me even when I'm forty and my body is starting to turn a little squishy*

- *He acts like our separation is a minor inconvenience*
- <u>*He left*</u>

By now, I'm practically fuming, my breath coming in short, angry bursts. Heat floods my cheeks, my chest tightening with every thought of him—of what he's done to me, to us, to Max.

I stop writing and glare at the list, the words blurring together as tears of frustration well up in my eyes. It's like every hurt, every disappointment, every broken promise is staring back at me from the page. My pulse quickens, and before I can think, I grab the notepad and hurl it across the kitchen. It hits the wall with a dull thud and falls to the floor, but the anger doesn't go with it. It stays lodged deep inside me, simmering, seething.

I stand abruptly, pacing the kitchen, my thoughts a chaotic swirl of rage and betrayal. Every step feels like a desperate attempt to outrun the pain, but it stays, shadowing me, refusing to let go. My hand reaches for my phone, my thumb hovering over Jack's name. The urge to call him, to let every bit of my fury explode through the phone, is so strong I can almost hear myself shouting.

But I stop. I catch myself just in time.

Calling him won't fix this. It won't change anything. It'll only give him more power over me, and right now, it's the last thing he deserves.

I lower the phone, my fingers trembling with restraint. Jack doesn't deserve my anger or my attention. Not anymore.

And maybe, just maybe, he never did.

I exhale, the weight of the realization sinking in. My anger doesn't vanish, but it shifts—morphing from a raw, uncontrollable fury to something more focused. More resolute.

I'm done with this. Done with *him*. And for the first time, it feels like the beginning of something new—something that's entirely mine.

PART THREE
LEARNING

CHAPTER
THIRTY-EIGHT

leave for Anaheim first thing Monday morning, watching as Las Vegas shrinks in my rearview mirror. The miles blur by, but I barely notice—I'm too consumed by the thought of seeing Daisy. She'll understand, I tell myself. She's always known how to make things better.

I call her from the road, my voice betraying the frantic energy I'm trying to suppress.

"I need to ask a favor, and I really need you to say yes."

Daisy pauses. "Okay..."

"I'm losing it here, Daisy. I can't stand another day in this house. I feel like I'm suffocating. Can I—could I come stay with you for a while? Just a few days?"

She hesitates, and I hear the crackling quiet on her end. "Oh, I don't—"

"I'm already on my way. Please." The word tumbles out, raw. I'm past pride. "I need to feel like I have control over something."

Daisy agrees, though reluctantly, but it's not until later, when I pull up out front of Mom's old place, that the weight of my hesitation settles over me.

It's strange seeing it again—Mom's old place. The worn stucco facade, the faded shutters that never did get replaced. It looks the same, yet so different without her. I don't know how Andy continues to live here.

I sit in the car for a moment, just staring at the front door. There's a lump in my throat, and I wonder if it'll go away when I see him. If he'll even answer.

Maybe this is a bad idea. Maybe I should've called first, but part of me thought just showing up would be better. Easier.

Taking a deep breath, I get out of the car and walk up the cracked path, trying to summon some courage. I knock softly at first, then louder. Nothing. I wait, shifting on my feet, then knock again. Still nothing.

I step back, glancing at the windows. His car is in the driveway, so I know he's home. I bite my lip, unsure if I should try again or just leave. My phone feels heavy in my pocket, but I pull it out and text him anyway.

> Hey. I'm in town. I stopped by the house...I'd really like to talk if you're up for it.

I stare at the message for a second, then hit send. I keep my phone in my hand, just in case he responds right away, but the screen stays blank. No typing bubbles. No dots.

My chest tightens as I look back at the door. It feels like I'm standing on the edge of something, but I don't know if I'm supposed to jump or turn away. I take one more step toward the door, willing it to open, for Andy to come out and say *something* —anything. But the door stays closed, and the house remains silent.

After a few more minutes of waiting, I sigh, heading back to my car. I don't know why I thought showing up like this would work. He's been avoiding me for months—why would today be any different?

I get into the driver's seat, closing the door with more force than I mean to. My fingers tap anxiously against the steering wheel as I debate driving to Daisy's. But just as I'm about to start the engine, I spot movement out of the corner of my eye.

Andy steps out of the side door, keys in hand, heading toward his car.

Without thinking, I shove the door open and call out, "Andy!"

He freezes, his shoulders tense, then slowly turns to face me.

His expression is guarded, the same wall he's been putting up for months still firmly in place.

I jog over to him, feeling my pulse quicken. "Why are you doing this?" I ask, breathless, standing in front of him now. "Why are you so determined to push me away?"

He lets out a sharp breath, looking past me instead of at me. "Hazel, we've been over this. We're not kids anymore."

"This isn't about being kids," I snap, my frustration bubbling over. "You're acting like our falling out didn't happen because of Mom's lie. I didn't know she was sick, Andy! She told you I knew, but she lied. I would've been there if I'd known."

"Why would she lie about that?" Then he shakes his head. "No, it...You weren't there when it mattered."

My chest tightens, but I force myself to keep going. "I'm going through a lot, okay? I could really use my brother right now."

Andy shakes his head, his eyes hardening. "You can't just come here expecting everything to go back to how it was. Yeah we were close, but it was a long time ago. Too much has happened..."

"I just want you to hear me out. Everything between us, all of this...it's because of her lie. I miss you, Andy. You're my brother. Don't you miss me, too?"

He looks away, his face unreadable, but the silence between us is heavy with everything unsaid. After a long moment, he speaks again, his voice flat. "Go, Hazel."

I feel a sharp sting of rejection, and I open my mouth to argue, but the look on his face tells me it's no use.

He's not ready. Maybe he never will be.

Swallowing the lump in my throat, I step back. "Fine. I'm going."

I walk back to my car, the weight of the conversation settling into my bones.

Daisy's house smells like apples and cinnamon, the way it always does, and I feel a fleeting sense of comfort as I step inside. Toys are scattered across the floor, the kitchen counter still cluttered with the remnants of breakfast. There's cold coffee at the bottom of the carafe. It's the chaos of a family home—a life I'm intruding on.

I make my way to what used to be the guest room. It's been transformed into a second kids' room, complete with bunk beds and glow-in-the-dark stars on the ceiling. Daisy had mentioned they were bursting at the seams in this house, but still, she loves it too much to leave. I drop my bags on the bottom bunk, where I'll be sleeping, sharing the room with Ava. It's cramped, but better than being alone in Vegas.

The house is quiet without Daisy here, and I feel like an intruder, even though I know she left the key for me under the mat. I set up at the kitchen table to get some work done, spotting the Wi-Fi password on a sticky note stuck to the fridge: *Coxhome45726* followed by *wewereonabreak*. It's so perfectly Daisy I can't help but smile.

Two hours pass, and soon I hear the garage door swing open. Daisy walks in with Ava and Charlie, who's taller than the last time I saw him. He barrels toward me, peppering me with questions—When did I get here? How long am I staying? Is Max coming?—while Ava clings to her mom, eyeing me warily. I can't say it doesn't sting a little.

Daisy pulls me into a hug, her blond hair brushing my cheek. But it's brief, and when she pulls back, she avoids my eyes. "How was the drive?" she asks, her voice tight.

"Terrible," I admit. "Not the traffic, just...being alone with my thoughts for four and a half hours. My brain's been spinning stories the whole way."

Daisy glances at the kitchen table, where my laptop and papers are strewn. "I'd offer to open a bottle of wine, but I've got homework to help with first." Her tone is casual, but there's a distance in it, like she's holding something back.

"Oh, let me clear my stuff," I say quickly, gathering my things. My chest tightens with disappointment. This isn't the warm welcome I'd expected.

I retreat to Ava's room, feeling a little ridiculous for being hurt. Daisy's got a life, a family, and responsibilities. I shouldn't expect her to drop everything for me. Still, I'd hoped for more than this.

An hour later, Daisy finds me sitting on the bottom bunk. "You've been hiding in here," she says, her voice soft but tired. She sits down beside me. "So...what happened? What brought on this impromptu visit?"

I exhale slowly, gathering the courage to lay it all out. "Jack got his own place so I could stay at the house," I begin. "But last week, I went to pick up something, and I saw this name and number on the fridge—someone named Everly. And then Max mentioned Jack was talking to some woman on the phone."

Daisy's expression doesn't change much, but her shoulders drop slightly. "I'm really sorry, Hazel."

I wait for more, for some sign of understanding or reassurance that I made the right choice by coming here. But nothing comes. It feels like she's trying to close a door on me.

I force a smile and tell her I'm exhausted and need to get some work done before bed. She nods, standing to leave, and I spend the rest of the night under the covers, listening to the sounds of her family in the other room—the clatter of dishes, the low hum of conversation, and eventually, the soft murmurs as she reads to her kids.

I try to eat a granola bar I find at the bottom of my purse, but it sticks in my throat. I lie there, staring up at the glow-in-the-dark stars, wondering if I made a mistake coming here. This isn't the comfort I thought I'd find. Daisy is distracted and distant. And it's not fair to ask her to choose between me and her life.

Later, when Ava comes into the room to change into her pajamas, I pretend to be asleep.

I probably should have stayed home.

CHAPTER
THIRTY-NINE

The next few days blur together in a haze of awkward exchanges and missed connections. Daisy is always on the move—rushing to work, wrangling her kids, or just too exhausted to hold a real conversation. I try to help out around the house, but whenever I pick up a dish or fold some laundry, it feels like I'm only getting in the way. I spend most of my time tucked away in Ava's room, working on the floor surrounded by Barbie dolls and half-finished craft projects, trying not to feel like a burden.

By Thursday, the tension is gnawing at me. I catch Daisy in the kitchen, chopping vegetables for dinner, the rhythmic slice of the knife filling the silence between us. She doesn't see me at first, too focused on her task, but I clear my throat, trying to break through the awkwardness.

"Hey," I say, leaning against the counter. "I was thinking... maybe we could watch a movie tonight? Like old times?"

Daisy looks up, her knife pausing mid-chop. Her eyes meet mine, and for a moment, I see a flicker of the friendship we used to have, the easy connection we've shared for so long. She smiles faintly. "I think it's a great idea."

The words are reassuring, but there's a strange distance in her tone, like she's somewhere else entirely.

That evening, we settle onto the couch, a bowl of popcorn

between us. The TV flickers to life, casting shadows across the room. We've chosen a rom-com, something light and nostalgic, but as the opening credits roll, I can't help but notice how quiet Daisy is. She's sitting beside me, but she feels a million miles away, her mind clearly elsewhere.

I glance at her, hoping to draw her back into the moment. "You okay?" I ask softly.

Daisy keeps her eyes on the screen. "Yeah, I'm fine," she says, but the words are hollow. There's no conviction behind them.

I don't push. I know her well enough to understand that when Daisy's in her head like this, she needs time to sort through her feelings before she's ready to talk. Still, the silence between us feels heavier than it should, and I can't shake the sense something is off.

The movie continues, the laughter and romance playing out in front of us, but it's hard to focus when Daisy is so clearly distracted. I nibble on a handful of popcorn, trying to ignore the growing unease in my chest.

When the credits finally roll, Daisy stands abruptly, gathering up the empty bowl. "I'm going to clean up," she says, already halfway to the kitchen before I can respond.

I follow her, leaning against the doorframe as she rinses the bowl in the sink. "You sure everything's okay?" I ask again, quieter this time, giving her space to open up if she wants to.

Daisy nods, but her back is to me. "Just a lot on my mind," she murmurs, her voice barely audible over the running water. She turns off the faucet, drying her hands on a dish towel, and glances over her shoulder. "I'm really sorry. It's just...things are hectic right now. I tried to tell you on the phone but—you didn't really give me any other choice but to say yes to you coming."

Oh!

"I know. I just... I needed you," I say, my voice breaking. "I thought being here would make things better, but..."

But you're making me feel like an inconvenience.

There's no point in pushing her, so I let it go. But the tension between us is unmistakable now, a growing chasm that neither of us seems willing to address.

I watch as she moves around the kitchen, her movements efficient and a little too controlled, as if she's trying to keep something at bay.

Finn comes in a few minutes later, his presence filling the room. He greets me with a nod, but his focus is on Daisy. They exchange a few quiet words—nothing unusual, just the kind of mundane conversation couples have about the kids and dinner—but there's something about the way they move around each other that feels off. Like they're carefully avoiding stepping on each other's toes, as if one wrong word might tip everything over the edge.

I watch them, a quiet suspicion creeping into my thoughts. Is there something going on between them? Something they're not saying?

Daisy's laughter rings out suddenly as Finn makes some light-hearted joke about the mess in the kitchen, but it doesn't reach her eyes. It's the kind of laugh that feels practiced, a sound she makes because it's expected, not because she's really amused.

As I watch them clean up together, moving around each other in a delicate dance of avoidance, the pit in my stomach grows. I've known Daisy and Finn for years, and seen them in their best and worst moments, but tonight, something feels different. Something is off.

I don't know if it's just the strain of life wearing on them, or if there's something deeper happening beneath the surface. But one thing's clear: the distance I'm feeling with Daisy isn't just between us—it's between her and Finn too.

I retreat to Ava's room again that night, trying to focus on work, but the uneasy feeling lingers. Whatever's going on with Daisy, I can't help but wonder if it's bigger than I realized. And worse, I wonder if there's anything I can do to help—or if I'm just another part of the problem.

———

On my last night in Anaheim, Daisy finally lets me help with dinner. It feels like a small victory, to have something tangible to focus on, to let my hands work through the knot of emotions I've been carrying all week. We chop vegetables side by side, the conversation light and meaningless—weather, TV shows, anything but the elephant in the room. I've long since given up on the hope we'll talk about what really matters. But I can't shake the disappointment clinging to me like a shadow.

After dinner, once the kids have disappeared into their rooms, it's Finn who finally breaks the silence that hangs between us. "How are you handling the separation?" he asks, his voice gentle, full of concern.

I swallow hard, feeling the words stick in my throat. There's a part of me that wants to spill everything—to unload the weight of my hurt, my confusion, my frustration. I want to tell him how the separation is tearing me apart, how Daisy's distance has only made everything harder. But before I can speak, I catch sight of Daisy out of the corner of my eye. She's staring down at her plate, picking at the scraps of dinner like they're the most fascinating thing she's ever seen.

A wave of hurt rolls through me, sharp and sudden. The person I came here to lean on is turning away. Again.

I force a smile, trying to keep it together. "I'm managing," I say, the words thin and brittle. Even I can hear how hollow they sound. "Just taking it one day at a time."

Finn nods, sympathy etched across his face. "If you need anything, just let us know, okay? We're here for you."

I glance at Daisy again, hoping—praying—she'll say something, offer some sign she's still with me, that she still cares. She meets my gaze, but her expression is unreadable, a wall I can't see past.

"Thanks, Finn," I murmur, my voice barely above a whisper. "I appreciate it."

He pats my shoulder. His touch is meant to comfort, but it only deepens the ache in my chest. As he starts to clear the dishes, I sit there in the lingering quiet, the weight of everything pressing down on me.

———

I leave Anaheim that night, slipping out of the house after everyone has gone to bed. I don't want any more awkward goodbyes or forced smiles. I just want to go. The door clicks softly behind me as I step out into the cool night air. My car feels both like an escape and a surrender.

The engine hums to life, the sound breaking the stillness. As I drive away, tears blur my vision, the freeway lights smearing into glowing streaks. I came here looking for comfort, for a refuge in the friendship that had once been everything to me. But now, all I feel is the cold emptiness of something slipping away—something I don't know how to save.

By the time I reach the edge of the city, the tears have dried, but the sadness lingers, thick and heavy. As the lights of Las Vegas come into view, the energy of the city pulses against my sadness. The contrast is stark—Vegas, with all its noise and flash, feels like the opposite of what I need right now. Yet, it's home. It's where I belong, flawed and painful as it may be.

I take a deep breath, the familiar skyline grounding me. I can't control what Jack does, or how Daisy reacts. I can't fix what's already broken between us. But I can decide how to move forward. I can decide what happens next.

The city lights, once harsh and overwhelming, now feel like a challenge—a dare. They're telling me this isn't the end, not for me. My story doesn't stop here. And as I drive into the heart of Vegas, I realize I'm ready. Ready to face it all—Jack, Daisy, the uncertainty of what comes next. Ready to confront the messy, painful reality of my life.

Because this time, I'm not running away.

————————

In the morning there is a text from Daisy:

> You didn't have to leave, you know.

But I did. I really did.

CHAPTER
FORTY

t's a Tuesday morning in mid-September, and the Las Vegas heat still clings to the air like a second skin, making me sweat through my shirt. I push the front door open with my shoulder, balancing the grocery bags in my arms, and the rush of cool air from inside wraps around me like a hug. The relief is instant. I drop the bags on the kitchen counter and stand still for a moment, letting the coolness sink in as I catch my breath.

For a split second, Jack slips into my mind, but I push the thought away before it takes root. This time, I don't linger in the 'what ifs.'

I focus on unpacking the groceries. One by one, I arrange fresh vegetables in the crisper, line up spices in the cabinet, and carefully organize pasta and canned goods in the pantry. It's a mundane task, but it feels oddly grounding. There's something about the act of putting things in their place that brings a small sense of control. Small steps, but somehow significant.

With the groceries tucked away, I roll up my sleeves, losing myself in the comforting rhythm of preparing a meal. The steady chopping of vegetables, the sizzle of garlic hitting the hot pan—it's familiar, soothing. The sharp, rich aromas fill the kitchen, and

I hum quietly as I stir the pot, the scent of tomato sauce and fresh basil curling around me like an invitation to breathe deeper.

It's funny, I think, how I've missed this—just the simple pleasure of making something with my hands, nourishing myself in a way that's more than just food. I reach for the flour, preparing fresh pasta dough, kneading it slowly, letting the repetitive motion work out the tension in my shoulders. My hands are dusted with flour, the countertop sprinkled with the mess of my labor. It's a good mess—a sign of life, of movement, of something more than just waiting.

The sauce bubbles away as I set the table for one. A single flower in a small vase takes up the center. The simplicity of it makes me pause, but instead of feeling lonely, the sight is oddly comforting. There's peace here, in the quiet, in this moment I've carved out for myself.

When I finally sit down to eat, twirling the fresh pasta on my fork, I savor the first bite slowly. The flavors bloom on my tongue, and it's delicious, but beyond that—it's a reminder.

I'm more than just the wife Jack knows, more than the person caught in the chaos of our separation. I'm still here. I can still create, still find joy in the quiet, still feel whole even when it's just me.

After lunch, I open my laptop and pull up Atlas's manuscript. After weeks of back and forth, of emails and revisions, he finally finished his draft. The champagne I sent him as a reward must have hit its mark—he'd emailed me a photo, holding up a glass with a grin so wide it filled the screen. I smile to myself thinking I should print it out and stick it to my wall. A reminder this is why I do what I do.

I settle by the window, the natural light spilling over me as I dive into his story. The hours pass without me noticing, the room shifting in shadows as the afternoon drifts by. When I finally stand and stretch, a sense of accomplishment settles over me. I close my laptop, leaving the story behind for now, but feeling lighter somehow.

I glance around the house, surveying the mess that's collected over the past few weeks. The kitchen counters are cluttered, and the living room is strewn with the signs of life moving on.

Upstairs, I know there's a toothpaste-splattered mirror waiting for me and stray hairs littering the bathroom floor. The toilets probably have rings in them by now, but I shrug.

And it's in this moment, surrounded by the quiet hum of my own space, that I realize I don't have to care. Not about the mess, not about the expectations I used to hold so tightly.

There's something liberating in this, in the freedom to let things be as they are without rushing to fix them.

Lately, it feels a little bit like winning.

———

I arrive at Amelia's house just as the sun dips behind the horizon, casting an orange glow over the quiet neighborhood. She greets me with a wide smile and pulls me into a hug, the warmth of it surprising me even after all this time. I can't help but notice Quinn standing in the background, her gaze lingering a little too long, her mouth a tight line.

In the living room, the usual group—Quinn, Jenny, and Lucy —are already settled in, their laughter bubbling through the space. Books are scattered across the coffee table, a sign that the discussion is about to begin. I squeeze in next to Jenny, who shuffles over with a friendly grin.

"All right, let's dive in," Amelia says, clapping her hands together with excitement. "What did everyone think of *Bright Young Women?*"

"I'm still reeling from the twist," Jenny says, her voice buzzing with energy.

I shift uncomfortably, guilt gnawing at me. I didn't finish the book—hell, I barely started it. "Yeah, that was...unexpected," I say, trying to sound convincing.

Quinn, ever watchful, raises an eyebrow at me. "Did you actually finish it?" Her tone is light but the undertone stings.

I swirl the wine in my glass, avoiding her eyes. "Not quite. Life's been...well, you know how it is."

Amelia cuts in before Quinn can say anything more. "No worries, Hazel. It happens to the best of us," she says, flashing me a reassuring smile. There's something about the way she steps in so effortlessly, the way she seems to know just when I need saving, that makes me feel seen. We've gotten closer since I opened up to her about Jack and everything falling apart, and she never makes me feel like I have to apologize for not keeping up.

The conversation picks up again, flowing easily as Jenny launches into a passionate analysis of the protagonist's motives. Lucy shares a passage that moved her, and Quinn, despite her earlier comment, adds an impressively insightful take on how the author explores societal pressure on women. I can't help but nod in agreement, impressed despite myself.

Amelia, with her usual charm, makes a witty remark that has us all laughing, the tension easing from the room.

It's evenings like this that remind me why I'm grateful for this little group—even with Quinn's lingering glances, I feel comfortable, part of something again.

As the night winds down and everyone starts gathering their things, Amelia stands by the door to see them out, her smile never faltering. I linger behind, offering to help clean up. The kitchen is still warm from the gathering, and as I start stacking empty plates and glasses, Amelia comes to stand beside me.

"How've you been feeling these days?" she asks softly.

I lean against the counter, letting out a long breath. "Better, I think. It's been...nice to have nights like these." I glance over at her, appreciating the way she asks without prying, how she's been such a steady presence since I opened up about Jack and Everly. She listens without judgment, without offering unsolicited advice.

She nods, wiping her hands on a dish towel. "I'm glad to hear that."

"I actually got out of town for a bit," I admit, feeling the need to share more. "Spent some time with Daisy in Anaheim, thinking it might help clear my head. But somehow, I feel worse."

Amelia looks at me with her wide, sincere eyes. "Oh?"

I sigh, feeling a lump rise in my throat. "It's like there's this... distance between us. Like she doesn't know how to just *be* there for me. I wasn't asking for much...just to be there with her. To not be alone. She didn't seem like herself, is all."

Amelia's expression softens, and she places a hand on my arm.

"Maybe it's like with Jack. She just doesn't know what to say or do because she's never been through it herself."

I nod, the weight of her words sinking in. "Maybe. But it still hurts."

"I know," she says softly. "But give her some grace. She's your best friend, right? She's probably doing the best she can."

I swallow hard, nodding. "You're right. I just…I can't help but feel a little hurt."

Amelia doesn't rush to respond, just lets my words hang in the air between us. The silence isn't uncomfortable, though. If anything, it feels like we've reached some deeper understanding, the kind that's hard to put into words.

We work in silence for a while, the clinking of dishes and the low hum of the dishwasher the only sounds in the room. It's easy and companionable—so different from the strained interactions I've been having with other people lately. I can sense the closeness growing between us, but I also can't help but think about Quinn, the way she'd been watching earlier, the way her eyes had narrowed when Amelia hugged me. I get the feeling she doesn't like how easily Amelia and I have clicked.

Once everything is cleaned up, Amelia turns to me with a thoughtful look. "I was thinking…I have a friend, Nathan, I'd love you to meet. I think you two would get along."

I shake my head quickly, feeling a twinge of panic. "Thanks, but I'm not really ready for that."

She smiles, unbothered by my response. "Okay. Just keep it in mind. No pressure." She offers it so gently, like she understands exactly where I am, and she's not trying to push me anywhere I'm not ready to go.

She doesn't push me. Doesn't remind me that Jack is out there exploring his options and that maybe I should, too. She simply lays out the option for me. An offering.

"Maybe one day," I say, half-smiling, knowing I'm probably just saying it to make her happy. But even so, it feels good to have the option laid out in front of me, even if I'm not ready to take it.

CHAPTER
FORTY-ONE

The next day, I go about my usual routine, but Amelia's words keep circling in my head like an insistent hum. Maybe it wouldn't hurt to keep an open mind about dating.

Dating. It feels strange, even thinking about it. Something I haven't done since...well, since Jack. We met so young, I'd barely had time to figure out what I wanted, let alone explore what else was out there. Now, I can't help but wonder what it would be like to meet someone different, to see who else I might connect with, even if just for a little while.

Would it be reckless? Maybe. But then again, what's wrong with a little recklessness at this stage of my life? I've been so careful, so rooted in stability for so long. Maybe I could use a bit of unpredictability. Not for love, of course—I'm not looking for that. But fun? Yes. Fun has been missing for a while now.

The idea of it teases me with a warmth I haven't felt in ages.

I imagine what it could be like. Meeting someone for coffee or a drink, exchanging stories, and sharing a laugh. No strings attached. Just two people enjoying each other's company. Companionship, I suppose. Even if it's brief. Even if it leads nowhere.

The thought of sharing moments with someone new—a conversation with fresh eyes, a dinner with no expectations—

sends a ripple of excitement through me. The Hazel of ten years ago would never have entertained this idea. But now? Now I'm curious. And maybe that's enough of a reason to dip my toe in.

Before I can change my mind, I find myself opening my laptop and typing "match.com" into the search bar. The site loads quickly, and the screen flickers with bright, welcoming profiles of strangers. A world of possibilities.

I hesitate only for a moment before creating an account, filling out the basics. No harm in seeing what's out there, right?

After I finish, I sit back, staring at the screen. Then, almost on impulse, I reach for my phone and type out a text to Nathan, introducing myself and asking if he's free on Friday night.

Why not? It's time to try something new. Even if it's just for the experience.

———

Having not been on a first date in over twenty years, I have serious reservations about the whole ordeal. But when it happens, it comes about so quickly, so naturally, it almost feels like fate pushing me toward something new. I curl my hair, apply lipstick, and slip into a skirt I haven't worn in years, pleasantly surprised it still fits. Something is soothing about the familiar ritual of getting ready, even though I can't shake the nervous flutter in my stomach.

When I arrive at the restaurant, Nathan is already there, leaning casually against the hostess stand. He's decently handsome—dirty blond hair and a neatly trimmed beard—but his wrinkled shirt immediately catches my eye. It's not a dealbreaker, but it feels like a small signal he hasn't put as much effort into this as I have. I think of the hour I spent fretting over my outfit, and a twinge of self-consciousness creeps in.

Maybe I'm overthinking things already.

"Hazel, right?" Nathan greets me with a bright smile, his handshake firm but not lingering. "Nice to meet you."

"You too," I reply, smiling back, though I already feel a slight disconnect. As we sit down and order drinks, I remind myself to relax, to go with the flow. After all, it's just one date.

"So, you're from Vegas originally?" he asks, leaning forward with interest.

"No, actually. I'm from Anaheim, but I've been in Vegas since college," I say, taking a sip of my drink.

"Ever miss it?"

I pause, thinking. "Sometimes. Mostly when the heat here gets unbearable. But I like it here. It's home now."

Nathan nods, but I sense he's not quite convinced. "Yeah, I'm still getting used to it. I moved here six months ago, and man, it's...intense. I mean, all the lights, the tourists, the noise. It's kind of overwhelming, don't you think?"

"It can be," I agree, smiling. "But there's more to it than The Strip. You just have to look for it."

He nods thoughtfully, but I can tell he's not entirely sold on Vegas, and a silence hangs between us. He quickly shifts gears, peppering me with rapid-fire questions. "So, what do you do for work? Hobbies? Any fun weekend plans?"

"I'm an acquisitions editor. I work with authors to develop their books. It's busy, but I love it. And when I'm not working, I'm usually with my son, or I'll spend a Saturday reading at a café or browsing bookstores. Pretty low-key."

A flicker of confusion crosses his face. "Amelia didn't mention a son."

"Oh." I glance down at my drink. "Yeah, he's eleven."

"Cool," he says, nodding slowly. "I didn't know if you were looking for, you know...anything serious."

"I'm not," I say quickly, sensing the tension. "I just want to have fun. See what's out there."

"Right, right," he says, his expression softening. "Well, I don't have kids, but I've got a dog. Golden retriever. Best decision I ever made."

"A dog sounds nice," I say, trying to bridge the gap, but I feel it widening between us. His enthusiasm for his bachelor lifestyle and my quiet evenings spent with Max couldn't feel more different.

We keep the conversation going, talking about everything from favorite movies (his are action-packed blockbusters, while I lean more toward character-driven dramas) to weekend plans (he's into hiking and sports; I prefer a cozy afternoon with a book). We're both polite, but with each passing minute, it becomes clearer that we're on very different wavelengths.

At one point, Nathan leans in, his voice lowered conspiratorially. "Honestly, I'm not much of a reader. I can't remember the last book I read cover to cover. But I guess working in publishing, you're reading all the time, huh?"

"Pretty much," I say, forcing a smile. "It's part of the job, but I enjoy it. I can't imagine not reading."

Nathan chuckles, rubbing the back of his neck. "I bet. I just like to be outdoors. I'll take a hike or a weekend camping trip over sitting still any day."

And there it is—another difference, laid out plainly between us. The kind of person who thrives in nature, always seeking adventure, and the kind who can lose herself in the pages of a book for hours. Neither is wrong, but they aren't easily compatible either.

As the evening winds down, the check arrives, and I offer to split it. Nathan hesitates for a moment but ultimately agrees. I'm not sure what I expected, but I feel oddly relieved. It makes things cleaner and simpler.

Outside, he walks me to my car. There's no lingering moment, no awkward attempt at a kiss. Just a polite, "Well, this was fun. Thanks for coming out."

"Yeah, it was," I agree, even though we both know there's no real connection here. "Take care, Nathan."

I slide into my car, and as I drive home, I'm not exactly disappointed. Instead, I feel oddly upbeat, like I've crossed some invisible threshold. It wasn't a disaster, and that's a win.

I text Amelia to let her know we didn't click, but I'm glad I went.

My first first date is a thing of the past.

Thank god.

————

It's a couple of weeks before I go on my next date. Max is, once again, with his father and so I shower and dress with the bedroom door wide open. I wear the same skirt I wore on my date with Nathan but opt to pair it with white sneakers as we're just meeting for a late morning cup of coffee. As we live clear across the valley from one another, we choose to meet somewhere in the middle, at a place downtown called Bungalow Coffee I've never been to.

A tall man stands and approaches me when I walk through the door. He's dressed in navy blue scrubs and Nike running shoes. He has the kind of hair you immediately want to run your hand through and kind eyes, which he centers on me.

"Hazel," he says. "Hi. I'm sorry for the scrubs, I have to head to work after this and realized a little too late I was overdue on doing laundry. Please don't take this as a lack of interest." He smiles self-consciously.

I don't mind the scrubs. In fact, they're kind of doing it for me.

Over piping-hot lattes, Robert tells me about himself: "I'm the eldest of three kids, both girls, so I'm naturally super protective of my sisters. One of them is a physician's assistant like me, and the other works in a chiropractic office. Born and raised in Vegas and can't imagine being anywhere else.

"I work a lot, which doesn't leave much time for dating, which pretty much explains why I'm forty-two and single." When he smiles, his eyes nearly close. He really does have the kindest eyes. "What about you? What's your story?"

My breath catches. Finally, I say: "Which chapter of my story are you interested in hearing about?" I sound confident but I am anything but.

"I mean, you're clearly beautiful and normal, which is harder to find in this city than you would think. How is it you're sitting here with me right now instead of at home with a husband and kids?"

Oh, and the date had been going so well...

"I'm sitting here with you...because I want to."

A flicker of uncertainty flashes across Robert's face.

I try again. "I don't—" The words catch like so many times before and the look on Robert's face is now one of pure confusion.

"I'm married," I say, unable to stop myself. "But it's complicated."

"Oh," he says. And this is where I lose him. It's a shame, really. He had such a nice head of hair. I'll probably spend the rest of my life wondering what it might have felt like to run my hands through it.

––––––––––

My third first date comes three weeks after the second, and for some reason, it feels promising. I'm unusually chatty—unlike my usual self on a first date, where I keep things light and measured. Tonight, with Dennis, the words just spill out. I'm either getting more comfortable with dating or losing my filter. Either way, I can't seem to stop talking, in a situation where I'd normally retreat.

As I pick at my ahi tuna salad (I really do like salads, despite how cliché it might seem), I dive into explaining my career—how I got into publishing, what excites me about books, the details of editing that most people would find boring. Dennis seems genuinely engaged, nodding and asking the right questions. It's flattering, almost. Then, out of nowhere, he surprises me.

"You know, I've been thinking a lot about the lack of BIPOC representation in literature," he says, brow furrowed. "It's shocking how little diversity there is. Don't you think it's kind of…systemic?"

The shift in conversation catches me off guard, and I freeze mid-bite. He's not wrong—it's an important topic, one I've discussed plenty at work. But this is a first date. Wasn't this supposed to be fun? Still, I can't lie.

"Absolutely," I say, setting my fork down. "Publishing has a long history of gatekeeping, especially for marginalized voices. There's progress, but it's slow."

Dennis leans forward as if we're in a heated debate. "Exactly! And it's not just in literature. It's everywhere—education, health-care, you name it."

As the conversation deepens, I realize this isn't the fun, light-hearted date I hoped for. Dennis is intense, carrying the weight of the world on his shoulders. His narrowed eyes and the way he leans in make it feel like we're dissecting global issues, not getting to know each other. I wonder if he even knows how to have fun or if every conversation leads to life's biggest injustices.

I try to steer us back to something lighter. "That's why I read fiction with happy endings," I joke, smiling. "Life's tough enough without having to relive it through books."

But Dennis doesn't smile. Instead, he frowns, like I've said something naive. "Don't you think fiction has a responsibility to address real issues? We can't just pretend everything's fine."

I inwardly sigh. There it is again—his seriousness. "I mean, sure," I say, "but sometimes people just need a break. Not everything has to be about fixing the world."

He looks at me like I've completely missed the point. "But isn't that what makes good art? It challenges us."

I don't disagree, but I also don't want to spend the night debating the ethics of fiction. "It depends on what you're looking for," I say, trying to stay neutral. "Sometimes people just want to be entertained."

The conversation stalls. The earlier ease between us evaporates. We finish our meals in silence, with Dennis still looking deep in thought, probably dissecting everything I've said. Meanwhile, I'm left wondering if this guy ever just...relaxes. It's clear he's passionate and thoughtful, but the idea of spending more time with someone who takes everything so seriously feels suffocating.

When the check comes, I offer to split it. Dennis agrees, though there's a slight pause, like he expected me to insist he covers it. I get the feeling he thinks paying would have put me in some sort of debt to him. But I don't feel like owing him anything —not after spending the night navigating his intensity.

Driving home, I feel full from the meal but empty otherwise. I replay the evening, wondering where it all went wrong. Was it me? Am I too blunt, too honest? Or was Dennis just not the right fit—too intense, too serious, too caught up in the world's problems to just enjoy the moment?

Maybe it's not them. Maybe it's me. Maybe I came into this with unrealistic expectations. I thought I just wanted someone fun, someone to make the lonely days a little less lonely. But finding the balance between fun and connection is harder than I expected.

At home, I sit with a latte and replay the night in my head. "Well, it started well, didn't it?" I mutter to myself. "Right up until he started lecturing me on the responsibilities of fiction."

I can almost hear Daisy laughing at me, telling me I need to relax. But I promised her I wouldn't lean on her so much.

———

After my fourth bad first date, seven weeks after finding out about Jack's new girlfriend from our son, I decide I'm done. If something is meant to happen, it will. No more forcing it. No more pretending I'm okay with being dragged into endless serious conversations that drain the life out of me.

In the car outside the restaurant, I delete my online profile.

CHAPTER
FORTY-TWO

I don't know why I'm driving toward Jack's apartment instead of heading home. I didn't plan to, but here I am, turning onto Hualapai Way, curiosity pulling me along. I don't even know what I'm hoping to see. Maybe a second car next to his, or the blinds open, giving me a glimpse of the life I'm no longer part of.

When I arrive, the blinds are shut and the apartment dark. It's past eight p.m., and Max should be in his usual routine—shower, teeth, reading in bed by nine. But everything feels off.

I wait, telling myself I'll only stay a few minutes. At eight-forty-five, Jack and Max finally pull up. Max looks tired, dragging his backpack, while Jack walks ahead, keys in hand, as if nothing's changed. I watch them go inside, and soon, Max's light turns on. That's my cue to leave, but I linger, gripping the steering wheel, resisting the urge to text Jack.

Where were they tonight? It's such a simple question, but I can't ask it. I drive home replaying their entrance, searching for a reason to feel less disconnected, though I know there's no valid reason, just the ache of being left out.

When I finally arrive home, the emptiness of the house settling over me like a heavy blanket. This time apart is complete bullshit. Nothing has changed except the fact Jack and I aren't fighting anymore—and that's only because we can't fight if we're not in the same room. The silence between us isn't peace; it's avoidance. And for what?

I think, not for the first time, that we should be under the same roof, hashing things out, instead of hiding from our problems in separate spaces. What's going to change between now and some arbitrary future date? When I turn forty, will I magically know how to care less or be more carefree? Will I suddenly become the woman who doesn't mind the ridiculously specific way Jack insists on loading the dishwasher? No. And Jack isn't going to stop being obsessed with his job, nor is he going to start looking at me the way he did when we were newlyweds. We're not going to be fixed by distance. If anything, this separation is just stretching the cracks wider.

The only silver lining in this whole fiasco is that Max is spending more time with his father. But even that feels bittersweet because it means I'm spending less time with him.

The urge to turn around and confront him hits me hard. I want to demand why we're pretending time and space will fix everything. But just as quickly, the feeling fades, replaced by a strange, welcome detachment.

Enough. Enough now.

And for the first time, I mean it.

I throw myself into work. It's my go-to when life gets tough—something I can control. The endless manuscripts and editing are a welcome distraction, immersing me in other worlds instead of my own.

A calendar reminder buzzes, pulling me back. Time for the weekly Zoom call. I close the manuscript, take a deep breath, and put on my professional smile as the familiar faces from Inklings appear on the screen.

"Good morning, everyone," I say. I glance down at the steno pad beside me where I've written a long list of manuscripts, each one a potential new acquisition for Inklings. The second list holds authors that aren't so lucky this time around.

"Morning, Hazel," Emma, our senior editor, replies with a

warm smile. "Let's dive right in. Any standout manuscripts we know are a hard pass?"

I clear my throat, looking again at my list. "Yes, actually. *Heartstrings and Stardust*," I say, "is compelling but also deeply flawed. The character development is inconsistent, and the plot meanders without clear direction."

Emma raises an eyebrow. "That's…okay. Any others?"

I sort through my list, feeling the weight of honesty pressing down on me. "*The Unwritten Horizon* is well-written, with strong characters and a gripping plot. But it's overly derivative, like the author read too many bestsellers and tried to mash them all into one."

A few of my colleagues exchange puzzled looks through the screen. Normally, I'd sugarcoat my critiques, balancing the negatives with the positives. Right now, that balance is impossible.

The room falls silent. I can feel the tension growing. This level of honesty is unsettling, even for me.

"Is there anything you actually like, Hazel?" James, our marketing lead, asks. He laughs as he says it but it's forced.

I swallow hard. "Yes, actually. *Echoes of Silent Waters*. It's raw and unpolished, but it has authenticity. The author's voice is unique, and the story has potential. It needs work, but I believe it will be worth it."

Emma nods slowly. "Thank you, Hazel. Your honesty is… refreshing, if a bit unexpected. We'll consider your thoughts."

As the meeting continues, I can't help but wonder how long this honesty thing is going to last. It's been months and I'm no closer to figuring out how to reverse it.

"All right," Emma says. She is suddenly chipper, seemingly happy to be done with the portion of the meeting where she has to converse with me. "Anyone else?"

The Zoom call ends, and I slump back in my chair, staring at the screen. Why did I have to be so brutally honest? I know I can't lie, but sometimes I wish I could just soften the blow.

My head throbs with the stress of it all, and I know I need a change of scenery. There's only one place that can help me clear my mind.

I head out the door, the thought of a warm latte and the hum of quiet conversation already soothing my nerves.

The moment I push through the doors of Foxtail Coffee, I feel a weight lift from my shoulders. There's something about this place that always brings me peace, like the scent of freshly ground beans and the low hum of quiet conversations are all I need to reset. It's my go-to escape whenever work starts to feel overwhelming.

Today, I order my usual black coffee, and to my surprise, my favorite stool is open as if it's been waiting just for me.

I slide onto the stool, pull out my laptop, and glance at the book I brought, wishing I could dive into it instead of tackling work emails. With a sigh, I settle into the familiar rhythm of answering emails, tapping away at the keyboard. It's not long before I sense movement behind me—someone standing too close.

"I'm sorry," a deep voice says, making me freeze. I realize my bag is on the only free stool. Flustered, I move it and look up into chestnut-brown eyes. There's something magnetic about him, though we've never met.

"Sit, please," I stammer, embarrassed. He smiles, sits, and the barista places his coffee in front of him. I try to focus on my work, but I'm distracted by how close he is. His presence feels tangible, and I catch myself staring.

Our eyes meet again, and he grins. I can't help but smile back.

"I'm Matt," he says, his voice smooth and amused.

I laugh nervously, turning to face him more fully, but in doing so, my knee knocks into his. "Sorry!" I laugh, awkwardly extending my hand before realizing the proximity makes it too weird. I drop it back to my lap, feeling like an idiot. "Hazel."

"Nice to meet you, Hazel," Matt says, and his smile widens. His teeth are straight and white, and I can't help but wonder if he knows how irresistible his smile is. He nods toward my laptop. "Are you a writer?"

"I wish. No, I'm an acquisitions editor," I say, relaxing just a bit. I like that he's interested.

"What exactly does an acquisitions editor do?" he asks, his voice genuine.

I smile as I explain my job, surprised by how easy it is to talk to him. There's no pressure, no need to hide anything. He listens closely, and when I ask what he does, he replies, "I'm in real estate. But tell me more about you."

I talk about growing up in Anaheim, brushing over my complicated relationship with my mother my time at UNLV, and becoming a mother, without mentioning Jack. The conversation flows effortlessly. We even share an almond croissant, and it feels comfortable—yet electric.

"If you could change one thing about your life, what would it be?" he asks, a playful smile on his lips.

I pause, surprised by the depth of his question. "So much for light and breezy, huh?"

He smiles wider, and I bite my lip to keep from grinning. The answer comes quickly. "I'd try to mend things with my mother before she passed."

Matt's expression softens. "That's tough. I'm sorry."

"Yeah, me too," I say, looking at my empty cup. He gives me space, then says, "I kind of wish I hadn't asked. I'm terrible at small talk."

I laugh. "You're doing fine."

"Your turn. Ask me something equally invasive," he says, blushing slightly.

I ask, "What's something you're working on in yourself?"

He thinks for a moment. "I'm trying to be more grateful instead of always wanting more."

I nod. "It's hard, with everything telling us we should want more."

We lean in, the connection between us growing stronger, feeling so natural, like we've known each other for much longer.

"You can't possibly be single, right?" he says, a playful gleam in his eyes. "Just tell me now and put me out of my misery."

I blink slowly, savoring the moment. "I'm not *single*," I say carefully, watching his face fall just a bit. "But I am…available. If you have time, I can explain."

As the afternoon light filters through the large windows,

casting a soft glow over everything, I find myself leaning in even closer, my breath catching as our fingers brush on the table. Matt's gaze drops to my lips, and before I can second-guess anything, we're both leaning in and then—

I'm kissing a man who is decidedly not my husband. And I'm loving every second of it.

I let the moment wash over me, the warmth of it, the electricity, the feeling of being wanted—truly wanted—for the first time in what feels like forever.

CHAPTER
FORTY-THREE

For the next two days, Matt takes up more space in my mind than my own to-do list. Like a love-struck teenager, I'm consumed by absurdly cliché thoughts: What's he doing? Who's he with? Could he possibly be thinking of me too? Suddenly, everything is Matt-themed. The barista's smile? Not as perfect as his. A random song on the radio? Clearly written about us. Even the way he leaned in before our kiss has become a mental GIF on infinite replay.

I float through my days with a bounce in my step, as if my sneakers came with a built-in serotonin boost. The summer heat has finally broken, and it feels like the universe hit "refresh" on my mood.

I've exchanged numbers with a man who isn't my husband.

That little tidbit sends a dangerous thrill zipping through me. I bite my lip to keep from outright giggling, but the smile creeping across my face isn't so easily contained. Somewhere between my car and the grocery cart return, I probably look like a woman who just won the lottery—or lost her marbles. Either way, I can't bring myself to care.

I review what I know about Matt. He works in real estate, admits to being bad at small talk, and has a passion for music and books. It's not much, but we've only just met. And yet, I feel like there's something more, something deeper just waiting to unfold.

I know it's complicated. He knows I'm married. He knows in less than five months, Jack and I are supposed to come back together and figure out what happens next. If I were Matt, I'd probably have run for the hills by now. But the fact he hasn't, the fact he still wanted my number, buoys me in a way I hadn't expected.

At work, my daydreaming starts to slip into everything I do. On Zoom calls, my name has to be repeated two, sometimes three times before I snap out of it. "Hazel?" someone asks again, pulling me back into reality. I apologize, pretending to be focused, but my mind is already drifting back to him. I'm there physically, but my thoughts are somewhere else—lost in the possibility of what could be.

Life feels absurdly surreal, like I've stumbled into a fairytale where, against all odds, I'm the lucky princess—minus the glass slippers and with significantly more emotional baggage. I know better than to start singing "Someday My Prince Will Come," but I can't help it. I haven't felt this kind of spark in years, and even if it's fleeting, even if it's just a tiny detour from reality, I'm savoring every second of this unexpected magic.

But, of course, doubt has to crash the party. Will I ever hear from him again? The thought sits in the corner of my mind like an uninvited guest, nibbling on my confidence. Matt knows everything—about Jack, about my complicated life, about the messiness of my not-so-happily-ever-after.

Maybe he'll decide it's too much drama for one lifetime.

And honestly? I wouldn't blame him. Who signs up for this kind of chaos willingly? Fairy godmothers definitely don't work overtime for that.

Three days after meeting Matt, I finally muster up the courage to text him...only to find out he's already beaten me to it.

> It was great meeting you the other day. Would love to see you again sometime. —Matt

A smile tugs at the corners of my lips, and I feel a pleasant warmth rising to my cheeks. How incredible it feels to be wanted, to be shiny and new to someone. I barely have time to process the feeling before another text arrives.

> I would have texted sooner, but my sister told me I had to wait at least two days so as not to appear too eager.

I grin, appreciating the mix of honesty and wit—and his proper use of a comma. My response practically writes itself.

> Honestly, I was feeling rather lukewarm about the whole night, but then you had to go ahead and hit me with a properly punctuated text.

The telltale three dots begin dancing on the screen, and a rush of anticipation floods me.

> Damn. And here I was thinking I'd dazzled you with my personality. Your killing me.

I laugh, catching the typo immediately. Just as I'm contemplating how to tease him about it, my phone rings. I answer without hesitation.

"I meant to type 'you're,'" Matt says, his voice quick and a little breathless. "That was obviously a mistake. Please don't judge me too harshly."

"Relax," I say, suppressing a laugh. "I was going to let it slide. But if there's another grammar slip, I'm afraid we're done."

"Noted," he replies, his tone lighter now. "So, if I haven't scared you off with my poor texting skills, how about dinner tonight?"

"Tonight?" I ask, letting mock skepticism creep into my voice. "That's awfully presumptuous of you—assuming I don't have plans."

"Call it a hunch," he says smoothly, the confidence in his voice making me smile. "I'll pick you up at seven."

"Well, aren't you bold," I tease.

"Bold enough to risk a second typo in this conversation," he quips.

I laugh, feeling a spark—a lightness I hadn't realized I was missing. "Fine. Seven it is. But for the record, you're already on thin ice."

"I'll bring my A-game," he promises, and for the first time in ages, I believe it might actually be true.

I glance at the clock on my computer. It's only noon.

Don't you dare obsess about this for the next seven hours, I tell myself. But even as I think it, I know I won't listen. In the five minutes since the call ended, I've already mentally run through half my wardrobe, debated whether to attempt the elusive flick of eyeliner, and wondered which perfume to wear—should I go with the classic sweet scent or the spicier one I impulsively bought at Nordstrom Rack?

By five, I'm in the shower, washing away the day's anxieties.

By six, I'm styling my hair, carefully applying my makeup. To my surprise, the eyeliner goes on without a hitch, as if tonight's good fortune extends to my winged liner technique.

At six fifty, I realize I'm starving, but I can't risk ruining my lipstick. I fold a piece of swiss cheese and honey ham into my mouth, chewing carefully, then rinse with mouthwash just as the doorbell rings.

Right on time—seven o'clock exactly.

When I open the door, Matt is standing there, and he's even more handsome than I remember. I feel a flicker of nervousness in my chest. He's well beyond my league, and for a brief moment, I wonder what he's doing here. But when his face lights up with a genuine smile, all of my doubts vanish.

"You look beautiful," he says, his voice soft, but full of admiration.

Oh! You're going to be trouble.

———

Matt's disarming smile makes it easy to lose focus, and I realize I've missed the last part of his story. I shake myself back to the moment.

"I'm sorry. What did you say?"

He laughs lightly. "I was telling you about a client I had to drop after she got caught going through people's belongings during showings—three times before I found out."

I bark out a laugh. "That's terrible!"

His grin widens, and I take in his features—chestnut-brown eyes, a square jaw with just the right amount of stubble, and a stylish haircut. He's the type of guy you'd look at twice and then rule out because he's too good-looking, like someone who never had to try hard for attention. I hope I'm not staring too long.

"So," he says, pulling me back, "how did you get into acquisitions?" He pops a fry into his mouth, and I love that he picked a burger place for our first real date. It feels casual and easy—not like he's trying to impress me with anything flashy.

I take a sip of my drink. "To keep it short, I love discovering new voices and helping authors turn raw potential into something extraordinary. It's the thrill of collaborating and bringing their vision to life."

He listens intently, his eyes full of genuine interest, which is refreshing compared to the halfhearted nods I usually get when I talk about my job.

"What do you like to read?" he asks, leaning in.

"Mostly literary fiction," I say. "But I'm open to anything if it's good. What about you?"

"Mysteries and thrillers," he replies, "but I like non-fiction too. It keeps me grounded."

I wrinkle my nose playfully. "Non-fiction isn't really my thing. Unless it's a memoir."

Matt's eyes light up, but then he hesitates. "Have you read *I'm Glad My Mom Died* by Jennette McCurdy?" Realizing the implication, he winces. "Oh, god. I'm sorry. I didn't think."

It takes a second for the weight of his words to hit me, bringing memories of my mother flooding back. The air between us shifts, heavy.

"Yeah," I finally say. "I've read it."

An awkward silence settles between us, thick and uncomfortable. I search for something to say, but my mind blanks.

Matt chuckles nervously, running a hand through his hair. "I'm terrible at small talk, apparently."

His attempt to lighten the mood works, and I smile. "Nah, you're doing better than you think."

The tension dissipates, and we're back to the comfortable rhythm we'd been building. The moment that could have derailed the night becomes a layer of connection, and Matt's vulnerability makes me feel more open and willing to see where this goes.

After dinner, Matt suggests a walk.

We stroll through a nearby park, our footsteps blending with the rustling leaves. We find a bench and sit down, the silence between us natural, not awkward. Matt turns to me, his expression tender.

"Hazel, I've been thinking about you a lot these past few days," he says softly.

I smile down at my hands, blushing. "I feel the same way."

Relief washes over his face as he reaches for my hand. We sit there for a while, holding hands and enjoying the quiet.

"I had a great time tonight."

"Me too," I say, feeling breathless.

He leans in, and our lips meet in a gentle kiss, full of promise. As we part, the thought crosses my mind that this is the start of something special.

Except it can't be.

I'm still married.

CHAPTER
FORTY-FOUR

The bell above the door jingles as I step into the salon, the familiar hum of hairdryers and chatter greeting me. The smell of shampoo and hairspray is comforting, like a place I've known forever. I wave at Carolyn, my hairdresser, who grins widely and beckons me over.

"Long time no see," she says, giving me a quick hug. I sit down and she lightly combs her fingers through my hair. "What are we doing today?"

"I need a change, Carolyn. A big one. Let's chop it," I say, surprising even myself with my boldness. I'm probably a little late to the game, seeing as the summer is coming to an end, but better late than never. I show her a photo on my phone of a woman with a gorgeous head of short, messy curls.

Carolyn's eyebrows shoot up, but she nods enthusiastically. "I love it. Let's do it."

I settle into the chair, watching her in the mirror as she gathers her tools. The chair squeaks as she pumps it higher, and I inhale deeply, feeling the excitement bubble up inside me. This is it, the next step to a fresh start.

Snip, snip, snip. The sound of the scissors cutting through my hair is oddly satisfying. Locks of hair tumble to the floor, and I feel lighter with each cut. Carolyn works quickly, expertly, chatting all the while about the latest salon gossip, but I'm barely listening. I'm focused on the reflection in the mirror, watching as I transform before my eyes. Even if I could keep up with her chatter, I don't trust myself to not say something incriminating. Best just to keep quiet.

Carolyn blow dries and curls my hair and then runs her fingers through the curls, pulling them apart. I barely recognize the person staring back at me. She's confident, hopeful, ready to move forward.

Carolyn steps back, admiring her work. "What do you think?"

I run my fingers through my new hair, feeling the silky strands brush against my shoulders. A smile spreads across my face, and for the first time in a long while, it feels truly genuine. "I love it, thank you."

She beams. "Anytime."

I step out of the salon, the sun warm on my face. The wind catches my new hair, heavy, as though carrying away the weight of the past. I feel alive and rejuvenated. Ready to take on whatever comes next.

At school pickup, the book club moms—having graduated from being referred to as the fifth grade moms—are excited about my new look, except for Quinn who smiles but says nothing. If she's still upset about my outburst months ago then so be it. I don't have the strength or desire to worry about what every single person thinks about me.

Max startles when he sees me. His eyes widen. "Whoa, Mom! Your hair! It looks awesome!"

I feel a warm glow inside, his excitement and approval making me feel even better about my decision. "Thanks, bud. I needed a change."

We say our goodbyes and head for the car.

"Did you do it because of Dad?" he asks.

I try not to laugh. "No, Max. I did it for me. Sometimes, we need to do things for ourselves to feel good and move forward."

He nods slowly, processing my words. "That makes sense."

Settled in the car, I feel a sense of peace wash over me. This new chapter, this new beginning, isn't just about moving on from the past. It's about embracing who I am and who I want to be, for myself and my son. And right now, that feels pretty amazing.

It's almost—*almost*—enough to take my mind off the fact that Andy hasn't responded to any of my texts in two months.

> Please. I'm all the family you have left.

> What kind of person doesn't respond to that kind of plea?

> What kind of person doesn't respect someone's wish for space...

————

My phone buzzes on the counter as I finish dinner, and when I glance at it, I see a text from Amelia.

> Come over for a glass of wine? I need to hear about your latest romantic escapades.

I grin. Wine and some girl talk with Amelia sounds like exactly what I need. I glance over at Max, still at the table, working through his math homework. He seems focused, but I know a change of scenery would do him good. And thankfully, Amelia's son, Reese, is always up for hanging out with him.

I text back.

> That sounds perfect. Mind if I bring Max?

Almost instantly, Amelia replies.

> Absolutely! Bring him over. Reese is dying for some company anyway.

"Hey, how'd you like to hang out with Reese for a little while?"

Max looks up, his pencil pausing mid-air. "Heck yeah. Can I bring my Switch?"

I nod. "Go grab it. We'll head over in a few minutes."

As Max rushes off to gather his things, I quickly clean up the kitchen, grab my coat, and throw my phone in my pocket. It's been too long since I've had a proper chat with Amelia, and this feels like the perfect excuse to unwind.

By the time we get to Amelia's house, Max is already bouncing with excitement. Amelia greets us at the door, a bottle of wine in one hand and a smirk on her face.

"You made it," she says, opening the door wider to let us in. "Reese is upstairs. Max, head on up whenever you're ready."

Max doesn't need any more prompting—he darts past us, already calling out Reese's name.

Amelia hands me a glass of wine and raises her eyebrows. "Now, spill. Tell me everything."

I laugh, taking the glass from her. "Oh, you're in for a story."

We settle onto the couch, the distant sound of video game chatter from upstairs fading into the background as we finally get down to what we're really here for: wine, friendship, and catching up.

Amelia leans forward, eyes bright with curiosity. "So, what exactly was wrong with Nathan? He's so handsome and intelligent, well-spoken. I'm trying not to take it as a personal failure there won't be a second date."

I take a sip of wine, trying to gather my thoughts. "Nathan was nice," I begin, carefully choosing my words. "But there just weren't any sparks."

Amelia raises an eyebrow, clearly perplexed. "No sparks? I thought he checked all the boxes."

I nod, feeling a little guilty for disappointing her. "He did, on paper. He was polite, considerate, and asked all the right questions...I don't know. There was no excitement, no real connection. By the end of the night, I didn't feel anything. In the past, I might have kept that to myself, smoothed things over to avoid awkwardness, but...I can't do it anymore."

Amelia tilts her head, curious. "What do you mean?"

Oh. Right.

"I mean, I can't lie. I can't pretend something is there when it's not. I used to do that, you know? In the past, I might have said all the right things, made it seem like the date went better than it did, maybe even agreed to a second one, just to avoid the discomfort of being honest. But now? Now, I have to be brutally honest —whether I want to or not." I swallow. "I mean, I feel like I have to be brutally honest."

Amelia's face softens in understanding.

"It was freeing in a way," I admit. "I didn't waste my time or his. I could have dragged it out, but what would've been the point? Nathan's a nice guy, but he would've never been right for me. Being honest kept me from settling for something that wasn't a good fit."

Amelia nods thoughtfully. "I guess that's a good thing then. Saves you a lot of time and trouble."

"Exactly," I say, feeling the truth of it settle in. "He's not the one for me, and that's okay. Unlike..." My voice trails off as thoughts of Matt slip into my mind, and I can't help the small smile that follows.

"Unlike?" Amelia's eyes light up. "Oh, do tell."

And so I do. I tell her about Matt. About the way his eyes crinkle when he smiles, and the scar on his knee from a childhood accident. I tell her how I'd forgotten what it felt like to have someone thinking about me, and how much I enjoy thinking about him in return. I even tell her how, for the first time in a long time, I can be myself with someone—warts and all.

Amelia listens closely, her expression growing more intrigued as I continue. "And he knows about Jack?" she asks, her voice tinged with surprise.

I nod. "Yeah, he knows about my...situation. And what's more, he gets it. He understands relationships aren't always black and white. He knows what we're doing—just having fun."

"Having fun," Amelia repeats, smiling knowingly. "Well, I'm happy for you. Even if it's not Nathan you're having fun with."

I laugh, feeling a sense of relief and gratitude for a friend like Amelia, someone who knows when to listen and when to nudge.

As we sip our coffee in comfortable silence, I can't help but feel like I've made the right choices—being honest with myself, with Nathan, and with Matt. I didn't settle for something that wasn't right, and in doing so, I've opened the door to something far more real.

———

After an hour of laughter and wine with Amelia, Max and I head home, the night calm and still around us. Once inside, the house feels quiet, a peaceful kind of silence. Max drops his backpack by the door and stretches, looking more tired than I realized.

"You had fun with Reese?" I ask, hanging up my coat.

"Yeah, we beat a boss level on *Super Mario*," he says, his eyes lighting up with a familiar pride.

"I'm impressed," I say with a smile, watching him as he yawns and rubs his eyes.

"Come here." I motion to the couch. He shuffles over, and without a second thought, leans into me, resting his head on my shoulder. I wrap my arm around him, the warmth of the moment filling me up as we sit quietly, just the two of us.

For a while, neither of us speaks. It feels like the way things used to be when he was smaller, when he'd snuggle close without thinking twice. I kiss the top of his head, feeling the familiar softness of his hair against my lips.

"You know I love you, right?" I whisper.

"Yeah, Mom. I love you too."

"And you know Dad loves you too."

Max doesn't say anything right away, but I feel him shift slightly, like he's listening more closely now.

"I know this is hard," I continue, choosing my words carefully. "With me and Dad being apart like this...I know it's confusing, and it's not easy."

Max is quiet for a moment, his small body still leaning into mine. Finally, he speaks, his voice barely above a whisper. "Yeah, it's weird sometimes."

"I know," I say softly, squeezing him a little tighter. "And it's okay to feel that way. Just know that no matter what happens, both Dad and I love you more than anything. We're figuring things out, but none of this changes how much we care about you."

"Okay," he whispers.

"Thank you for always being such a good kid," I say softly.

Max doesn't say anything, but I feel his small hand gently squeeze mine.

CHAPTER
FORTY-FIVE

The restaurant is cozy and dimly lit, with candles flickering softly on each table. Matt and I sit across from each other, our conversation flowing easily as it has for the past hour. He leans forward, eyes intent on mine, and asks, "Can I ask you a personal question?"

I nod, feeling a flutter of nerves. "Sure."

"What was your relationship with your mom like?" His tone is gentle, but the question hits a sore spot. He must have known it was delicate by the way he braced for my response.

I take a breath, looking down at my hands before meeting his gaze again. "It was...complicated," I say slowly, feeling the weight of the words. "She wasn't there for me growing up. When I left for college, I didn't look back. Now that she's gone, I have all these regrets, all these things I wish I'd said to her while I still had the chance."

My voice wavers, but I push through. "It's hard to grieve for someone who wasn't there for you."

Matt reaches across the table, his hand covering mine, warm and steady. "I'm sorry, Hazel."

"It is. And then there's Andy—my brother." I feel my chest tighten, like this is the real conversation I need to have. "He's been so distant since...everything with Mom. He's pulled away, and the worst part is, I think it's my fault. Like maybe he thinks I've been avoiding him, avoiding the family. I can't shake the feeling he believes something terrible about me."

Matt's brow furrows, and he leans in a little more. "Why do you think that?"

"The silence," I say softly, feeling the weight of Andy's absence. "He's barely said anything since Mom died, and it feels like... I don't know, like he's blaming me. The thought he could think something so terrible about me, that I'd ignore him when he needed me—it's hard to get past."

Matt listens, nodding thoughtfully. His presence is steady, and for a moment, I just let the quiet between us settle. Then he speaks, his voice low and calm. "You know, sometimes silence doesn't mean what we think it does. When my aunt passed, I withdrew from everyone. Not because I was blaming them, but because I didn't know how to deal with my feelings. I pushed people away because I didn't know what to say, or how to process my grief."

I let his words sink in. "So...you think maybe Andy's not blaming me? That he's just...processing?"

Matt shrugs. "It's possible. It's hard for some people to communicate grief. He might not know how to come to you right now, and it's easier to pull back than confront those emotions. It doesn't mean he thinks badly of you."

I feel something shift inside me. "I've been so stuck on the idea he's mad at me, or disappointed in me for not being there more. But I never thought this might just be a part of his grieving process." I wince. "God, I feel really selfish."

"You're not selfish," Matt says gently.

We sit quietly for a moment, the air between us filled with the unspoken weight of everything we're both working through. I feel lighter, though—not entirely fixed, but like I've taken a step forward.

"Thank you," I say quietly.

Matt squeezes my hand gently.

When we finally leave the restaurant, walking side by side, I realize something important has shifted. It's not just that Matt understands me—it's that he's offered me a new way of looking at my pain.

At this moment, I know I can trust him with more than just surface-level emotions.

As we walk, I glance at him and feel a familiar pull. It's not just attraction anymore—it's trust. I know now, with certainty, I want to sleep with him. Not just because of chemistry, but because I feel safe with him, safe enough to let my guard down completely.

I catch his eye, and he smiles, that easy, disarming grin. And for the first time in a long time, I don't feel like I'm carrying the weight of everything alone.

After spending the evening with Matt, feeling both lighter and more grounded than I have in weeks, Saturday arrives quickly, bringing with it the familiar buzz of my book club meeting.

It's only because of Jenny's obsession with Elin Hilderbrand that we read *The Rumor* as our next pick for the book club. I found the book deliciously juicy and look forward to hearing how Quinn will try to pick it apart because it's not as literary as what we usually read.

There's a platter of gourmet cheeses, a bowl of shiny olives, and a pitcher of what I've been told is Amelia's famous sangria. I grab a sliver of bread and slather it with some herb-infused butter before settling into my favorite armchair.

Jenny is already talking animatedly about the book, her hands gesticulating wildly. "I just love the way she captures the essence of Nantucket," she says. "It's like you can feel the salty air and hear the waves crashing."

I nod in agreement, even though I've never been to Nantucket. The book did make it feel incredibly real. I've always felt you can distinguish an excellent writer from a good writer by how well they capture the scenery.

I take a sip of sangria, savoring the blend of fruits and wine. "It all felt real," I add. "Like I was peeking into their real lives, full of secrets and all."

Quinn leans back in her chair, a smirk playing on her lips. "It was entertaining," she says. We wait for more, but evidently, this is all she wishes to add to the conversation.

As Amelia reads a passage aloud about Madeline feeling betrayed, it strikes a chord, cutting deeper than I'd like to admit. I remember having the same thought when I read that passage for the first time—how betrayal can creep in so quietly that you don't even notice it until it's already cracked something fundamental.

Something has shifted between Daisy and me, something I can't quite name. We used to share everything—our wildest dreams, our silliest fears—but now there's a wall between us.

The void where her laughter used to fill the space feels unsettling.

My phone buzzes on the table, and I half hope it's Daisy. But it's just another work email. I sigh and lean back in my chair, the weight of the silence between us growing heavier by the day. Have I been too caught up in my own world to notice the signs earlier? Or maybe I did something without realizing it, some-thing that pushed her away.

I pick up the book again, but my heart isn't in it. The story only serves as a painful reminder of how fragile friendships can be, and how easily they can splinter under the weight of unspoken truths and hidden emotions. I know I need to talk to Daisy, to ask her what's going on. But the thought of confronting her, of possibly hearing something I don't want to, fills me with a dread I can't shake.

I flip a page, my eyes scanning the words without really seeing them. I can only hope, like the characters in the book, that Daisy and I can find our way through this. That the bond we've built over the years is strong enough to withstand whatever is causing this rift. I close my eyes, feeling hopeful, even as uncertainty gnaws at the edges of my heart.

The conversation around the room ebbs and flows—favorite characters, plot twists, and half-baked literary theories floating between us. At one point, Quinn and Jenny launch into a heated debate about what defines "literary fiction." I glance at my phone, feeling the urge to do something—anything—to bridge the distance with Daisy.

Without thinking too much about it, I compose a text.

> Me again. I'm sure it's just in my head, but I get the feeling you're ignoring me. I'd love for you to call or text me to tell me I'm wrong!

I hit send before I can second-guess myself.

CHAPTER
FORTY-SIX

I awaken to the sound of my mother's voice echoing in my dreams, pulling me from sleep. My heart pounds as I blink into the dark, disoriented. Where am I? What time is it? The unfamiliar blurs, then clears—I'm in my bed. The clock reads ten p.m. Only ten? Amelia's sangria must've knocked me out, leaving a gritty aftertaste in my mouth.

I reach for my phone, hoping, half-dreading, to see a reply from Daisy. Nothing. The empty notification screen stabs at me.

Something feels wrong. It has to be. My mind swirls with a hundred scenarios, and I can't just sit back this time, like I did with Jack, letting things slip away. If Daisy is avoiding me, I'll force the issue. I'm ready to—

My phone rings. FaceTime. Daisy. Relief floods me so fast my hand shakes as I swipe to answer.

"Hey!" I blurt, trying to sound casual, like I wasn't seconds from spiraling.

"Hi." Daisy's face appears, her eyes tired, lines on her forehead I hadn't noticed before. Something's off. I can feel it in the way she holds her shoulders, in the too-long silence. "Sorry I've been quiet," she says finally, but there's no warmth.

My heart sinks. She's not calling to smooth things over. She's calling to…what? I brace myself, forcing a smile, expecting excuses about work or the kids. Instead, she says, "Hazel, I…I need to be honest with you."

My stomach drops. "Okay…" I barely manage.

She sighs, glancing away, probably toward Finn for support. "I'm feeling overwhelmed. By you."

My stomach churns. "By…me?" I stammer. "You said to call when I needed you."

Her shoulders sag, her voice soft but firm. "I did. But, Hazel, I can't be your main source of support anymore. It's too much."

Her words hit me like a slap. I switch the phone to my other hand, wiping my sweaty palm on my pants.

"What do you mean too much? This isn't drama—this is just me."

She flinches, glancing down, and I know she means it. "I'm not saying you're drama, Hazel. But I don't have the emotional space right now. I'm sorry."

The silence stretches unbearably. I swallow hard, fighting tears, trying to keep my voice steady. "So, what are you saying?"

"I need some space," she says, her voice cracking. "I'm sorry."

It feels like a punch. Memories of our friendship—sleepovers, endless talks, laughter—flood my mind, now distant, unreachable. How did we end up here?

"I'm sorry too," I whisper, barely holding it together.

She nods, giving me a weak smile. "Thank you for understanding."

And then she's gone. The screen goes black, leaving me staring at my reflection, cold and empty. Tears blur my vision and spill down my face, soaking my shirt collar.

I can't think about Jack, Daisy, or the way everything's unraveling. Not tonight. Not when I'm already fraying.

In desperation, I text Matt, skipping any pretense:

> What's your go-to routine to shake off a bad day?

Minutes later, my phone buzzes.

> If you're having a bad day, we could hang out. Maybe I could help.

His offer is tempting, but something inside me says I need to handle this alone. Still, his message soothes the storm in my chest.

> Thanks, but I think I need to tackle this one
> solo. I guess I was just missing you.

I hit send before I can overthink it, my heart pounding. Seconds feel like hours before his reply lights up my screen.

> That's nice to hear. You just made my night.

Relief washes over me. Somehow, knowing Matt's there makes everything a little more bearable. The tension loosens, and for the first time in hours, I feel like I can breathe.

His next message comes:

> When can I see you again?

> Tomorrow.

Matt wants to see where I live.

The thought makes me uneasy at first, a twinge of nerves tightening in my chest. But when the doorbell rings and I open it to find him standing there, holding a bottle of wine, the tension dissolves. His easy smile and the casual way he stands on my doorstep—like he belongs here—puts me at ease. He's dressed like me tonight, in a simple T-shirt and medium-wash jeans, a reminder that we're both choosing comfort, not pretense.

As he steps inside, I'm suddenly aware of the intimate details filling my space—the art on the walls, the books scattered on the shelves, even the faint scent of the toast I burned this morning and tried to mask with too much air freshener. But as his eyes meet mine, all those worries fade.

"You cut your hair," he says, stepping closer. He reaches out and brushes his fingers through a lock of my hair. There's a softness in his touch, but I can feel a slight tremble in his hand. His thumb lingers on the edge of my hairline, and I can't help but notice the way his eyes darken as he watches me. "I like it. You look...different. In a good way."

His fingers fall away, leaving a lingering warmth behind. "Thanks."

In the kitchen, Matt makes himself at home, casually opening the wine while keeping his gaze on me. There's an intensity in the way he watches, like he's trying to learn everything about me without saying a word. His presence is magnetic, and I feel my body responding to it, an unspoken pull drawing us closer.

He pours the wine, handing me a glass, and leans back against the counter, his eyes still fixed on mine. "You know," he says with a grin, "you're not what I expected."

"Oh? What did you expect?" I ask, taking a sip of wine.

He shrugs, the grin deepening. "I don't know. You're so... mysterious. But being around you, everything feels so easy. I didn't expect that."

There's a crackling energy between us, a subtle, growing tension that makes every word and gesture feel charged with meaning. I can sense the attraction hanging in the air, like an unspoken promise, making the space between us feel smaller and more intimate. I don't want to break the moment.

He steps forward, closing the gap just a little. "You surprise me," he says, his voice lower now, more serious. "I feel like I'm constantly learning new things about you."

The way his eyes sweep over me, slowly, deliberately, sends a shiver down my spine. "You're pretty good at reading people," I manage to say, my voice a little breathless. "What do you think you've learned so far?"

He takes another step closer, his gaze holding mine. "I've learned you like things a certain way. You notice the details. And..." His eyes flick to my lips for just a second before locking back onto mine. "You're more guarded than you let on."

I can't help but smile, feeling the tension between us tighten like a string ready to snap. "Maybe," I say, taking a step back just to keep the space manageable.

Matt's attention shifts to the room around us, as if noticing my home for the first time. He glances around, taking in the art, the decor, the way everything is arranged. "It's exactly how I pictured it," he says, swirling the wine in his glass. "But...maybe a little cleaner."

I laugh, feeling lighter, the tension between us momentarily softened by the easy banter. "I spent two hours cleaning today. I couldn't let you see the real chaos."

He chuckles and wanders into the living room, his fingers grazing the spines of books on the shelf. "Still, it feels very *you*," he says, turning back to me. "Comfortable. Warm. Lived-in."

The compliment sends a thrill through me, though I have to suppress a laugh. "My hu—Jack...did most of the decorating," I admit, a slight blush creeping up my neck. "Except for my bedroom. I made the space exactly how I wanted."

At this, Matt's eyes spark with interest. He sets his wine glass down on the coffee table and walks toward the stairs. "Let me see," he says, his voice a mix of curiosity and challenge.

My pulse quickens, and I find myself hesitating. Not because I don't want him to see it—but because of how badly I do. There's a weight to his words, a teasing intimacy in the way he's asking like he's not just talking about the decor.

I feel my breath catch as I follow him up the stairs, the distance between us shrinking with every step. When we reach the top, I open the door to my bedroom, letting him step inside. He pauses, glancing around, and then turns back to me, his gaze smoldering, the air between us electric.

"It's perfect," he murmurs, his voice low. His eyes sweep over the room, but I can tell it's me he's really looking at. "Just like I thought it would be."

He takes the wine glass from my hand and grasps the sides of my face. He makes no attempt to move, only watches me watch him. He opens his mouth as though he's about to say something but seems to change his mind.

For a split second, I worry he's going to pull away.

That is...until he kisses me.

When we finally pull apart, breathless, his forehead rests against mine. Suddenly, I feel sober.

Matt seems to recognize the thoughts running through my head. *Not here.*

He follows me into the guest room—a room I have no real attachment to. He steps closer, the heat of his body drawing me in as the space between us disappears. No more words. The chemistry that's been building all night finally boils over, and when his hand touches the small of my back, pulling me closer, I don't resist.

Our faces are inches apart, and without thinking, I lean in and kiss him. His response is immediate, lips meeting mine with a hunger that sends heat rushing through me. The kiss deepens, and I lose myself in it, in the feel of his hands sliding around my waist, holding me close.

It's not just attraction—it's a connection, something deeper, something that feels inevitable.

Everything seems to happen in slow motion: the removing of our clothes, our mouths exploring each other's bodies, the cries of joy. Of lust. Of desire.

And then I fall on top of him, breathless.

Oh.

CHAPTER
FORTY-SEVEN

I close the front door behind Matt, a warm, contented smile lingering on my lips. Our night together was everything I'd hoped for—intimate, tender, and freeing in a way that made me feel weightless. As I lean back against the door, I let the memory of his touch, his words, linger a little longer before pushing off to head toward the bedroom.

I hum softly, floating through the house, basking in the afterglow. My body feels light, my mind calm. I head to the closet to grab something more comfortable to sleep in, still humming to myself as I move aside a stack of sweaters. That's when I spot it— a folded piece of paper tucked in the back corner.

Curious, I pluck it out, not thinking much of it. It's probably old, something I shoved away ages ago. But as I unfold it and see the handwriting, I freeze.

It's not mine.

It's Jack's.

A chill washes over me, stark and sudden. I sink onto the edge of the bed, the warmth from moments ago evaporating, replaced with an uneasy weight settling in my chest. I stare at the familiar slanted script for a second before I start reading, my breath coming in shallow bursts.

- *She's messy. Can't keep her spaces tidy.*

- *She takes everything too personally.*
- *She doesn't talk to me anymore—like she used to.*
- *She didn't cry at her mother's funeral.*
- *We stopped having real sex. Good sex.*
- *She honestly thinks I bullied her into having a baby.*
- *Sometimes I think she cares more about the fictional characters in her books than me.*
- *Too emotional lately.*
- *The fucking dishwasher.*
- *We're not attracted to each other the way we used to be.*
- *She used to be more fun and carefree.*
- *She overthinks everything to death.*
- *She's always looking for things to improve, ways to improve. Can't she just appreciate the good things? If she were happy, she wouldn't be chasing all these other things.*
- *Is she even in love with me anymore?*
- *Am I even in love with her anymore?*

The words blur in front of me as the sting of betrayal starts to settle in. I grip the paper tighter, my heart sinking as each accusation lands with more weight than the last.

I should feel something. Anger. Hurt. Rage.

But instead, there's nothing. Just a hollow ache in my chest echoing louder with every second. I set the paper down gently, as though dropping it any faster would break me.

My eyes drift around the room, landing on the small pieces of my life that seem almost foreign now. The mirror hanging crookedly on the wall, the fake tulips I'd placed on the nightstand for a splash of cheer, the sock still sitting on the floor, left out of place. All the imperfections Jack hated.

His words should cut deep, but they don't. I don't feel broken. What I feel is worse. Numb. Numb like the cold of a winter morning before the sun rises. Numb like I've already been through this and now there's nothing left to feel.

It's as though I've become weightless again, but not in the same way as before. Now it's a drifting, hollow sort of weightlessness, the kind that makes you wonder if you've floated too far from yourself to ever come back.

Daisy, Andy, Jack—they all want space. From me.

I swallow hard, the silence pressing in. It's suffocating now, different from the quiet bliss of before. This time, the silence carries a bitter finality, an answer to questions I didn't know I had.

I hum a tune from my childhood that rises unbidden to my mind. *One of these things is not like the other...*

CHAPTER
FORTY-EIGHT

use the carpool lane for the rest of the week, unable to face the other moms. I can't bear the thought of turning another person against me. Not now. But by Saturday, Amelia's patience seems to have run out and she practically demands I come over for coffee.

I sit in my car outside her house, gripping the steering wheel so hard my knuckles turn white. My mind races with a hundred reasons not to go inside. What if my problems are suddenly too much for her?

I can't deal with all this drama anymore.

I close my eyes, trying to muster the courage to get out of the car. I have to do this. I have to talk to someone. See someone. I can't keep avoiding everyone, pretending everything is fine when it's not. Taking another deep breath, I finally open the car door and step out. The air hits my face, and for a moment, it feels refreshing. Like maybe I can do this after all.

I walk up to Amelia's door, each step feeling heavier than the last. With a shaky hand, I press the doorbell and wait.

Inside, the familiar smell of coffee instantly wraps around me, comforting and inviting. Amelia leads me to the living room, where we sit on her cozy, overstuffed couch. She hands me a mug, and I take it, feeling the warmth seep into my hands.

"So, what's going on?" she asks gently.

I'm tempted to say nothing. To pretend the call with Daisy never happened. It's not like Amelia is going to ask me outright if Daisy and I are okay, in which case I will be incapable of lying.

I want to say everything is fine, but everything is far from fine, and even if I could lie, I'm not sure I would be able to this time. I could remind her Jack has his own apartment, that our son is splitting his time between our places, and that we decided to take this break from one another to help our marriage, but everything that's happening seems to be in direct contrast. I could also remind her that, after losing my mother to cancer I never knew she had, my brother, the only family I have left, refuses to speak to me. And that, now, I've pushed away Daisy, too.

No, I am decidedly *not* fine.

And so I do the only thing I can do to avoid answering her question: I change the subject, pretending I never heard her at all.

"We always talk about me," I say. "Tell me what's been going on with you."

It works, but only briefly, because after Amelia tells me about the constant battle she's having with her husband over the household chores and the new language that Reese has brought home from school—"He said, 'Mom, why you cappin'?' And I was like, 'Could you please use proper English when speaking to me?'"—she levels her gaze on me in a way I know means she isn't about to let me off the hook this time.

Amelia refills my cup. "Spill it. I know something is bothering you."

I consider evading her question again, but the truth is I'm dying to have someone to talk to, and I didn't want it to have to be Matt.

"It's Daisy. She'd been avoiding my calls and texts for a while, but we finally talked about it the other day. She said I'm overwhelming her."

"She said that?"

I nod. "She told me she doesn't have the emotional space to take on my problems."

"I don't know what to say." Amelia looks conflicted. "I can see how that would hurt you to hear, but I also understand she's probably doing what's right for her."

"Everyone is pulling away from me." It hurts to admit this. To be so vulnerable.

"I'm still here. And you have *Matt*." She says his name like we're a bunch of teenage girls at a sleepover, about to paint each other's nails.

Naturally, my face flushes. Even when I'm not opening my mouth I still can't keep a secret.

Amelia's words are a balm to my wounded heart, and for the first time in days, I feel a glimmer of hope. Emboldened by her support, I draw a deep breath and decide to confess the one thing I've been reluctant to admit.

"I slept with him."

For a moment, Amelia is silent, processing what I've just told her. I brace myself for judgment, for disappointment, but instead, she smiles. And then she's laughing.

"Hell yes, you did!"

When I laugh, it's as though all the tension is immediately released from my body in one giant *whoosh*. I feel it leave, feel the relief from it being gone.

Amelia leans in. "Now, tell me everything." Her laughter is infectious.

"Well, it was earlier this week. He came over to the house… there was wine…and well, one thing led to another."

Amelia's eyes widen with excitement. "Details, Hazel! You can't just leave me hanging with 'one thing led to another.'"

I laugh again, feeling more at ease. "Okay, okay. So, I was showing him the place and at one point he followed me into the guest room. There was this moment where we just looked at each other, and it felt like the world stopped. Next thing I knew, we were kissing."

Amelia gasps dramatically. "Kissing! And then?"

"And then," I continue, feeling a blush creep up my cheeks, "it was all so…intense. Like we couldn't get enough of each other."

She claps her hands together, grinning. "And? How was it?"

I bite my lip, trying and failing to fight back a smile. "It was amazing. Everything just clicked."

Amelia's expression is one of pure delight. "I love it!"

I sip my coffee.

"Now," she says with a mischievous glint in her eye, "how about we celebrate your confession with some ice cream and a rom-com?"

"Sounds perfect," I agree.

We raid the freezer, digging out a tub of chocolate fudge brownie, and then settle on the couch. After a short debate, we decide to watch *Sleepless In Seattle* because Meg Ryan and Tom Hanks are rom-com royalty.

Halfway through the movie, she says: "I won't ask you what sleeping with Matt means for your marriage."

I lift my empty bowl in salute. "I appreciate you."

———

The room is dim, the only light coming from the small lamp on my nightstand. Matt and I lie side by side, the warmth of our recent intimacy still lingering in the air. His fingers trace lazy patterns on my arm, and I feel a sense of calm I haven't felt in a long time.

I'm thinking of initiating round two when he moves to get out of bed.

"Where are you going?"

"Coffee," he says.

I lean my head back against the headboard and listen to the sounds of him in the kitchen below, thinking how easy it has been to slide him into my life. Thinking how difficult it will be when it comes time to say goodbye.

He isn't gone long before he reappears with two cups of coffee in hand. I sit up in bed and accept one gratefully. I don't know how he does it but his coffee is always better than mine, even though we're using the same beans.

"Everything served to you in bed tastes better," he says. "Simple fact."

I murmur in agreement.

"What are your plans for the day?" he asks.

I sip my coffee slowly. "I've got a couple of contracts to review and an edit I've got to finish off. Nothing I can't do right here in this very spot."

"I was hoping you were going to say that."

After coffee, Matt makes toast with avocado, which we eat in bed. He brings me a fresh cup of coffee and then I settle in to work. Matt reads beside me, and the sound of him turning the pages of his worn paperback soothes me.

"Thank you for being here by the way. For the...distraction."

He lifts a brow. "Is that what I am?"

Yes. But I can't say it.

Thankfully, he doesn't seem to be looking for a response as he kisses me quickly before returning his attention to his book.

"I've been wanting to ask, how are you feeling about everything?" he asks an hour later, his voice breaking the comfortable silence.

I push my laptop aside, ready for a break, and turn to face him. How honest is too honest?

"I think I'm still a little numb."

Matt's eyes are full of understanding as he looks at me. "I know it's been hard, Hazel. You've been through a lot."

Going through. Present tense.

"This is probably a stupid question but have you tried reaching out to your brother again?"

I nod, a heavy stone in my stomach. "Almost daily. And nothing. It makes no sense."

He sighs. "Everyone grieves differently," he reminds me. As though I could forget.

I drop my head back against the headboard, closing my eyes. "Shouldn't he be thinking about me even a little? Shouldn't he be concerned about how I'm handling this? I know we aren't close now but there was a time I was all he had. And he was all *I* had. Mom was always working or out or just avoiding us as best as she could. Sure we had a roof over our heads and enough food on the table but she was still *terrible*, Matt.

"The only reason I got through it was because of Andy. He was my rock, my support.

"We talked about getting out of Anaheim all the time. We were going to do it together. But he didn't come with me when I left for college. He could have but he didn't, and I'll never quite understand why."

Matt pulls me into his arms. I pull in a deep breath, breathing in the scent of my soap he'd washed himself with last night. "Family can be complicated. You just have to keep trying."

We lie there for a moment, the silence filled with a sense of sadness I know I won't easily be able to shake. It's a far cry from how I felt waking up next to Matt earlier this morning.

"And this thing with Daisy...I don't know. It's a lot."

Matt presses a gentle kiss to my forehead. "I'm here for you, whatever you need."

A warmth spreads through me from his words but is quickly extinguished by my next thought.

In only four more months, Jack will be home.

CHAPTER
FORTY-NINE

The following week, Max finds me in bed with a book and climbs in next to me, wanting advice about Lindsey. I'm rendered momentarily speechless, having forgotten the way time continues to move on regardless of what is happening in your life. My son is now twelve. He won't climb into my bed for much longer, or even come to me for advice as willingly—certainly not about his romantic life. Soon his friends' feelings will mean more than mine, and their advice will hold more weight. If I so much as blink, he'll be eighteen and heading to college.

I put my book down and I listen.

The week after, Matt and I spend every spare moment we have together. There's something freeing about being with him, knowing it can never be more than sex, never be more than fun. It feels dangerous. Wrong in the best kind of way. When I'm not with Matt, I miss Daisy. I think of her all the time. Twenty or thirty times a day, something happens and I think, *I have to tell Daisy.* But then I recall her words: *I can't deal with all this drama anymore.* I turn to Amelia for support more and more, trying to fill the Daisy-shaped void in my life.

The week after that, Emma, Inklings senior editor gives me the go-ahead to acquire *Echoes of Silent Waters* I pitched in an earlier meeting. I email the author right away to set up a Zoom call. I find a way to avoid telling her I had once referred to her manuscript as "raw and unpolished."

Time passes, and I do my best to keep up.

———

Sundays always come around too quickly. Sending Max off to his father's has become a ritual in contradictions—part of me hates watching him go, knowing he's stuck in this back-and-forth shuffle, but another part of me feels a guilty sense of relief. When he's gone, I can just be Hazel. Not "Mom—Hazel." Just Hazel.

Max trudges into the living room with his overnight bag slung over his shoulder, the weight of the past few months etched on his eleven-year-old face. His usual energy feels dampened today, and I can see the telltale signs of weariness creeping in.

"Don't forget to pack your swim stuff," I remind him. "Your lesson's on Tuesday, so Dad will take you."

Max pauses, his hand tightening on the strap of his bag. A flicker of something—annoyance, maybe—passes over his normally sweet expression. He's quiet for a moment too long.

"Everything okay, bud?" I ask, keeping my tone light.

He shrugs, not meeting my eyes. "Yeah...it's fine."

But I can tell it's not fine. I've suspected for a while now that this arrangement—the constant moving between houses—has been wearing him down. And now it's right there, on his face. But he won't say it. I know Max well enough to know when he's trying to protect someone, even if it's me or Jack.

I kneel to his level. "Max, if something's bothering you, you can tell me. I won't be mad."

He glances up at me, then away again. "It's just...I don't like packing all the time. It's annoying. I wish I didn't have to."

There it is the crack in the armor.

I try to hide the sting of guilt in my voice. "I know, sweetheart. It's hard moving back and forth all the time."

He fidgets with the zipper on his bag. "Yeah, I just like it when things stay the same. Like, when I'm here for a few days, I get used to it, and then I have to switch again."

I nod, feeling the weight of his words settle in my chest. "I get it. I do. Would you want to stay here for a while? Just to give you a break from all the moving around?"

As soon as the words are out of my mouth I know I shouldn't have said them—not until I speak to Jack first.

Max looks relieved, but hesitant. "Maybe... but Dad wouldn't like it."

"We'll talk to him, okay? We'll figure it out."

Max gives a small nod, then disappears into his room to grab the last of his things. As soon as I hear the door click shut, I pull out my phone and start typing.

> I know we're not supposed to talk, but we need to talk about Max

I hit send and wait. It doesn't take long for the typing bubbles to appear.

> What's wrong?

> I think he's getting tired of moving back and forth all the time. It seems like it's beginning to wear on him.

A few seconds pass before his response comes in.

> He told you that?

I try not to sound pretentious.

> He didn't have to. I can tell. I think maybe it would be better for him to stay at the house with me for a while.

Little bubbles pop up again, then disappear. They reappear, and finally, his message comes through.

> I don't know if it's a fair solution.

Okay...he's not wrong. But I'm not ready to give in that easily.

> Do you have any other ideas?

When Jack doesn't respond, I add:

> I'm not trying to punish you, Jack. It's just a
> suggestion. You can see him whenever you
> want. I'm just trying to tell you what I see. At his
> age he needs stability.

There's an even longer pause this time. When his message finally arrives, I can almost hear the anger in his words.

> I'm not sure that's the best option. I understand
> what you're saying but I think that having equal
> time with us is most important.

I breathe deeply before replying.

> He's exhausted, Jack. I'm sure you've noticed
> how tough this arrangement is on him. Just for
> the rest of the break, let him stay at the house.

There's a long silence. I stare at the screen, willing Jack to understand. Finally, his message appears:

> I'm sorry but I don't agree.

I quickly type back.

> Please think about it. For Max's sake. Let's make
> this easier on him.

The typing bubbles appear, then vanish again. After what feels like an eternity, Jack's reply comes in.

> Feelings aren't fact. It feels like you're trying to
> push me out, Hazel.

I respond.

> I'm not. I promise. I'm just trying to do what's
> best for Max.

There's no response for a long time. I can picture him, sitting in his apartment, struggling with this. Finally, his message appears.

I'm sorry, but no.

An hour later I see Jack's sedan pull up out front of the house. He honks once, as usual, and moments later Max comes down the stairs, overnight bag in hand. At the door, I kiss him goodbye.

"Be good for your dad," I say. And then, because I can't help myself—and maybe because I'm still smarting a little from our earlier text conversation—I add, "Don't let him get away with being on the phone all the time this week."

Max is halfway through the doorway but turns back to me. "Well, it's good maybe. He was talking to a therapist."

This...I am not expecting. "He told you that?"

Max nods. He seems proud to have told me this information. Proud he knew something I didn't. "You always say everyone could use therapy, right?"

I attempt to relax my facial muscles and form a smile. "That's right. Good for him."

Max continues down the front walk. "Bye, Mom."

I close the door and listen for the sound of Jack's car pulling away. For a moment, I just stand there, my hand resting on the doorknob.

Jack's earlier words echo in my mind. *Feelings aren't fact.*

Yeah, he's in therapy all right.

On the one hand, I'm thrilled. Good for him for wanting to dig through to the root of his problems. Good for him for working on becoming a better version of himself. Good for him for being so self-aware.

But if I'm being honest—and I have no other choice but to be —a small part of me worries I'm not doing enough with our time apart. Not if he's in therapy working with a professional...

Silence settles around me like a soft, comforting blanket. It's funny how this once-familiar silence used to feel so foreign, so empty. Only months ago, the house echoed with the absence of Max's laughter and the steady hum of his presence. I would pace the halls, unsure of what to do with myself, trying to fill the void with noise, with distractions.

But now, I feel a lightness in the quiet. I turn and walk into the living room, letting the serenity wash over me. The house feels different when it's just me—not lonely, but peaceful. I take a deep breath, the kind that fills my lungs and makes my chest feel expansive. It's a reminder that this time is mine, a chance to reconnect with myself.

I head to the kitchen, my mind already drifting to the manuscript I need to finish reading. There's a sense of freedom in knowing I can spend the entire evening lost in another world without interruptions. I make a cup of decaf tea, the ritual soothing in its simplicity. The kettle whistles, and I pour the hot water over the tea bag, watching the steam rise in gentle curls.

With my mug in hand, I settle into my favorite chair by the window. I open my laptop and begin to read, the words pulling me in, but not before I take one more look around. The house is quiet, but it's a good kind of quiet. It's a space where I can breathe, where I can just be.

——————

The next week feels like three. It's as though I've split into two different people: the mom who packs lunches and does school pickup and drop-off and helps with homework and kisses my son goodnight, and the other woman: this suddenly wild and free character who is desperate for her time away from parenting, her time out with her new friends and romantic interest—her chance to be someone she has never been. There is a lightness to me during these weeks that fuels me, pushing me through, and filling me up before I must become a parent again.

I do my best not to think about Max. I try to let him be Jack's problem.

CHAPTER
FIFTY

NOVEMBER

Though the city looks no different, November arrives with a rush of cool, fresh air that reminds me what it's like to be alive. I quicken my pace, eager to reach the gates before the final bell rings, ready to find the others. I've just finished this month's book, and the urge to talk about it bubbles up inside me.

But as I approach the familiar semi-circle of moms, something feels off. The usual hum of chatting is there, but there's a weird tension clinging to the air like a chill that refuses to lift. Amelia waves, her face lighting up with her usual warmth. "Hey!" she calls, weaving through the small clusters of parents to meet me.

I pull my jacket tighter, trying to block out the crisp air.

Then I notice Jenny and Lucy. They're always friendly, but today there's something off about their smiles—too eager, too bright. Jenny's eyes widen slightly as I come closer.

"Hi, Hazel! How are you?" she asks, her voice just a touch too high, too forced.

"I'm fine," I answer automatically, but my voice lacks the usual conviction. I can't lie, not even to make them feel better. I try for a smile. "How about you?"

"Oh, you know, busy with the kids and all," Jenny replies, waving her hand, but the gesture feels awkward and unnatural.

Lucy jumps in, her tone overly enthusiastic. "Yeah, same here. Have you read anything interesting lately?"

I blink at her, surprised by the sudden shift. Normally we'd talk books, but this... this feels rehearsed. "Just the usual submissions at work." The truth slips out before I can stop it. I'm not sure why I feel the need to downplay it, but I can't lie, not even about something as harmless as books.

Before I can ask more, Quinn, who normally avoids me, strides over with an almost friendly expression—something I've never seen on her face before. "Hi," she greets, her voice missing its usual edge. "How's everything?"

"Fine," I say, but I can't help the questioning tone creeping into my words. My eyes flick between the three of them—Jenny, Lucy, Quinn—all wearing smiles that don't quite fit. Amelia, beside me, seems oblivious.

"What's going on?" I ask, blunt and direct, unable to keep the question in. The silence following is deafening.

Jenny clears her throat and glances at Quinn, who in turn looks at Lucy. Finally, Lucy speaks, hesitant, her voice barely above a whisper. "Oh, it's nothing, really." But I can tell she's lying.

And I can't stand lies. I shift uncomfortably, feeling the need to pull back, to escape before the tension thickens. But before I can press them any further, Max comes bounding out of the school doors, waving his colorful craft project.

"Mom! Look what I made!"

I seize the moment. "Amazing!" Relief washes over me as I turn my back on the women and walk toward the car with Max, his bright project in hand.

I glance back once, but only briefly. Whatever they're not saying, I'll deal with later. For now, Max is all that matters.

———

They know.

About Jack, my mom—all of it.

They must.

I feel it in every lingering glance, every unanswered text. I can almost hear the whispers in the spaces between words. I don't dare go near the school. The mothers, the teachers—anyone who might recognize the storm brewing behind my eyes. Their stares, their questions, their sympathy—it's too much. So, I stay hidden.

From bed to bath, bath to bed, I move like a ghost haunting the life I used to live. I tell Emma at Inklings I have food poisoning. She doesn't push. I skip the bi-weekly acquisitions meeting, the emails pile up, simple ones—questions about edits, scheduling Zoom calls—and I can't bring myself to answer. I'm buried under it all, suffocating in shame.

Wine has become my companion. Half a bottle, maybe more, two nights in a row. It dulls the edge, but it doesn't silence the thoughts. I go to bed tired and hollow, and I wake up the same.

I dream of my mother again. She's in the kitchen, standing at the stove like always, stirring pasta. When she turns to me, spatula raised, her eyes meet mine—soft but heavy with the weight of something unspoken. Her mouth opens, and I brace myself for the words I've been desperate to hear in the eleven months since she died.

But before she can say anything, I wake up.

I can't face anyone. Not the moms at the school, not my colleagues, not even myself. So, I stay far away—far from their prying eyes, from the knowing looks that cut deeper than words.

———————

By the time the next book club meeting rolls around I've all but made myself sick with worry. The only reason I've even come tonight is because, after numerous texts, Amelia has convinced me if any of the other women knew anything, she'd have heard about it by now. These were the same women who told her about Reese's teacher's Only Fans account the same hour they found out. The same women who knew Max was new to the school that year the first morning I walked him up to the gate.

But as I step into Amelia's living room for the book club

meeting, I still can't shake the feeling of dread that's settled in my stomach.

The usual buzz of conversation greets me, but it feels different tonight—hushed, cautious. Amelia meets my eyes with a tight smile, and I force myself to smile back, trying to ignore the knot of anxiety tightening inside me.

I take a seat and listen to the familiar voices of Jenny, Lucy, and Quinn, but there's an undercurrent of something I can't quite place.

The awkwardness at school the other day was positively *not* in my head.

As the discussion begins, I try to focus on the book—some story about three best friends spending a summer in Greece that has been given Reese Witherspoon's stamp of approval—but my mind keeps drifting, replaying the strange interactions at school pickup.

Finally, during a lull in the conversation, Jenny clears her throat. "So, Hazel, how have you been holding up?" she asks, her voice overly sympathetic.

The sound my fist makes when it meets with the book in my lap even surprises me. As does the wave of pain that floods through my right hand.

"Enough! Someone tell me what is going on."

Eventually, Jenny speaks up, her voice hesitant. "We heard you and your husband split up."

Her words hang in the air, and for a moment, everything seems to stop.

Quinn leans forward, her face a picture of concern. "And about your mom."

The words hit me like a punch to the gut. My heart starts to race, and I feel a flush creeping up my neck. "What?" I manage to say, my voice barely above a whisper.

I feel Amelia's hand gently squeeze my arm, a silent show of support. My mind races as I try to process what Jenny just said. The information isn't a surprise to me—after all, I lived through it—but the fact it's now public knowledge feels like a violation of my private life.

I exhale slowly, feeling the weight of their gaze on me.

Amelia's grip tightens briefly on my arm before she lets go, her eyes wide with concern. "I didn't say anything, Hazel. I promise."

I force a smile, trying to muster some composure.

Turning back to the others, I see a mixture of sympathy and awkwardness in their expressions. "I don't know where you heard that," I say, my voice sharp and unyielding. "But my personal life is..."

I see Jenny open her mouth to say something, but I cut her off. "I don't appreciate my private matters being the subject of gossip."

Quinn's face flushes, and she looks away, but not before I catch the guilt in her eyes. "We didn't mean to pry; we were just worried about you."

"Worried?" I repeat, my tone icy. "If you were truly worried, you'd have come to me directly, not whispered behind my back."

I glance at Amelia, who looks just as confused and out of place as I feel. "I swear, Hazel, I didn't tell anyone."

"Then how does everyone know?" I say, my voice rising with a mix of anger and hurt.

The room falls silent. No one meets my gaze. Jenny looks down at her hands, Quinn shifts uncomfortably in her seat, and Lucy avoids my eyes altogether.

"I don't know," Amelia finally says, her voice weak.

I stand. "This is why I don't trust people," I say, my voice breaking. "This is why I don't have friends. They always disappoint me. I don't know why I thought this time would be any different."

Amelia looks devastated, her eyes filling with tears.

I know now I shouldn't have said anything to Amelia. Never confided in her. Maybe I shouldn't have even joined the book club to begin with. This was supposed to be my safe space, a place where I could open up, but now my most personal pain has become gossip.

I feel the weight of their concern, their pity, pressing down on me, and I wonder how much of my life will become fodder for their next conversation.

"I shouldn't be here," I say. "I should never have joined in the first place."

I walk out of the house, my vision blurred with tears, feeling the lowest I've felt in a long time. I was foolish to think I could open up, to believe people could be different.

I make it to my car before I hear a voice behind me.

"Hazel, wait!" Amelia calls, her voice pleading. "Please, I swear I didn't say anything to them."

I spin around, my frustration boiling over. "Really, Amelia? Because somehow they know! My private business is now schoolyard gossip, and you're the only one I told!"

Amelia's face falls, and she looks genuinely hurt. "Hazel, I would never betray your trust. I don't know how they found out, but it wasn't from me."

"Then how did they know, Amelia?" I snap, my voice rising. Tears well up in Amelia's eyes, but I don't stop. "I thought I could count on you. I thought you were different. But I guess I was wrong."

Amelia reaches out, her voice breaking. "Hazel, please, believe me. I didn't—"

"I don't want to hear it," I cut her off, sounding strangled. "Just...stay away from me."

With that, I close the car door.

Trusting people has only ever led to pain and disappointment, and this is just another bitter reminder.

CHAPTER
FIFTY-ONE

At home, I slam the front door, the sound reverberating through the empty house, but it doesn't bring the relief I crave. My chest heaves with a storm of anger and hurt. I try, and fail, to push away the argument with Amelia, to forget the sting of knowing the secrets I've kept—fought to keep —are out there now, exposed like raw nerves. But her words play on a loop in my head, each repetition cutting deeper.

I grab my phone, hands shaking, and scroll to Andy's name. He has to pick up. He *has* to. "Come on, pick up, pick up," I mutter as the ringing drags on. But it goes straight to voicemail. Of course it does. It always does.

"Andy, it's me," I say, voice cracking as I struggle to keep it together. "Look, I don't even know why I'm calling. You never pick up. Never. Do you even care?" I pause, swallowing hard against the lump in my throat. "We should be grieving Mom together, but here I am, doing it all alone. Jack left, did you know that?"

I take a shaky breath, the words tumbling out faster now, hot and bitter. "You're my brother. You're supposed to be here for me, but you never are! I'm so tired of being the one who always tries. I'm done, Andy! Don't bother calling back because I won't be waiting anymore."

I hang up, my hands trembling, and toss the phone onto the

couch. The dam breaks, and the tears I've been holding back flood out, unstoppable, soaking my cheeks. The weight of it all—Jack, Mom, Daisy, Andy—it's like an anchor dragging me down, leaving me drowning in disappointment.

I stumble to the bedroom, the walls closing in around me, the silence of the house louder than any argument. I don't even bother changing out of my clothes, collapsing onto the bed as the tears slow, leaving behind an emptiness that feels like it's carved itself into my chest. The anger burns out, and what's left is a hollow ache that won't go away.

I stare at the ceiling, the distance between me and Andy a chasm I can't cross. I've tried and tried again, but I can't bridge it. Not anymore.

Sleep doesn't come easily. I spend hours circling the drain of my disappointments, replaying every conversation, every moment where someone let me down. By the time exhaustion finally pulls me under, the last thing I see is Andy's distant gaze, fading into the dark.

———

I'm ripped from a dead sleep by the shrill ring of my phone. I groggily reach for it, squinting at the screen. Unknown number. I swipe to answer, my voice thick with sleep. "Hello?"

"Is this Hazel Greenwood?" a woman's voice asks, professional but with a note of urgency.

"Yes, this is she."

"I'm calling from St. Joseph Hospital in Anaheim. Your brother, Andy Danler, was brought in tonight after being involved in a car accident."

I shoot upright in bed, my heart racing. "Oh my god. Is he…is he okay?"

"He's stable, but he was asking for you."

"He asked for me?" Hope rises like a quiet flame in my chest. "What was the name of the hospital again?"

"St. Joseph."

I scramble out of bed, already slipping a shirt on over my head.

"I-I'm in Vegas, it's going to be a while until I can be there."

"I'll make a note for the doctors. Please drive safely."

I hang up, my hands shaking as I pull on jeans and a sweatshirt. My mind is a whirlwind of fear and panic. Andy, my brother. I have to get to him.

I grab my keys and run out the door, my thoughts racing faster than my feet.

For a long while I don't think, I just drive. The dark, empty roads blur past me. But then my chest tightens with the memory of Mom, the words I never got to say hanging in the air like a ghost.

What if this is it? What if Andy dies before we can fix things, as Mom did? I couldn't handle it again. Not with Andy.

Tears sting my eyes, but I blink them away. I can't lose him. Not now. Not ever. I press harder on the gas pedal, urging the car to go faster. The fear gnaws at me, a cold, relentless ache. I picture Andy lying in a hospital bed, injured and alone, and a sob catches in my mouth.

"Please be okay," I whisper to the empty car. "Please, Andy, be okay."

I have to see him. I have to tell him I care that we'll fix things. I can't let him go, not like Mom.

Not without making things right.

PART FOUR
HEALING

CHAPTER
FIFTY-TWO

'I've never walked the empty halls of a hospital in the middle of the night. It's confusing, almost: the quiet, the stillness, the lack of usual activity. I'm shown to Andy's room immediately upon arrival, no trouble with visiting hours. My heart pounds, the adrenaline from the drive still coursing through me. Through the crack in his blinds, I can only just make out the very beginnings of the sunrise.

I stand there for a moment, just watching him. Andy, my brother, lying there with a scraped and bruised face and a broken left leg, but otherwise intact. Relief floods through me.

I sit down in the chair beside his bed, my fingers trembling as I reach out to touch his hand. He's still asleep, his breathing steady, and for a moment, I allow myself to hope that this will be the wake-up call he needs. Maybe this accident will make him realize how much we need each other; how much I need him.

The first rays of sunlight start to filter into the room, casting a soft glow over everything. Andy stirs, his eyelids fluttering open. I hold my breath, waiting for his reaction. His eyes meet mine, and I force a smile, trying to hide the tears threatening to spill over.

"Hey," I whisper, my voice cracking. "I'm here."

He blinks a few times, groaning as he shifts slightly in bed. For a moment, I think I see a flicker of something in his eyes—

recognition, relief, maybe even gratitude. But then he looks away, past me.

"I'm so tired," he mutters, his voice rough from sleep.

"Shh, it's okay. Go back to sleep."

I sit beside Andy's hospital bed, listening to the steady beeping of the machines and watching the slow rise and fall of his chest. The room is dimly lit, casting long shadows that dance across the sterile white walls.

My phone is a cold weight in my hand, and my thumb hovers over Jack's name in my contacts. He should know Andy has been in an accident. He would want to know. But we're not supposed to be communicating. We've already broken the rule a couple of times and it's never ended well.

The thought gnaws at me, twisting my insides into a tight knot.

I glance at Andy, his face pale and peaceful, as if he's merely sleeping off a long day. My eyes flick back to my phone, the screen now dark, waiting my decision.

I wish I could call Daisy. She, too, would want to know. But she's made it abundantly clear she needs space from me...just like Jack...and Andy.

Maybe I should call Matt instead. He would understand, would know what to say to make this unbearable wait a little less suffocating. But even as I think it, I know it's Jack I want to talk to. It's Jack who would understand the depth of my fear, the weight of my worry.

I close my eyes and take a deep breath, letting my thumb hover over Jack's name once more. But I can't reach out to him. I shouldn't.

My thumb moves away from his name and I scroll to Matt's instead. I hesitate, and then I tap on his name, pressing the phone to my ear.

The line rings, and with each ring, I feel a little more of the tension ease from my shoulders. Matt answers on the third ring, his voice warm and familiar, ringed with sleep.

"Hey," I say, my voice trembling slightly. "I just wanted to let you know I'm in Anaheim. I got a call late last night that Andy was in a car accident."

As I fill Matt in, I glance at Andy again, my heart aching. I'll tell Jack later, I promise myself. But for now, I need Matt.

"Do you want me to come?" he asks. A part of me wants to say yes, to have him here, his solid presence a comfort in the sterile hospital room. But another part of me hesitates.

I glance at Andy. "No, no, that's okay." It would only...complicate things.

After I hang up, I feel a little better, the weight of my worry slightly lifted. But the room feels unbearably silent again.

I check the time. It's early, but there's a chance Jack might be awake. But before I can do anything, the door to Andy's room swings open, and a nurse steps in.

She checks the monitors and makes notes on her chart.

"I—I don't know anything. How did this even happen?" I say, my voice sounding small even to my own ears.

"I don't know the details, just that he was involved in a car accident. Though, if he were driving, his injuries would be quite different." She gives me a reassuring smile. "But he's stable. That's a good sign."

Stable.

Absolutely *nothing* is stable.

————

It's a few hours before Andy opens his eyes again. When he does, he looks at me, blinking, his entire body still.

"What are you doing here?" His voice is hoarse. He clears his throat roughly.

I frown. "I got a call that you were in an accident. The nurse said you were asking for me. I was so worried about you. I thought you'd—"

"It must have been the painkillers," he says, cutting me off.

I ignore the jab. "What happened?"

He shakes his head and I close my eyes. I had hoped it wouldn't be like this. I'm not so naive to have expected him to welcome me with open arms, but I thought he would feel some kind of comfort in my having dropped everything to drive here to be with him.

I can see now how wrong I was.

"Andy."

He shakes his head again, and then tries to turn away from me but winces, going still.

He looks so despondent, so vulnerable, I can't help myself when I say, "I still don't understand why you have been pushing me away."

He sighs, a long, weary sound seemingly carrying the weight of the world. "Hazel, you can't fix everything. Some things are just broken."

"I refuse to accept that. We *aren't* broken!"

He swallows. "Okay, then I am."

"Then let me help you. We're family, we need to stick together."

"Family," he repeats bitterly, not looking at me. "Sometimes family is the problem."

His words cut deep, and I feel a sob rising. "Andy, please. There's so much we need to talk about. I—"

"Do I look like I want to talk right now? I'm lying in a fucking hospital bed, barely able to move. You ambushing me like this isn't helping anything." He finally turns to look at me, his eyes cold and distant. "I don't want to talk about Mom. Not with you, not with anyone. Just...leave it alone."

I feel the sting of rejection, the frustration of not understanding why he's pushing me away. "I don't understand why you're doing this. Why you continue to shut me out."

He closes his eyes, taking a deep breath. "Just go home, Hazel. As you can see, I'm alive and well."

I sit there, stunned and heartbroken, as he turns away from me again. I don't know what to say, what to do. All I can feel is the crushing weight of our broken relationship and the fear it might never be fixed.

CHAPTER
FIFTY-THREE

I don't go home. I barely leave Andy's side. Only when I know he's asleep do I use the restroom and wander off in search of food. When he's awake, we do not speak, though I try. I push for him to speak, to explain what's happened, to open up, and he continues to push me away. I've never before felt so helpless. So utterly out of control.

Except—no, it's not true. I've felt this before, after Mom died. But I can't think of that now. Can't fall apart when Andy needs me, even if he can't admit he does.

Instead of talking, we watch bad TV on the too-small television set in the corner of the room and read from trashy magazines I borrowed from the waiting room. I wish I'd thought to bring a book with me...and a change of clothes. After a day and a half in the hospital, I'm no longer smelling the freshest, a fact Andy must be working hard not to comment on, even as I see his nose wrinkle when I lean over him to adjust his pillow.

"I'm not an invalid," he sneers.

"Just admit you're glad I'm here. That you're not alone."

"I told you to go home, didn't I?"

I ignore him and begin to read aloud the latest gossip concerning celebrities we don't particularly care about: So and so is sleeping with someone new and some pop star's "distinct

238 | RACHEL DEL GROSSO

streetwear chic style" is being dissected by the media. I expect Andy to tell me to stop, but he doesn't.

It's the closest to him I've felt in years.

At dinnertime, the nurse who has been in and out all day, witnessing Andy do his best to ignore me, takes pity on me and brings me a salad from the cafeteria. It settles noisily in the pit of my stomach.

Soon after, loosened by painkillers, Andy falls asleep, and I take the opportunity to get some air.

At a nearby Starbucks, I clean my underarms—and other areas—with sticky soap and wadded-up toilet paper and change into the itchy crewneck sweatshirt and slightly tight jeans I found at a local Ross store. There's not much I can do about my hair.

On my way out, I double back and order a flat white and black coffee. I'll see which the nurse prefers and drink the other one myself. Except when I get back to Andy's room there's a nurse I don't recognize buzzing around him.

"Where's Eva?" I ask.

The new nurse turns to me. "Shift's done. I'm Christina. I'll be here for the next twelve hours."

I look down at the drinks in my hand and then set them both on the table between myself and Andy. I'll drink the flat white now and save the coffee for the morning.

Except as soon as I've emptied the flat white, I go right for the black coffee. And then jittery and not thinking entirely clearly, I text Jack.

———

I awaken the next morning to the sound of Andy cursing a blue streak at poor Christina who, granted, looks like she's seen and heard it all before.

"You have to stay still," she says. She turns to me. "He pulled out his IV overnight."

I watch her work. Andy continues to mumble obscenities under his breath.

"I'm sorry," I tell her, "He's not usually like this. It's just...he's in a lot of pain from the accident, and we recently lost our mother..."

I stop talking when I see the way Andy is looking at me.

"Now why on earth did you feel the need to tell her that?" he growls.

Oh, because I can't lie. Didn't I tell you? And while I'm at it I should tell you that Jack and I are on a break from our marriage and Daisy thinks my drama is too much to handle right now? Oh, and the new friends I made turned out to be nothing but gossips who can't be trusted. How's that for honesty? You should try it sometime.

But what comes out is, "Well, it's the truth."

Christina touches me briefly on the shoulder as she passes by. "I'm sorry for your loss."

I'm sorry for your loss.

In terms of acknowledging the pain and sorrow a person is going through, it kind of feels like a cop out. You can always tell when you're in the company of someone who understands the depth of your grief. There's a look in their eye, or maybe it's a certain way they speak or stand or make you feel, or how they listen to you. Whatever it is, it's obvious they too know loss personally. Deeply.

Christina has experienced loss.

Andy and I have experienced loss.

He just refuses to talk about it.

Andy groans and shifts uncomfortably, his movements awkward and deliberate. "This is ridiculous," he mutters. "I can't even sit like a normal human. You'd think I'd mastered the art of being pathetic by now."

"Can I help—"

"Yeah, you can go home."

"I'm not going to do that."

He sighs, rolling his eyes. "Of course you're not. Because that would make my life too easy."

I say, "I don't care what you want right now, Andy. I'm family, and this is what family does. They stay, they help, they love. They *talk.*"

"Talk? Oh, good, my favorite pastime." He smirks weakly, gesturing to his cast. "Because when you're a guy with a broken leg and zero dignity, *talking* is definitely what you're looking forward to."

"I'm not going to talk about Mom."

"I didn't say you have to talk about her."

He narrows his eyes. "But that's what you want, right? That's why you're here—cornering the guy who can't escape, just to have your moment?"

I say, "I'm sorry if it seems like that's what I'm doing. It's not my intention."

He raises an eyebrow. "So why *are* you here, Hazel? And don't say 'to help,' because you know I'm not a charity case. Well, okay, I *look* like one right now, but still."

I hesitate before answering. A hard, painful lump settles in my throat. I say, "I didn't get to speak with Mom before she died." I stumble over the last word. After all this time it still doesn't feel quite real. "I couldn't let it happen with you."

"Well, as you can see, I'm very much alive."

I frown slightly. "I don't understand you. You know I didn't know about Mom's cancer. I've made that very clear. So this whole grudge thing you have against me has gone on long enough."

"Grudge?" He lets out a dry laugh. "I'm not holding a grudge. I just don't feel like unloading all my emotional baggage on you." He glances down at his cast and adds, "I've already got plenty weighing me down."

I can't help but snap, "We used to tell each other everything!"

Andy laughs bitterly. It's a terrible, hurtful sound. "We were kids, Hazel. Life was simpler when the worst thing I had to worry about was you stealing my fries."

His words land with the intended effect, and for a long moment, I just sit there staring at him, unsure of what to say. Eventually, I find the words.

"Doesn't mean we can't be close again."

He snorts. "Yeah, sure. Just like riding a bike. Except my bike is broken, and I keep falling off. A lot has changed since then."

I laugh. He has no idea. "Agreed. And?"

He considers me for a moment before saying, "Hazel, please. I don't want to talk about this."

The silence stretches out, taut and heavy, until I finally nod. "All right. We won't talk about it now."

He gives me a small, grateful smile, though it doesn't quite reach his eyes.

I can't help but hope that someday the walls between us come down. But for now, all we can do is take it one step at a time.

CHAPTER
FIFTY-FOUR

L ater, when Andy falls asleep, I slip out again.

This time, I buy a mass market paperback copy of *Romancing Mister Bridgerton* from CVS and then visit a bakery where I purchase two chocolate croissants right before they close for the night. It's not the same as the cheap Pillsbury ones Andy and I used to make back in the day, but it's something.

Back in his hospital room, I read, waiting for him to wake. My phone, which I've left on silent for days now, buzzes where I've left it in my purse. I'm surprised to see a message from Amelia, doubly surprised to see one from Quinn right above it. I select Amelia's first, my stomach tightening, the memory of our last argument still fresh.

> Hey. Missed you at the book club tonight.
> Listen, I'm really sorry again about everything. I swear, I had nothing to do with the other ladies finding out. Please, let me know if you're okay.

I read the message twice, my thumb hovering over the screen. The fight we had feels like a gaping wound, and seeing her name only makes it ache more. I can almost hear her voice, the worry and sincerity in her words. She's always been straightforward and honest, and I'm tempted to believe her.

I know she didn't mean for things to blow up like they did,

but it doesn't make the betrayal sting any less. I'm not sure if I'm ready to forgive her yet. But the concern in her message softens me a little.

I type a quick reply, too exhausted and angry to lie—even if I could.

> I'm fine. With my brother in the hospital.

She follows up quickly with a response, but I ignore it and tap on Quinn's name.

> Amelia said she hadn't heard from you in a while, and you missed book club. I guess I'm just checking to make sure you're okay. I know I'm probably one of the last people you want to hear from right now but—

I delete the text without reading the rest. And then I delete the conversation with Amelia as well.

I put the phone down and close my eyes, pulling in a deep breath. Andy's machines continue to *beep beep beep*.

———

Three nights spent sleeping sitting up in a hospital chair is doing my neck in. This time, I wake up with a pain shooting between my shoulder blades so bad I'm rendered momentarily immobile. Andy is already awake and looks at me with little pity as he attempts to shove what looks like a stretched out coat hanger beneath his cast.

He motions to the book sitting atop my purse.

"I take it that's for me," he says.

I don't even look at him when I say, "If I knew what kind of books you were into I could have gotten you something."

"Fair point."

"So," I say. "What kind of books are you into? Or is that too personal of a question?"

He narrows his eyes in a way I believe is meant to appear

menacing, but only serves to remind me my fun-loving brother is indeed still in there somewhere.

"Crime and thrillers, mostly. The bloodier the better."

"I could"—I motion toward the door—"go see what I could find?"

He hesitates for a moment too long, revealing his true desire.

I stand. "Can I get you anything else while I'm out?"

"Yeah. See if you can find a doctor to tell me when I can get the hell out of here."

I roll my eyes. "Oh, there's a chocolate croissant in the paper bag on the table there. It's from last night so no guarantee it will be any good."

He peers into the bag. "What, no Pillsbury crescent rolls?"

Then he smiles—a soft, familiar curve of his lips, the kind of smile that would drive me crazy as a kid because it meant he was about to drag me into some trouble, but today, it's different. It's warmth and mischief and everything I've been desperate to see. In this sterile room, where everything feels distant and wrong, that smile feels like coming home. I hadn't realized how much I missed it until now.

His smile is *everything*. It's hope.

———

Early afternoon light filters through the window, casting a warm glow over the book in my lap. A knock on the door pulls me from my reading. I turn to see a nurse carrying a large bouquet of flowers and a small brown package. The vibrant colors are a stark contrast to the blandness of the room.

"Flowers for you," she says with a smile, placing them on the table beside me.

Andy snorts. "Figures, I'm the one in the hospital you're getting flowers."

I reach for the card, assuming they're from Matt, but when I open the envelope, my breath catches.

My hands tremble slightly as I unfold the letter tucked inside. Quinn's handwriting is neat, almost too perfect, as if she had carefully crafted every word.

Dear Hazel,

I hope these flowers brighten your day, even just a little, and that your brother is doing well.

I owe you an apology, and I can only hope you'll find it in your heart to forgive me.

I glance at Andy before continuing.

I overheard you and Amelia at the coffee shop that day. That's how I found out about you and Jack separating...and about your mother.

I shouldn't have eavesdropped, and I definitely shouldn't have told the rest of the girls. I can't really begin to explain why I did it, only I know now it was out of jealousy. And for that, I'm truly sorry.

The words blur as tears well up in my eyes. It was Quinn! She had known, and she'd told everyone. Which means Amelia was telling the truth...

I can't undo what I did, but I want you to know I regret it deeply. I never meant to hurt you.

Quinn
P.S. I figured you might need something to read. Here's our next book for book club.

I fold the letter, my mind racing. Anger bubbles up, but it's quickly followed by a wave of exhaustion. I've been running on fumes for days, and this feels like just another burden to bear.

I take a deep breath, trying to steady my emotions. Forgiveness seems like a distant concept right now, but holding onto anger won't help Andy, and it won't help me. For now, I'll focus on Andy. Everything else can wait.

This is why, when Matt asks again if he should come to the hospital, I tell him no, even though the thought of him wrapping me in the warmth and safety of his arms is enough to bring me to joyful tears.

I notice Andy staring at the flowers.

"Those look like apology flowers," he says. He's very astute; this one.

"They are."

He says, "What did Jack do now?"

I hesitate, trying to think of a way around telling him the truth. Not because I don't want to—I'm desperate to feel closer to him—rather I don't want to scare him off. It's really the first personal question he's asked me the whole time I've been here with him.

"That bad, huh? I thought he had all the power in your relationship. Maybe the tides have finally turned."

A year ago I would have thought this an odd thing for him to say, but I see the truth in it now. I see how I'd allowed myself to be swallowed up by Jack more and more as the years went by. I see that all I knew was him, being his girlfriend and then his wife and then the mother of his son. I *had* molded myself around this other person—person*s*, actually, never realizing the importance of ensuring I didn't lose myself in the process.

"Things are complicated with me and Jack right now."

I hold my breath, waiting to see if Andy will press for more information.

He looks down at his hands in his lap before meeting my gaze once again. "Whatever it is, you two will get through it. Forgive him for whatever it is he's done to require sending flowers across state lines"—I don't bother to correct him for fear he'll stop talking—"you have a life that so many people would kill for."

I'm stunned into silence. Does he mean a life *he* would kill for? Granted we haven't been close for a while; I was never under the impression he desired a so-called normal life like mine. If I ask him, would he—

I say, "A life *you* would kill for?"

He pulls his bottom lip into his mouth before answering. "Well, yeah," he says quietly.

I match his tone. "I never would have guessed."

"There's a lot you don't know about me," he says, though not unkindly.

I must tread carefully. "What else don't I know?"

He pauses, his eyes searching mine as if deciding how much to reveal. "A lot," he finally says, the weight of years of untold stories in his voice. "It's just been easier to keep different parts of my life separate. Mom, work...you. Maybe I thought it was easier this way. Maybe I was just scared."

I lean forward, trying to bridge the gap between us. "Scared of what?"

He shrugs. It's a small, almost defeated motion. "Of being vulnerable. Of letting people in and them not liking what they see."

Because I've spent years doing the hard work of looking at my life, my childhood, my motivations, I know this is because of our mother, and it breaks my heart.

If she were still around, I'd want to scream at her for this—for making him feel like he had to hide who he really was, for making us both feel like we had to tiptoe around her judgment. But she's not here to yell at, and it wouldn't fix anything anyway.

I study Andy, the way his shoulders hunch as if he's carrying the weight of something far heavier than just his cast. He's always been the easygoing one, the one who could brush things off with a laugh or a joke. But here he is, cracking open just a little, and I can see how much he's been holding back. How much I've missed.

"Andy..." I say softly, unsure how to even begin. "I've never seen you like this."

His eyes flicker up, meeting mine with a wry smirk. "Well, I'd say 'lucky you,' but here we are."

"I'm serious."

"So am I," he quips, gesturing toward himself. "This is the deluxe Andy experience—brooding, vulnerable, and immobile. Act now, and you might even get a side of sarcasm."

I roll my eyes, but his humor doesn't entirely mask the weight in his gaze. "Why didn't you tell me things were this bad?"

He shrugs, leaning back with exaggerated nonchalance. "I

don't know, Hazel. Maybe I didn't want to ruin your perfect perception of me as a charming, carefree genius."

"You're not charming."

"Ouch," he says, placing a hand over his heart. "You wound me. But that's fine—I've got a leg for that."

Despite myself, I let out a small laugh. "You're deflecting."

"Of course I'm deflecting," he says, his smirk softening. "It's my thing. Some people bake, some people knit—I deflect."

"You don't have to do that with me," I say quietly.

He pauses, the air between us growing heavier. Then, with a theatrical sigh, he says, "Hazel, if I stopped deflecting, who would I even be? Just some guy with a broken leg and a weirdly supportive sister? I'd be unrecognizable."

I shake my head, a faint smile tugging at my lips. "You're impossible."

"And yet," he says, raising an eyebrow, "you're still here."

For a moment, we sit in silence, the weight of everything unsaid lingering in the air. Finally, Andy breaks it with a sigh. "You know, I've always admired you. Your strength, your resilience...your ability to sit through my nonsense without strangling me."

I blink, caught off guard. "Is that your way of saying something nice?"

"Don't get used to it," he says with a crooked smile.

And just like that, the space between us doesn't feel quite so wide anymore.

"Thank you," I manage to say. "You know the same could be said for you."

"What have I done with my life?" He groans. "I have a job I don't particularly like, a dog I adore but who nearly killed me, and the only reason I own a house is because my mother died and left one to me."

The only thing I can think to say is, "How did your dog nearly kill you?"

He sighs. "I was out walking him when I got hit."

I pull in a breath. "Is your dog okay?"

"Gunnar? Oh he'll outlive me, I'm certain of it."

Realizing I've leaned forward in my chair so much I'm about to fall out of it, I shuffle back, pressing my back firmly into the chair. I look at the flowers once again, losing myself in thought. When I re-emerge from my thoughts, Andy is asleep.

CHAPTER
FIFTY-FIVE

Andy begins talking before I even realize he's awake.

"Always with your nose in a book. Some things never change."

I've started reading the book Quinn sent, *Fiona and Jane*, about the strained friendship of two Asian women trying to find their place and joy in America. I was pulled in from the first paragraph and am already debating if I should slow down and make it last longer.

I glance at Andy with a smirk. It's nearly nine; he out-slept even himself today. I get up and open the blinds to let some sunlight in. He groans like a vampire meeting dawn.

"I can't argue with that, really. Reading has been the one constant in my life."

"What were those books you used to carry around everywhere? They were practically falling disintegrating."

"Probably some *Sweet Valley High* book," I say, wistfully. "I read those all. Multiple times. I basically lived in Sweet Valley."

"I never understood how you could read the same books over and over. Doesn't it ruin the suspense? Like watching a rerun of a game where you already know the score?"

The answer is simple, and I tell him so. "They were something I could trust. No surprise endings, no plot twists that ruined everything. It counted for a lot."

I pretend to consider it. "Yeah, thank god you weren't a plot twist."

"Oh, please. I was totally a twist. The fun kind. Like the one where the quiet neighbor turns out to be a secret spy."

"Or where the charming guy thinks he's clever, but he's really just sweet and predictable."

He grins. "You'd read that book again, wouldn't you?"

I nod. "Every time."

"Listen..." he says.

I sit up straighter, my heart rate rising. This is it; I know it. He's finally ready to talk.

"It was hard after you left for school. Mom took it personally."

"I wasn't aware she had enough self-awareness to come to that conclusion." The words are out of my mouth before I have the chance to wonder if they might derail this conversation before it's even begun.

Indeed, Andy shoots me a look of warning before saying, "She was trying. You know...to be better. But you had met Jack by then and seemed so entrenched in his life. It was clear you had a new family and weren't interested in ours anymore."

"What?"

"That's what it felt like."

"Or that's what she led you to believe."

His gaze falls. "Maybe both."

The beeping of the monitors is the only sound for a while, creating a rhythm that seems to underline the gravity of the moment.

I draw in a long breath, my eyes fixed on the white sheets of his bed. "The plan was always to get out of Anaheim...away from Mom. It was the right thing to do for me, and I stand by that."

"I know."

"So why didn't *you*?"

He hesitates. "She was trying to be better and I...I guess I wanted to believe she could be. So I stayed. Maybe I was trying to be better right alongside her."

"Did it work? Did things improve?"

He nods. "They did. She struggled but, overall, yeah, things were better."

"I'm happy to hear that, Andy. I am."

"When she got sick...she tried to reach out to you and you ignored her. It was a tough time for us."

I try to temper the anger that begins to bubble in the pit of my stomach. "I told you...you should have tried harder, Andy. I thought she was just trying to pull me back into her bullshit. I'd worked hard to separate myself from all that. If I'd had any idea she was sick..." I trail off.

Andy sighs. "I know. And there's nothing we can do about it now, but...all I had was Mom. I clung to her because I was scared. I needed her. Things were different after her diagnosis. *Mom* was different. She needed me and...we became closer. A lot closer. So when she died—"

Oh.

"You were lost," I say.

"Yeah." He looks down at his hands. "I just couldn't handle it. The pain was too much, so I shut it out. I tried not to think about it."

"Which is why you pushed me away."

I can see the pain in his eyes, the guilt that's been eating at him all these months. He doesn't have to respond; I know I'm right.

"I'm sorry," he says, finally looking at me. "I was so wrapped up in my own grief I didn't bother to think about how you might be hurting, too. You're my sister, I should have been there for you."

Tears well up in my eyes as I reach out and take his hand. "We're both hurting, Andy. We're both lost. But we have each other. We can move forward together."

He squeezes my hand. "I'm sorry," he says again.

I nod, the weight of the past lifting slightly. We've opened the door to our pain, but also to our healing.

Suddenly, he says, "I was so mad at you when you left." His gaze is harsh and questioning and I immediately want to look away, to run from the discomfort, but I don't. I stay and I watch him watch me and I don't look away.

"And I was mad at you for not coming with me," I say. And then my gaze trails along the length of him, taking in, once again, the bruises and scratches, the broken leg, the resigned look on his face. He was hit by a car for god's sake!

I stand suddenly. "Why were you out walking so late?" I want to scream at him for being so stupid, but I'm just so glad he's okay. To think I came so close to losing him too...

"I was in a difficult place...with my thoughts. I thought the walk might help; I wasn't really thinking beyond that." He stops, seemingly to gather his thoughts. "I was listening to this one song over and over—"Dixie Road" by Lee Greenwood. I don't know if it was one of Mom's favorites or what but I have this fading memory of her singing along to it."

"I don't think I know it," I say.

To my surprise, he starts to sing.

"'My heart goes drifting down a dusty dixie road...'"

Oh.

It's the song from my dreams, the one my mother was humming as she cooked.

I say nothing, my head trying to wrap itself around this information. The beeping of Andy's machines continues. I think of all the people who hate hospitals, hate the smell or the endless brightness, or maybe what they represent. But I find hospitals comforting—just the fact that they exist should anything happen to us.

Andy says, "I think I was just searching for a connection to Mom where I could picture her smiling, you know? I was letting my sadness run through me because I was tired of trying to fight it off. Maybe walking alone with just your dog gives you the confidential surroundings required to quietly fall apart."

I close my eyes. "I tried to be there for you, Andy. You—"

"I wouldn't let you. I know."

I'm quiet for a moment before saying: "You should have called me. You should have known I wouldn't ignore her being sick."

"I know."

"And it's—"

He casts his eyes downward. "I know."

"I didn't get to say goodbye," I whisper.

We sit in silence, the past finally finding its way into the light.

A nurse comes in to check on Andy and leaves again, and still we do not speak.

I pick up my book to read, which I do for only a few moments before I notice Andy watching me. Studying me, really.

"She loved you," he says, and I blink, desperate not to begin crying. His voice is raspy, each word a struggle. "I know she had a lot of trouble showing it, but she did."

I swallow hard, my throat tight. "It didn't feel like it," I manage to whisper, my gaze fixed on the floor. The linoleum tiles are a drab gray, matching the mood that's settled over us.

Andy reaches for my hand, his grip weak but reassuring. "She was dealing with so much. It wasn't about you. It never was."

"Andy. I was her kid. Her daughter. She should have tried harder. You said it wasn't about me but it was. It should have been!" I look at him, tears spilling over despite my efforts. His eyes, mirrors of my own, are filled with a sadness echoing my own. "If she loved me, why didn't she ever tell me?"

Andy sighs, a long, pained exhale. "She didn't know how. She wasn't raised to show love. But it was there, Hazel. I promise you; it was there."

The dam inside me breaks, and I lean forward, resting my head on the edge of his bed. Andy strokes my hair, a gesture so gentle it almost hurts. We stay like that, the unspoken words between us filling the room, heavy and freeing all at once.

"I miss her," I whisper into the sheets, my voice cracking. I know it doesn't make any sense, but it's the truth.

"Me too," Andy says. "Every day."

"I missed her even when she was alive. I thought—" I swallow. "I thought we'd have time to fix things."

Andy's hand moves to my shoulder, where it rests. "I know."

I stand suddenly, almost out of breath. "I need...I need some air."

I practically sprint out of the room and down the hall. I'm turned around, unable to locate an exit. I take a right and then a left and stop in my tracks.

He's here.

He steps through the doorway, his eyes immediately finding mine, and without a word, he crosses the space between us and pulls me into a tight hug. I bury my face in his chest, finally allowing myself to let go of the tears I've been holding back.

"It's going to be okay," he murmurs, his voice soothing. "I'm here now."

In this moment, the rules don't matter. All that matters is I'm not alone, and Jack is here.

CHAPTER
FIFTY-SIX

The room is too small for the three of us, but with Andy asleep between Jack and me, we are calm and poised. Reserved. My temperature rises and falls with every passing minute, unable to regulate itself in Jack's presence. It is wonderful to have him here, even if I haven't asked him to come. There was a part of me that wondered if, when he saw my message, he might call me, but I never imagined he'd drive all the way out here.

I want to know where Max is and what Jack has told his boss in order to get the time off to be here with me, but I won't ask him. He might accuse me of not knowing how to take care of his son. He's done it before.

I can't even recall what I said in the message, but he has determined it necessary to come.

Now, we try not to look at one another as Andy's machine beeps between us.

Jack looks good, different but also very much the same. He's shaved recently, maybe that morning. I can see where he's nicked his chin. When we were first dating, he'd rub his freshly shaved cheek against mine like he'd seen his father do to his mother when he was a young boy.

For the briefest of moments, I allow myself to imagine him doing so now. I don't hate the thought.

"You didn't have to come," I say. But again, I can't recall if I've explicitly asked him to or not.

"I know I didn't."

"But I'm glad you're here."

"It's no problem."

"I don't know what to say."

Jack looks at me through his lashes. "It's good to see you. You look good. I like the shorter hair."

He's lying, of course. I haven't had a proper shower in days and, just yesterday, I resorted to washing my hair in the sink of Andy's bathroom. At least I'd remembered the emergency concealer stick I left in my purse and applied it below my eyes where dark circles had sprouted.

Still, I try not to dismiss his comment, because I've come to realize I should take my compliments wherever I can get them. That's something no one ever warns you about growing older—that the compliments dry up. The attention too.

We fall into silence again. Between us, Andy continues to sleep.

We are still quiet when a nurse comes in to check Andy's vitals. It's Eva again. She meets my eye before she leaves the room. I'm not certain what she's trying to communicate, but it shakes something loose within me.

"Why did you come?"

Jack seems surprised by my question. "What do you mean? Andy is family."

"Okay."

"You said you were glad I came."

"I am," I admit.

He shrugs as though to say, *Well, there you go.* But it answers nothing. Andy is my brother. Sure they've known each other for twenty years but it's not as though they're close. Andy is clearly my problem, not Jack's, who is...well, I don't quite know what we are at the moment. Married? Separated?

"Where's Max?" I ask, unable to stop myself.

"He's with my parents."

Of course he is, I don't know why I hadn't thought of that

from the beginning. Sue and Michael would have answered Jack's call on the first ring, happy to help.

I look at Jack again. I'm terrible at this.

What are we? I want to say. Because you're here and you look amazing and it's making me feel confused. A person doesn't drive all this way for someone they don't care about. I want to ask what it means that he's here, but my lips aren't working and nothing sensical is bound to come out of them anyway.

"Hazel," he says at the exact time I say his name. We laugh, the tension in the room easing. "Could we find somewhere private to talk?"

I motion to Andy. "You mean you don't want to talk in front of Andy?"

He shrugs. "I wouldn't put it past him to be faking sleep so he can listen to our conversation."

With his eyes still closed, Andy mumbles, "Dammit, Jack."

Jack says, "You haven't changed at all, man." Which is an odd thing to say considering it's been a long while since either of us felt as though we knew him.

I follow him out into the hallway, which isn't really all that private. I guess the point is that Andy won't hear us.

"I wasn't going to say anything, but I can't help it. I'm so sorry. I…" For a moment, it looks like he might reach out and take my hand in his. I would have let him. "I went about this all wrong. This…separation."

I feel the tip of my ears grow hot. "What are you saying?"

"I'm saying I shouldn't have left. It wasn't the right thing to do. I have—I have no idea what I'm doing!"

Frustration suits him, makes his rugged features even more so. I want to reach out and massage the frown line between his eyebrows.

But even as I feel myself physically softening to him, I know the answer is not that simple. It's not as easy as falling into his arms, apologies spilling from our lips. Damage has been done here, and there's no way to ignore it.

Then, he reaches out and takes my hands, just as I thought he might. "I booked a hotel room for the night. Come back with me, have a shower and a real night's sleep and we can talk."

It's a tempting offer, one that would be so easy to give in to. But as happy as I am to see Jack here, I can't leave Andy. Not yet.

I give Jack's hand a light squeeze. "I agree we need to talk, but now's not the time. I want to be here for my brother."

"I get it," he says, looking forlorn.

I make sure to look him straight in the eyes when I say, "Thank you for coming."

———

I wake up to the pale morning light filtering through the curtains, as if even the sun is reluctant to start the day. My body feels like lead—a hangover, but make it emotional. I turn my head toward Andy, who's stirring like a character in a movie who's *definitely* about to drop some heavy dialogue.

"Morning," he mumbles, rubbing his eyes like someone auditioning for the role of Exhausted Guy #3.

"Morning." The silence stretches between us, the awkward after-party of yesterday's conversation still raging in our heads.

Andy shifts in his bed, wincing slightly as he props himself up on one elbow. Only a few more hours now until he's discharged.

"So...you and Jack," he begins, his voice carefully casual but his expression full of nosy determination. "What's the deal there?"

I sigh, feeling a familiar knot tighten in my chest. How do I even begin to explain?

"The truth? Things were bad. Like, sitcom-marriage-in-season-four bad. We stopped talking, stopped respecting each other. It fell apart. Jack moved out and got his own place. The idea was to take a break until my fortieth birthday, give ourselves space."

Andy's mouth falls open slightly. "Wow."

"That was the plan, but now...I don't know. He's seeing someone."

"*No!*"

I wince. "But so am I. Kind of."

"*Kind of?*"

"Fine. I am."

He looks down at his hands, silent for a moment. "But you still love him, right?"

"Of course I do," I reply, my voice breaking slightly. "But sometimes love isn't enough to make a marriage work. We have to figure out if we're still compatible, if we still want the same things."

Andy's eyes meet mine, filled with a mix of sympathy and frustration. "I wish there was a way I could help."

I reach out and squeeze his hand. "You being here, talking to me...it does help. More than you know."

He squeezes back, offering a lopsided smile. "Well, I'm here under duress, but hey, glad I'm pulling my weight."

I nod, feeling a glimmer of hope amid the uncertainty. "You have no idea just how much."

For the next hour, Andy and I read our books, comfortable in each other's company. Every so often, like we did when we were little, we read each other snippets from our books.

"'In her New York years, Fiona had lost touch with Jane. She wondered now if it had been on purpose, the way she let the time between returning Jane's phone calls, her emails, stretch out languorously,'" I read.

I look at Andy pointedly.

He shrugs, noncommittal as ever. A few moments later, he begins to read a line from his own book, a James Patterson novel I found at the drugstore.

But then the door opens, and I look up to see Jack. He's freshly showered, dressed in trendy jeans and a green hooded long-sleeved shirt that brings out the color of his eyes. Despite everything, despite the tangled mess of our relationship, my heart skips a beat. I'm glad he's here. His presence is a comfort, a reminder that not everything is broken beyond repair.

"Hey," he says softly, his eyes meeting mine. There's a complicated mix of emotions there, but I choose to focus on the warmth.

"Morning" I reply, smiling.

He nods and steps further into the room, glancing at Andy, who gives him a small nod of acknowledgment. Surely Andy is thinking about everything I've just told him.

"I was going to get some coffee, does anyone want anything?"

Andy shakes his head as I say, "Coffee would be great."

Expecting a nurse, I'm taken by surprise when Matt steps in. He scans the room before his gaze locks onto mine, and my heart skips—not with the frantic anxiety I felt moments ago, but with pure joy. That joy quickly dims into concern.

Jack.

"Hi," I say, leaping from my chair. "What are you doing here?"

His eyes flicker to my brother. "I wanted to make sure you were okay, that Andy was okay."

Andy raises an eyebrow, intrigued. "And who's this?" he asks, sounding much like the brother he is.

I feel a blush creeping up my cheeks. "This is Matt. He's..." I don't bother to finish my sentence.

"Nice to meet you, Andy," Matt says, stepping forward to shake his hand. Andy looks amused as he shakes Matt's hand.

"Can we talk?" I ask Matt. I need a moment to process everything. He nods, and I lead him out into the hallway, closing the door softly behind us.

Once we're alone, I turn to him, emotions swirling. "I can't believe you're here."

Matt's presence catches me off guard—his determination, his care. He drove all this way, not for some casual fling, but for me. For something real.

"I wouldn't be anywhere else," he says, his voice gentle. "How are you holding up?"

I sigh, leaning against the wall. "It's been rough, but better now. Andy and I...we finally talked. Really talked."

"That's good to hear," Matt says. He reaches for my hand and squeezes it tenderly. His touch is reassuring, grounding me.

The elevator dings behind us, and I glance over, my breath catching when I see Jack step out, two coffees in hand. His eyes land on us—on Matt, standing close, holding my hand—and something shifts in his face. His grip on the coffee cups hardens.

"Hazel," he says, voice strained, teetering on the edge of something dangerous.

The air thickens between us, the tension snapping into place. I don't know how to handle this—there's no manual for this situation. No set rules for what to do when your husband finds you with someone else. And not just anyone, but the man you're sleeping with, while Jack's got someone else waiting for him back in Vegas.

"I...uh..." I stammer, then force myself to introduce them. "Jack, this is Matt. He came to check on me."

Jack's gaze flicks to Matt, his face unreadable, though something dark passes through his eyes. Jealousy? Hurt? Maybe both.

"Check on you?" Jack's voice cuts, sharper than I expect, and I wince.

For a split second, we all just stand there—me, caught in the middle of this unbearable tension, Matt's hand releasing mine as if he's suddenly too aware of Jack's eyes on us. Jack catches this too, his expression hardening as the unspoken passes between them.

"I can go if this isn't a good time," Matt offers, his eyes finding mine.

I freeze, unsure what to say. My heart races, torn between them.

"I'll go," Matt says, taking a step back before I can respond.

"No, wait," I call, but he's already turning to leave.

A wave of frustration and sadness hits me—this wasn't supposed to happen. I didn't want them both here, facing off in this sterile hospital hallway.

Jack watches him go, his eyes heavy with confusion and something deeper—something that twists in my chest. He turns back to me, his expression hardening again. "Hazel, we need to talk."

"Not here," I plead, my voice barely a whisper. "Please, not now."

Jack's jaw clenches, the frustration simmering just beneath the surface. "Fine. But we are talking about this."

I nod, feeling the weight of it all pressing down on me. "We will. Just...not yet."

He studies me for a long moment, as if searching for something—an explanation, a justification—but all he finds is my uncertainty. He hands me one of the coffees, his hand lingering on mine for just a second too long before he lets go. The brief contact feels like a question neither of us is ready to answer.

"I shouldn't have come," he mutters, more to himself than to me. "I didn't expect…"

"I didn't know Matt was coming," I rush to say, as if that could fix anything. The words feel hollow and inadequate.

Jack looks at me again, and I can see it—how he's struggling to hold back what he really wants to say. His eyes are searching for something he's not sure he wants to find. But then, just as quickly, his expression shifts. The hurt is still there, but something else clouds it. Resignation, maybe. Bitterness.

And then I remember—he has Everly. He has someone waiting for him back in Vegas. He can't possibly be upset with me, not when he has someone else.

But Jack's eyes meet mine, and the hurt is there, plain as day.

"I'm glad Andy's okay. I guess we'll talk when you're back."

His words hit me harder than I expect, and before I can say anything more, he walks away, leaving me with the coffee and the wreckage of whatever this is.

CHAPTER
FIFTY-SEVEN

A ndy is asleep when I return to his room. I'm relieved to
have a moment to process what I'm feeling without
having to do so in front of him. But I can't sort through
my thoughts, can't separate one from the next. I was so touched
to see Jack walk into the hospital last night, but then the moment
Matt walked in this morning, all I could think about was the fact
that Jack was coming back. That he would see me with Matt—
which he had.

Jack's reaction made little sense given he had Everly at home,
probably wondering where he'd run off to. This is what I find the
most confusing of all.

I pick up my phone to call Jack, but it's already ringing, a call
coming in from Matt.

I slip into the bathroom to answer it.

"Hey," he says. And I know. I know why he's calling, what he's
going to say. "I just wanted to say again how glad I am your
brother is okay, and that you two seem to have worked things
out." He hesitates and I find myself holding my breath. "Listen, I
think it's pretty obvious I really like you, but...I knew what I was
getting into with you. What could happen. So I really shouldn't
be surprised by what just happened, but..."

He pauses again and my throat feels tight and swollen.

"I think...this was just supposed to be fun. We should end

things now...before it gets more complicated. You're obviously still in love with your husband and I shouldn't be the guy to get in the way. I won't be."

"Matt," I say, my voice catching. "I...I don't know what to say."

"You don't have to say anything. I just wanted you to know where I stand. It's not fair to any of us if we keep going like this."

I inhale deeply, trying to steady my emotions. "I understand. I really do. And I'm sorry if I led you on or made things more confusing."

"I knew what I was getting into that day at the coffee shop," he says. "I just couldn't help myself."

I smile down at my lap. Even as he's ending things with me he still has a way of making me feel seen and appreciated. Wanted.

"Take care of yourself, okay?"

"Okay," I whisper, feeling a mix of relief and sorrow. "You too, Matt."

We hang up and I stare at my reflection in the bathroom mirror. The woman looking back at me is a mess of emotions, but beneath the confusion, there's a glimmer of clarity. I need to figure out what I really want and who I want to be with. And I need to do it for myself, not because of anyone else.

I splash cold water on my face, the universal reset button for bad decisions and existential crises. It doesn't fix anything, but at least I look *slightly* less like a train wreck. Stepping out of the bathroom, I try to tread lightly, hoping Andy's still asleep. But no —he's wide awake, propped up like he's about to conduct an interrogation.

"Well?" he says, smirking like the Cheshire Cat. "Are you going to spill it, or do I have to drag it out of you?"

I groan, rubbing my temples. "I'm still trying to figure it out myself."

"Your *husband* caught you with your *boyfriend*," he says, grinning like he's just delivered the punchline of the year.

"Thank you, Andy," I deadpan. "That's exactly the helpful commentary I needed."

"But it's so fun."

"You want me to break your other leg? Make it a pair?"

"You look like Mom when you're annoyed," he says, and then we're silent for a moment, taking in his comment.

"It's hard for me to picture her," I say softly. "I mean, from before I left."

He shrugs. "Maybe it's better this way."

"Maybe."

A nurse knocks and walks in. I look up to see it's Christine.

"Time to get you out of here," she says with a smile. Sending healthy patients home must be a bright spot in her job. "Just give us a couple of hours to get your discharge papers together." She looks from Andy to me. "I have a good feeling about the two of you. You're both going to be okay."

I'm sorry for your loss.

I manage a small smile. "Thank you, Christine. For everything."

When she's gone I say, "You going to be able to manage on your own at home? Because, if you want, I've got a nice spare bedroom—"

"Slowwww your roll, sister. Let's take this one day at a time."

"Okay," I say. But only because I have to.

"But maybe you could help me get home and settled in? I mean, if you have the time."

"For you, Andy, always."

————

There's nothing like coming home. The familiar creak of the front door, the faint scent of laundry detergent still lingering in the air—it usually brings a sense of comfort, a kind of exhale I can't find anywhere else. But today, it feels different. Hollow. The silence of the house stretches too far, the absence of footsteps, voices, and life weighing heavily in the stillness.

It's not just the house that's empty. I feel the emptiness too, gnawing at me from the inside.

I take a deep breath but the usual relief doesn't come. I head straight for the shower, craving the sensation of hot water on my skin, hoping it will wash away the weight of the past five days. The sound of the water hitting the tiles fills the bathroom, a rhythmic escape from my thoughts. I step in, letting the heat wrap around me, and close my eyes as the steam rises around me, cocooning me in something that feels like peace.

Maybe I was wrong—maybe coming home isn't the best feeling after all. A long, hot shower wins every time.

I let the water work its magic, scrubbing away the layers of exhaustion and emotion that cling to me. The sharp words with Andy, his disappointment cutting deeper than either of us wanted to admit. The look in Jack's eyes when he saw me with Matt—hurt, confusion, a sadness I hadn't expected to see from him. And then Matt...Matt, who had driven all that way, only for us to unravel in the end.

I let those moments fall away, each one rinsed from my skin, disappearing down the drain. I let it go. Or at least, I try to.

As the water cools, I step out, grabbing a towel, and catch my reflection in the foggy mirror. My face looks tired, but there's something else there—something I've been avoiding. The truth. The decision I've been turning over in my mind for days, unsure of how to face it, unsure if I even want to.

The next two days blur by in a haze of busywork, as if alphabetizing my spice rack will magically sort my life out, too. I unpack, make coffee, and wander aimlessly through rooms that feel too big and way too quiet. Every time I pause, the unanswered questions creep in, lounging on the furniture like smug houseguests.

I tell myself that if I stay busy enough, the answers will fall into place. Spoiler: they don't. They just hang there, mocking me in the silence, waiting for me to pull myself together.

And then Jack's text arrives, landing with the grace of a brick through a window.

> Hey. Just wanted to make sure you're home safe. When can we get together to talk?

I stare at the message, my heart sinking. I know what he wants: clarity, closure, maybe even an adult conversation. But clarity feels about as achievable as running a marathon in stilettos right now.

I hold my phone, my thumb hovering over the screen. The

truth? I don't know what to say. The truth about the truth? I don't know if I'm ready to have this conversation.

I take a deep breath, my fingers finally moving to type.

I need more time.

The words feel final as I hit send. There's no anger in them, no blame—just honesty. It's the first honest thing I've said in days, maybe longer. I sit with the weight of it, letting the truth settle in my chest. I'm not ready to face Jack, to face us. And I'm not sure when I will be.

For the first time in a long while, I don't feel guilty about it. There's a strange comfort in the uncertainty, in allowing myself the space to not have all the answers right now. I deserve that much, at least. I deserve the time to figure out who I am, what I want, before I try to make sense of what's left between Jack and me.

As I set my phone down, the house is quiet again. But this time, the silence doesn't feel so oppressive. It feels like space—space to breathe, to heal, and maybe, someday, to decide what comes next.

CHAPTER
FIFTY-EIGHT

DECEMBER

Eight days before Christmas, it snows in Las Vegas, blanketing the ground in a soft white. Families flock to Mt. Charleston for a chance to frolic in the snow. Others stay close to home, snapping photograph after photograph in their own front yards. History dictates the snow won't last long, and everyone wants to take advantage.

It's only the second time Max has ever seen snow. I record a video of him trying to make a snow angel in the backyard, and then I lie down next to him and try to make one of my own. The smile on his face is magnetic, and I know this is one of those moments I could live in forever, that I will play on repeat over and over again in years to come.

But then he says, "I wish Dad was here with us," and I pinch my eyes shut, pained.

Jack has been texting, asking to see me, to talk, but I've been putting it off. Sometimes I worry he'll show up at the house, but so far he's respected my space. Even still, at times, I think it might be the easiest way. For him to force it out of me. Otherwise, I might continue as I have for a week now: overthinking and over-analyzing. To make matters worse, Max has recently been asking if we can spend Christmas together as a family. I don't have the heart to tell him that my conflicted heart can't handle such a thing.

As the snow continues to fall, creating a serene and almost magical atmosphere, Max and I finish making our snow angels. We sit up and watch the flakes drift down from the sky, the silence between us filled with unspoken emotions.

Suddenly, Max's face lights up with an idea. "Mom, can we have a snowball fight?"

"You know it!" I say, pushing aside my swirling thoughts about Jack. For now, I want to focus on Max and this unexpected and very temporary winter wonderland. We scoop up snow, forming them into small snowballs. Max giggles as he throws the first one, and I can't help but laugh as it hits my arm. We play for what feels like hours, our laughter filling the air.

As we catch our breath, my phone buzzes in my pocket. I ignore it at first, but then curiosity gets the better of me. It's another text from Jack.

> I know you're busy, but can we please talk soon?
> It's important.

I sigh, feeling the weight of his words. Max notices my distraction and pauses, looking at me. "Is it Dad?" he asks quietly.

I nod, not wanting to lie to him. "He wants to talk, but I'm not sure what to say yet."

Max looks down at the tiny mound of snow he's been shaping. We've used up most of the snow in the backyard *and* front yard. "Maybe you could just listen to him," he suggests softly. "He misses us, too."

His words hit me like a punch to the stomach. He's right. Maybe it's time to stop avoiding the inevitable conversation. I owe it to Max, to Jack, and to myself to face this head-on, no matter how difficult it might be.

We head inside to prepare some hot cocoa. Max sits at the kitchen table, his face still flushed from the cold. "So what do you think about Christmas? Can Dad come over?" he asks hesitantly.

I pause, considering his question for what feels like the millionth time. "Maybe," I say slowly. "But first, I need to talk to your dad and see where things stand."

Max nods, a flicker of hope in his eyes. "Okay."

———

When Jack enlists Max's help to convince me to meet with him, I know he's reached a point of desperation. It feels like a move from someone grasping for something—anything—to fix what's broken between us, and it leaves me more unsettled than I want to admit.

What I needed was space. Space from everything that happened at the hospital, space from Jack's lingering words. *I shouldn't have left. It wasn't the right thing to do.* Words that hang in the air, heavy with meaning, but confusing too. What does he want from me? He's with Everly now. Isn't that where his focus should be?

Max comes bounding back up to the door, cheerful and oblivious. "Dad wants to know if you want to have dinner with him tonight."

I feel a flicker of something—anxiety, frustration, maybe both. "Remind him I have plans tonight," I say, trying to keep my voice neutral. "That's why you're going over there tonight instead of tomorrow."

Max nods, ready to relay the message, but I stop him, a wave of uncertainty crashing over me. "Wait—don't tell him I have plans. Tell him it's book club."

I don't want Jack to get the wrong idea. I don't even know what his idea is, really. He's dating Everly—so why does it feel like he's trying to pull me back in?

I stand there after Max leaves, my mind racing. Jack's intentions confuse me. Why is he pushing for this when he's with someone else? Does he want closure, or is there something more he's not saying? And more importantly, what do I want?

The questions swirl unanswered, leaving me standing in the doorway, more uncertain than ever.

"Got it." He disappears through the door, leaving it wide open. With a sigh, I reach out and close it. Once I'm sure he's pulled away from the house, I send Jack a text.

> I'll see if I can make plans for Max to visit with
> Reese tomorrow night so we can talk.

I hit send before I can change my mind.

After a quick shower, I head to Amelia's. My mind is racing as I drive the familiar path, and I try to take deep breaths to calm my nerves. Having missed the last book club meeting because of Andy's hospitalization, tonight I have to face the fallout from the last time we all gathered. Accusing Amelia of spreading rumors about my personal life was not my brightest moment, but I'm hopeful that if I'm open and honest—as though I have any choice but to be—then she will forgive me.

I haven't decided quite how to handle Quinn just yet.

As I reach Amelia's door, I hesitate for a moment, taking one last deep breath before ringing the bell. Amelia answers with a warm smile that doesn't quite reach her eyes. When I notice I'm the last to arrive *again*, I have to actively push back against the thought that they gathered early, on purpose, to talk about me before my arrival.

The conversation quiets as I enter.

"Hi, guys," I say, trying to sound cheerful. I place the wine and cookies I've brought along on the coffee table and take a seat. When Amelia offers me a tight-lipped smile, I know it's time to address the elephant in the room.

"Can I just—" My voice trembles slightly, "I wanted to thank you all for your support while Andy was in the hospital. It meant a lot to me. And...Amelia."—I turn to face her directly—"I owe you an apology. I'm sorry about how I spoke to you the last time we were together. About blaming you for...well, you know."

Amelia's face softens. "Thank you, Hazel."

I turn to Quinn, who looks to shrink under my gaze. "I got your letter, Quinn. Along with the book and flowers. Thank you for those, and for being honest with me."

From the corner of my eye I see Jenny sip her wine as Lucy's eyes dart back and forth between Quinn and myself.

"I accept your apology, and, if you can work through whatever caused this—whether it's anger or jealousy or maybe you just don't like me—I'd like to stay a part of the book club. This group has come to mean a lot to me."

In a show of tenderness that, before Anaheim would have been more surprising than anything that has happened in the last ten months, Quinn moves from her chair and sits down beside me. Her right hand curls around my left wrist.

"I really am sorry. I'll do my best to make it right."

We're silent for a few beats until—

"Enough of the love fest, can we get back to the drinking and talking about books portion of the evening?"

I bite back a smile. "Sure, Lucy." I settle back into my seat, grateful for this chance to move forward together.

Amelia leans forward in her chair. "I thought the friendship between Fiona and Jane was so realistically written. It felt like I was peeking into their lives."

Lucy nods in agreement, setting down her wine. She seems particularly excitable tonight. "Yes! The way their relationship evolves over the years, with all its ups and downs...it felt very authentic. It reminded me of some of my own friendships." She looks pointedly from Quinn to me and, despite everything, we all laugh.

Jenny flips through her copy of the book. "I like how the author didn't shy away from showing the complexity of the girls' emotions. There were moments when I felt frustrated with them both, but that made them feel more real."

Quinn, who has been quietly listening, says, "Emotions are a bitch."

We dissolve into laughter once again, any awkwardness from earlier in the evening long gone.

"Did we like the alternating perspectives?" Amelia asks.

I nod, feeling a sense of camaraderie in our shared appreciation for the book. "It gave us deeper insights into their thoughts and feelings. Both sides of the coin and all that."

Amelia smiles and leans back. "I think this was a great pick for book club. There's so much to unpack and discuss."

Lucy reaches for a cookie from the plate on the coffee table. "And it was beautifully written. Some of the passages were just so poetic."

We all fall into a comfortable silence for a moment, sipping our drinks and reflecting on the book. It's these moments of connection and shared experience I cherish most about our book club.

As we continue to discuss the themes, characters, and our personal takeaways, I feel grateful for the friendship and the chance to explore new stories together.

I feel grateful to my mother for, in her own way, teaching me the importance of forgiveness.

For Andy, for extending his forgiveness my way.

"Here's to another great read," I say, raising my glass. The others join in, and we clink our glasses together, smiles all around.

What I'm meant to learn from Jack and this whole *situation* remains yet to be seen.

CHAPTER
FIFTY-NINE

I stand outside Foxtail Café, the familiar scent of roasted coffee beans mingling with the sharp winter air. Ten months have passed since Jack and I agreed to step back from our marriage—ten long months of distance, confusion, and the quiet unraveling of everything we once were. Now, we're here to do the hardest thing of all: talk about whether we can still save what's left.

The holiday lights glitter around me, making the moment feel both surreal and painfully grounded. Christmas is just days away, and the warmth of the season contrasts sharply with the cold uncertainty between us. Inside, at a corner table I've sat at countless times, I wait for my husband to sit across from me—not as the man I used to know, but someone else entirely, someone who might ask me about Matt.

I see him through the window. His movements are hesitant, as if crossing the threshold feels like a final step toward the inevitable. Our eyes meet, and for an instant, it's like we're both suspended between who we used to be and who we are now. A strained smile flickers across his face, and I rise to meet him, my heart pounding in my chest.

"Hi," he says, voice tight, uncertain.

"Hi." We exchange a quick, awkward hug, and I gesture toward the table. "I ordered your usual."

There's a silence that follows, heavy with unspoken words and unasked questions. I wrap my hands around the mug in front of me, trying to find comfort in its warmth. Jack clears his throat, breaking the silence.

"So...how are you?" he asks, his voice gentle but filled with the weight of the months we've spent apart. "How is Andy?"

"He's good, yeah." I exhale slowly. "I've been okay. It's been... different." I look at his hands on his coffee cup before lifting my gaze to meet his. "You?"

"It's been strange," he says, a small, almost nostalgic smile tugging at his lips.

I nod, struggling to fight past the tight knot in my throat. The café bustles around us, but it's almost as though we're in our own little bubble, filled with memories and the uncertainty of what comes next. I take another deep breath, steeling myself for the conversation that lies ahead.

Jack's eyes are focused on his coffee, and I can see the tension in his shoulders. Finally, he looks up, his gaze meeting mine.

"I have to admit," he begins, his voice trembling slightly, "seeing you with Matt at the hospital caught me off guard. I was...I was jealous. There's no other way to put it. I can't stand the thought of you being with someone else. I—" He stops himself, looking torn.

My heart aches at his confession. I see the raw emotion in his eyes, the vulnerability he's laying bare. He takes a deep breath and continues, "I miss you, Hazel. I don't need another two months apart to know what I want."

I suck in a breath and hold it.

"I want to call things off. I want to come home."

His words hang in the air, heavy with hope and uncertainty. I swallow hard, feeling a knot in my stomach.

"What about Everly?" I ask, my voice barely above a whisper.

Jack looks puzzled. "Everly?"

I feel a surge of anxiety. I didn't want to bring this up, but now I have no choice. "Please don't lie to me. If these past ten months have taught me anything it's that we've been lying to each other for a long time without even really knowing it." I power on. "During one of your weeks in the house, I had to go back for something I needed for work. You were at work," I admit, my voice shaking. "I saw the note on the fridge."

His confusion deepens. "What note?"

"Her phone number," I say, my throat tightening. "Everly. 702-555-0135."

"You memorized the number?"

I say, "Who is she?"

Jack's eyes widen in realization, and then he barks out a laugh, a sound that's both relieved and incredulous. "Dr. Everly," he says, still chuckling. "She's my therapist, Hazel."

I stare at him. "Your therapist?"

"Yeah," he says, his laughter fading into a gentle smile. "I've been speaking to her a couple of times a week for a while now. She's been helping me understand myself better. Understand *us* better."

Relief washes over me, mingled with a touch of embarrassment. "I thought..." *I thought you'd been sleeping with someone else, which is why I...*

Matt.

Jack reaches across the table, taking my hand in his. "I want to come home, Hazel. I want to work through this together. No more misunderstandings. Just us."

Matt takes the wine glass from my hand and kisses me. Everything seems to happen in slow motion: the removing of our clothes, our mouths exploring each other's bodies, the cries of joy. Of lust. Of desire. And then I fall on top of him, breathless.

I look into Jack's eyes, seeing the sincerity and hope there. But it's not as simple as he makes it out to be. All this time I thought he'd been—unfaithful isn't the right word, not when it comes to us, to our arrangement. I thought he'd been with someone else, which is the only reason I even began to be open to the idea of seeing someone other than my husband. And now, to hear Everly is a therapist and not some lithe goddess in a flowy dress...

I pinch my eyes shut. "Jack," I say softly. "I need to tell you something, but I don't think this is the right place."

His eyes search mine for a moment, then he says, "I'll see you at home, then?"

Home.

I nod. What else is there to say?

Jack sits on the edge of the couch, his posture stiff. It is at once disarming and entirely normal to see him inside the house again. "What is it you have to tell me?"

I let out a steady breath, the words tasting bitter on my tongue. "I've...I slept with someone else."

His face remains unreadable, but I see the flicker of pain in his eyes. "Matt."

My nod is almost imperceptible.

"How many times?" he asks, his voice steady but laced with hurt.

I want to lie, to soften the blow, but I can't. "It was...we were together for a few months." My voice cracks, and I look away.

The silence that follows is unbearable. I can see the hurt etched into his features, hear it in the way he breathes.

"And you thought I was with Everly," he finally says, his voice strained but calm. I watch his face change as he seems to work through his thoughts.

"I did...but I'm not excusing what I did. I acted on my own volition. It was something I wanted to do, and so I did it." The second the words are out of my mouth I want to take them back. "I'm sorry to be so blunt."

Jack works his jaw back and forth.

My words hang in the air, offering no comfort. I want to reach out, to apologize again, to explain, but I know it's too late. The damage is done.

Without speaking, Jack rises from the couch and fetches himself a glass of water, which he drinks down before turning back to me. There are tears in his eyes, and mine grow wet immediately.

"What you said earlier, that we've been lying to each other for a long time without even really knowing it? I think you're right. I was disappointed for a long time, and then it morphed into anger, and instead of staying and doing the hard work, I took the easy way out. Or at least I thought I did." He swallows. "Dr.

Everly has me digging pretty deep into the 'why' behind my actions, so I can develop a better sense of myself and change behaviors that have been holding me back. Not only that but she's helped me to understand you better."

My head is spinning, a messy tangle of thoughts. "So your black shirt...you weren't trying to impress anyone?"

Jack looks thoroughly confused.

"Your black shirt...the one you called your lucky shirt..." The one I'd pictured thrown over someone else's chair in someone else's bedroom.

"Oh, Hazel." He lets out a sharp laugh, his expression one of amusement. "It's my favorite shirt, that's all. It feels like every other shirt I own is too tight across my stomach. You know how I am about that area..."

I'm quiet for a moment before saying, "I'll be right back."

Upstairs, I find the note where he'd hidden it beneath his stack of sweaters and carry it with me downstairs. I set it on the table between us.

We're not attracted to each other the way we used to be.

She honestly thinks I bullied her into having a baby.

At first, Jack looks at the paper like he doesn't know what it is, but slowly, realization dawns on his face. He closes his eyes momentarily before settling them on me.

"I want you to know this isn't how I feel. I wrote this back when...Hazel, I was angry when I wrote it," he says. "We've both said and done some things we wish we could take back, but we can't. It's all out there in the open now. The question is, what are we going to do with it?"

Is she even in love with me anymore? Am I even in love with her anymore?

Jack's eyes search mine, and I can see the mixture of emotions there—pain, regret, a flicker of hope. "We've both made mistakes."

For a moment, we just stand there, the weight of those mistakes hanging between us. Then, tentatively, I take a step forward. "Do you think this is fixable?"

"I do. But it's going to take time. And effort. But...I want to try. I want to find a way to make things right."

Matt.

"You weren't...with anyone else?"

"No," he says, and my stomach clenches. I'm happy to hear this—thrilled, really—but it only serves to make me feel worse for not being as strong as he has been.

As though he can read my thoughts, Jack pulls me against him. With my chest pinned against his, he holds me as I cry.

CHAPTER
SIXTY

We sit on opposite ends of the couch, the silence between us louder than anything we've said in months. The weight of everything we've been through presses down on me—resentment, regret, and those brief flickers of hope that always seemed just out of reach. The room feels stifling, like the air itself is waiting for us to finally confront the truth we've been avoiding for so long.

For the first time in what feels like forever, we're not dodging the conversation. We're not strangers in our own home. We're here, together, about to be brutally honest.

"I'd like to show you something else, if I could," Jack says quietly, his voice tentative.

I watch him reach into his jacket pocket and pull out a small, worn notebook. He flips through it with careful hands, and for a second, I can see the nerves in the way his fingers tremble slightly. He finds what he's looking for and holds it out to me, his eyes a mixture of hope and fear.

"Read this," he says.

I take the notebook from him, my hands shaking just enough to notice. My eyes land on the page—a list scribbled in different colors of ink, some lines faint, others bold. I start at the top, my heart pounding in my chest.

- *her 'that's what she said' jokes*
- *her inability to sneeze quietly*
- *waking up next to her*
- *her morning bedhead*

I look up. "What is this?"
"Isn't it obvious? Keep reading."

- *the way she licks her finger before she turns the page in her book*
- *her cold feet on my calves*
- *how her tongue peeks out of her mouth when she's deep in thought*
- *the way she hogs the covers*
- *the sound of her voice*

My mouth has gone dry.

- *her mouth*

"I added the last one just last week," he says, his voice low. He takes my hand and pulls me down to sit on the couch next to him. "I've missed you so much."

He flips to the next page of the notebook. I see more of his handwriting. Pages and pages of it.

- *We tell stupid jokes that only we could possibly find funny.*
- *At our best, we can finish each other's sentences.*
- *Our beautiful son.*
- *I sleep better when she's next to me.*
- *She never says no to dessert, and I love that about her.*
- *The way she changes out my bathroom towel every weekend without fail.*
- *She embraced my family as her own from the very beginning.*
- *She's compassionate and steadfast.*
- *We talk openly and honestly about money.*

- *We're not the kind of couple who asks each other for permission to live our lives.*
- *My life is better with her in it.*
- *No one has ever loved me the way she has.*

Each one is a reminder of the little things that make us, us.

Tears well up in my eyes, blurring the words on the page. I look up at Jack again, and he's watching me intently, his own eyes glistening.

"In case you needed a reminder of how much good there is here," he says. "I could have filled the entire notebook."

I reach for him. His touch is warm and familiar, and I feel a spark of hope. "I'm sorry," I say, my voice barely above a whisper. "For everything."

"These are the kind of lists I wrote when I stopped being so angry," he says. I think of my own lists, saved on my computer. Maybe one day I'll show them to Jack, but not right now.

We sit in silence for a moment, absorbing the gravity of the situation.

"We can do this," he says, squeezing my hand gently. "One step at a time."

I smile through my tears, squeezing back. "We have to be honest," I say. "But not like before. Not out of anger. It has to be out of love."

Jack steps closer. "I can do that. Can you?"

A laugh escapes me. "Absolutely."

And then I do the most honest thing I've done in months: I kiss my husband. I kiss him until our lips are chapped and swollen.

Eventually, I pull away from the kiss, breathless, but there's still so much I need to say. My lips tingle, swollen from the honesty in our touch, but the words that have been trapped inside me for years are pushing to the surface.

"Jack," I begin, my voice trembling, "I've held so much back. I've spent so much time trying to convince myself everything was fine, that I was fine. But I wasn't."

His eyes search mine, a softness in them that wasn't there

before. "I know," he says quietly. "You've been carrying a lot on your own."

I nod, swallowing hard. "I've come to realize I spent a lot of time pouring myself into being your wife, and into our life together. The problem is, somewhere along the way, I lost pieces of myself." I push out a steady breath. "I need to find a balance."

He says, "Okay."

"I never felt like I could ask for more. I thought if I did, I'd be seen as ungrateful. Like I wasn't enough for you, or maybe I wasn't enough for myself. But I need more, Jack. I need more from you, from us." My voice cracks, and I wipe a stray tear from my cheek. "I need to be seen. Not just as a mother or a wife, but as Hazel. The person I was before all of this."

He stays silent, his brow furrowed, taking it all in. "What do you need from me?" he asks.

"I need us to be partners again. I need us to dream together, to make decisions together. And I need space to be myself, too, without feeling guilty for wanting it. I don't want to feel like I'm failing you because I need things for me. We've lost sight of who we are, Jack. I need us to figure it out together."

He nods slowly, processing. "I've been learning a lot about us," he says after a moment, his voice steady. "In therapy...I realized just how much I shut down when things get hard. I think I'm protecting you, protecting us, by keeping everything inside. But I see now it only pushed you away. It made you feel alone."

I nod, biting my lip to keep from crying again. His words hit home in a way I didn't expect.

"Do you remember the night we went out to dinner with Milo from your work? You spent the whole evening ignoring me, and then at home you said..." I stop, unable to finish the sentence, the hurt still raw.

Jack's face falls, and his grip on my hand tightens. "Hazel," he breathes. "I'm sorry. I've thought so much about that night. He runs a hand through his hair, his face full of regret. "I was in a bad place. Work was overwhelming, and I was trying to impress Milo, trying to make it seem like I had everything together because I wanted the promotion so badly. You didn't deserve that."

"I just need to know you see me as more than just some woman who's there to make you look good."

"I do," he says, his voice thick with emotion. "I see you, Hazel. And I'm so sorry for how I treated you. It wasn't fair, and it wasn't right. I was...I was so lost in my own insecurities, and I took it out on you. But I promise, I see you now. I see how much you've been holding back, and I want to do better. I will do better."

He pauses, then adds, "That's part of what I've learned in therapy. I need to be more present, and more aware of how my actions affect you. I've spent too much time trying to be perfect on the outside, and it's cost us too much. I don't want to lose you because I was too blind to see what was happening right in front of me."

We sit in silence for a moment, the air between us shifting, growing lighter. His words, his apology, they soothe something inside me that's been aching for years. But it's not just his apology I needed—it's his understanding. His recognition of how he hurt me, how we got here.

"The thing is...I don't need you, Jack. But I do want you."

I lean my head against his shoulder, feeling the warmth of his body, the familiar scent of him. It feels like home, but different. Lighter.

"I love you," he says quietly. "I've always loved you."

"I love you, too," I whisper.

And I know it's not a lie.

CHAPTER
SIXTY-ONE

I sit on the porch steps, feeling the cool concrete beneath me, and look out at the desert landscape of Las Vegas. Even on Christmas Day, the city looks the same as it always does, the surprise snowfall having only lasted twenty-four hours. The sun is starting to set, casting a golden glow over the sparse plants and rocky ground. It's like a metaphor for my own life, a life that's been barren and is now finding a way to bloom again.

Jack joins me, sitting close but not touching. It's a tentative closeness, a new beginning after our time apart. While we seem to be well on our way to figuring ourselves out separately, we now need to figure out how to be together again.

"I missed this," he says, breaking the silence. His voice is soft, wistful.

"Me too," I reply, glancing at him with a small smile. It's true. Despite everything, I missed him, missed us.

From inside the house, I hear the sound of Max, laughing as he chats with his grandparents, no doubt rejoicing over his mound of gifts. The sound brings warmth to my heart, a reminder of what's important.

My phone buzzes in my pocket, and I pull it out to see a text from Andy.

Still on for tomorrow?

I smile and type back quickly.

Absolutely.

"I think it's great you're going to go see your mother together."

"It's a start," I say. I take a long, calming breath, the dry desert air filling my lungs. "I have a lot to say to her that I never got a chance to."

I turn to face him. "I haven't dreamed of her in weeks now," I say suddenly. It's a thought I've been sitting with for a while but haven't voiced out loud.

Jack looks at me, his expression a mix of curiosity and concern. "How does that make you feel?"

Yeah, this guy has definitely been seeing a therapist.

"Peaceful, actually," I admit. "For so long, I thought I needed to understand why things happened the way they did. But now, I think it's okay I don't have all the answers. I think I can heal without them."

He reaches out and takes my hand, giving it a gentle squeeze. We sit there, hand in hand, watching the desert as the sun begins to set. There's a sense of new beginnings, of healing, and of hope. And for the first time in a long time, I feel like I'm exactly where I'm supposed to be.

After a moment, Jack looks over at me. "You should know I quit my job."

"Good," I say, not bothering to hide my amusement. "You'll find a company that respects you."

"What's this about a book club, by the way?" He tips his head sideways.

I smile. "I made some new friends."

"Atta girl," he says, grinning widely.

"Don't do that," I say, playfully elbowing him. "Don't be smug."

He holds up his hands. "I wouldn't dream of it."

"Daisy told me I needed some new friends."

"She's a smart girl. How is she doing anyway?"

I feel myself physically deflate. I've been giving her the space she asked for, but it hasn't been easy.

"Turns out she wasn't the only one who needed some space from me." I look at him pointedly.

Jack sighs. "I've already admitted it was a mistake," he says. "As for Daisy, she'll come around. You two have far too much history."

"I hope you're right. She just needs time, like we did."

Jack's hand tightens around mine, a silent promise of support.

"Max seems happy," he says, breaking the silence once more. His eyes are fixed on the horizon, but I know he's thinking about our son, about the future we're rebuilding together.

"He is," I reply, my heart swelling with a mix of love and determination.

The desert night wraps around us, cool and comforting. I notice that, under his coat, Jack is wearing his lucky black shirt.

Eventually, he stands, pulling me up gently with him. "Come on, let's go back inside," he says softly.

I follow him into the house, where Max is on the floor, surrounded by his new toys, showing them off to his grandparents. His laughter fills the room, and I catch his eyes as he looks up and waves me over.

"Mom! Look what Grandma and Grandpa got me!" Max holds up a small drone and I try not to cringe. I crouch down beside him, taking it in my hands, pretending to inspect it carefully.

"Awesome," I say, grinning as I hand it back to him.

"Wanna see me fly it?"

"Of course, let's see what this thing can do."

Max eagerly sets up the drone, and soon it's buzzing around the room, hovering slightly too close to Grandma's lamp before veering wildly toward the Christmas tree. "Careful, Max," I say, half-laughing, half-nervous as he tries to steady it. "We should probably take it outside."

"I got it, I got it," Max insists, completely confident.

Just as Jack leans down to give Max some advice, the drone makes an unexpected turn—straight toward his head.

Thwack!

The little drone bounces off Jack's forehead, dropping to the floor as Jack stumbles back, rubbing the spot with an exaggerated wince.

Max's eyes go wide in horror. "I'm so sorry!"

I bite my lip to keep from laughing, but the sight of Jack standing there, bewildered, with a drone-marked forehead is too much. A giggle escapes me.

Jack, recovering quickly, gives Max a playful scowl. "You've got good aim."

Max's nervous expression breaks into laughter as he realizes his dad isn't mad. "Good thing you don't have to work tomorrow." Max jokes. We dissolve into laughter.

Jack picks up the drone, hands it back to Max, and crouches down beside him. "Okay, let's try again—but outside this time."

Max nods enthusiastically, already refocused on flying the drone again.

I lean into Jack, who wraps an arm around me, shaking his head in amused disbelief. "Of all the places that thing could've gone..."

"It must've known," I tease. "It's drawn to you."

He kisses my forehead and then, after wrapping himself in his jacket, follows Max outside. Soon, I hear the muffled buzz of the drone and the sound of laughter.

I feel, for the first time in a long time, that everything is truly going to be okay.

———

Christmas night wraps around our house like a warm blanket. Jack and I sit on the couch, the silence between us comfortable yet charged with a hint of uncertainty. Max is tucked in bed, his little snores a reminder of the joy today has brought.

I glance at Jack, his face partially illuminated by the soft light from the Christmas tree. "It's been a good day," I say, my voice barely above a whisper.

He nods, his eyes meeting mine. "Yeah, it has." There's a softness in his gaze, a warmth I had almost forgotten.

We sit there for a moment, the room filled with the faint scent of pine and the remnants of a hearty Christmas dinner. I feel a knot in my stomach, a mix of nerves and hope. "Jack," I start, unsure of how to continue. "Will you stay tonight?"

He doesn't hesitate. "I was hoping you would ask." He kisses the top of my head, and I close my eyes, savoring the feeling of being held by him again.

We eventually make our way upstairs, the house quiet except for the creaks of the floorboards under our feet. I check on Max one last time, his little face peaceful in sleep, before we head to our bedroom.

It feels both strange and familiar to be here with him, but as we settle into bed, I feel a surge of hope. This is the first step, a tentative beginning.

Jack pulls me close, and I give into his warmth, feeling the weight of the past ten months begin to lift. Then he kisses me, and his name comes as a purr from the depths of my throat he swallows whole.

"I missed this," he murmurs, his breath warm against my ear. And then Jack peels off my clothes and shows me just how much he's missed me.

———

I wake up to the soft morning light filtering through the curtains. The room feels unusually warm and comforting, and I realize it's because Jack is beside me. His steady breathing, the warmth of his body—I am home again. I exhale, savoring the moment.

I slowly sit up, careful not to wake him. I glance around the room, my eyes landing on the clock. It's early, too early for Max to be up, but I know he'll be bouncing into the room any minute now, eager to start the day.

Slipping out of bed, I step quietly to the window and peek through the curtains. The city outside is still and quiet, a rare sight for Las Vegas. I turn back to look at Jack, still sound asleep, and a smile spreads across my face.

As I head to the kitchen to start breakfast, I feel a strange sensation wash over me. It's like a weight I didn't even realize I was carrying has been lifted.

I blink, the room blurring for a moment. Standing here in the soft glow of the morning, I realize something has changed. I can feel it deep inside me.

I love cleaning bathrooms.

And then, tentatively, I try to say it out loud.

"I love cleaning the bathrooms," I whisper.

It's a lie.

I laugh, the sound filling the quiet kitchen. It's not just the spell that's been broken. It's me, too. I'm free.

Jack stirs and calls out groggily from the bedroom, "Hazel? You okay?"

I walk back to the bedroom, a spring in my step. "I'm more than okay," I say, sitting down on the edge of the bed. "Just thinking about chores."

He smiles sleepily, reaching out to take my hand. "Of course you are," he says, his voice filled with warmth and sincerity.

"It's good to be back," I reply, squeezing his hand.

We sit there for a moment, just enjoying the quiet togetherness, until Max bursts into the room. I watch as he registers Jack's presence.

"Dad?" His brows furrow. I want to reach out and smooth the lines out with my thumb.

"Morning, bud."

Max studies us for a short moment before saying, "Can we have pancakes?"

Jack and I exchange a knowing look, a shared smile that says everything we don't need to put into words.

I watch him follow our son out of the bedroom, my gaze landing on the armchair in the corner of the room. It's there; his lucky black is shirt thrown over the armrest.

Oh.

CHAPTER
SIXTY-TWO

A ndy is the first one out of the car. I can tell by the way he pulls his coat more tightly around him it's colder than we thought. He finds Mom's grave easily and crouches down before her headstone. I let him have his time with her. I can't begin to imagine what he is saying to her. I'm not sure I'll be able to find my own words when it comes time.

Eventually, Andy waves me over. I slip out of the car, the cool winter air filling my lungs as I try to steady myself. He is beside me, silent but supportive. It's the day after Christmas, and while others are enjoying the holiday cheer, we're here to face the past.

The cemetery is quiet, the soft rustling of leaves the only sound for what feels like miles. I've been dreading this moment, yet I know it's necessary. A wave of emotions crashes over me—anger, sorrow, regret. I kneel, tracing the letters on her tombstone with my fingertips.

"Hey, Mom," I whisper, my voice trembling. "It's been a while."

I stand by my mother's grave, the cold wind biting at my cheeks as I stare down at the headstone. It's simple and elegant—just as she would have wanted. But it feels wrong, too final. I've carried the weight of our fractured relationship, the silence, the distance, and now, it's permanent. There's no chance to fix it, no chance to say what I should have said.

Andy stands beside me, his hands in his coat pockets, quiet

but present. Our relationship is still fragile, but the anger has thawed, leaving space for something new—tentative, but hopeful.

"I didn't expect this to be so hard," I say, my voice barely above a whisper. It's the first thing I've said since we got here.

Andy looks at me, his expression softer than it's been in months. "It's okay."

He moves a few feet back, giving me space but staying close enough to offer comfort. I glance at him, and he nods a silent encouragement.

"I'm sorry it took so long to get here," I continue, tears welling up in my eyes.

The memories flood back—our fights, the harsh words, the distance I put between us when I left home for university.

"I hated you for so long and blamed you for everything," I admit, my voice barely audible. "You were a terrible mother, but now maybe I understand you were doing the best you could with the skills you were given by your parents."

Andy steps closer, placing a hand on my shoulder. His presence grounds me, giving me the strength to keep going.

"I always thought we'd have time to fix things between us, but I should have known there are no guarantees in life. I shouldn't have waited so long. I shouldn't have waited at all," I say, my voice breaking. "We never got to say all the things that needed to be said. And now, it's too late."

I bow my head, the weight of my regrets heavy on my heart. "I wish I could tell you I understand now, and I forgive you. I hope you can forgive me too."

The silence around us is deafening, but in it, I find a strange sense of peace. It's not the closure I wanted, but it's something.

Andy squeezes my shoulder as I cry and cry, finally finding the release I so desperately needed.

Eventually, I stand up and turn to my brother. "Thank you for being here with me," I say to him, my voice raw. "And thank you for—"

"Oh no you don't," he says, biting back a smile. "We already had our moment in the hospital. That's all you're getting from me."

"You're the absolute worst brother," I say. The lie feels foreign and wrong on my tongue.

As we turn to leave, I take one last look at the grave. "Bye, Mom," I whisper. And then we walk back to the car in silence, the weight of the past still heavy but somehow lighter than before.

I hear her before I see her. A small, timid voice calling my name. "Hazel."

I stop and turn, and there she is—Daisy. My heart skips a beat. What is she doing here? I glance at Andy, and he nods slightly, a silent confirmation it's his doing.

"Daisy," I say, my voice filled with a mix of surprise and confusion. "What are you doing here?"

She takes a tentative step forward. "I needed to see you, Hazel. I needed to apologize."

I'm caught off guard, the sting of her rejection still lingering. "Apologize?" I echo, unsure of what to say.

She nods, her expression earnest. "Yes. I'm sorry. For pushing you away, for saying there was too much drama surrounding you. I was wrong."

Swallowing feels like trying to force down a hard, stubborn knot of emotions.

She glances at Andy, then back at me. "Andy filled me in on everything. He told me you'd be here. Seeing you here, facing your past like this...I realized I needed to face mine too."

I swallow hard, my emotions swirling. "What do you mean?"

She takes a deep breath. "Your problems with Jack...I think they scared me. No—they *definitely* scared me. They made me worry about my own marriage. I found myself looking at Finn differently. Analyzing everything he did or didn't do. Every little argument we ever had. It made no sense. And instead of dealing with my fears in a healthy way, I did the only thing that made sense at the time. I pushed you away. It was just easier to blame you, to distance myself, than to confront what was really bothering me."

Her words hit me like a ton of bricks. Hearing her say it now, I feel a strange mix of anger and relief.

She smiles a little, tilting her head. "You've had a lot going on,

Hazel. I didn't mean to push you away. I just needed a little room to breathe."

"I get it now," I say, my voice thick with emotion. "I do. I've been dealing with a lot...But I've been selfish. I didn't stop to think about what you needed."

Daisy reaches over and takes my hand. "You're not selfish, Hazel. You've just been hurting."

I bite my lip, tears welling in my eyes. "I'm sorry."

She squeezes my hand, her smile warm and genuine. "We're okay. We'll figure this out."

We stand there for a moment, the weight of the last few weeks slowly lifting. I feel lighter, as though the distance between us is finally closing.

"You want to get some coffee?" Daisy asks.

I breathe deeply, trying to process everything. This isn't what I expected when I came here today, but maybe it's exactly what I needed.

She steps closer, and we embrace, both of us crying now. The weight of the past feels a little lighter, the future a little brighter.

I smile. "That sounds perfect."

CHAPTER
SIXTY-THREE

FEBRUARY

On the morning of my fortieth birthday, I am awoken by the sun streaming through the blinds, painting the room in soft morning light. I was dreaming of my mother. The same dream I had in the beginning, right after she'd died, of the two of us standing in her kitchen as she stirs pasta on the stove. She turns to face me, a spatula in her raised hand. I watch as her mouth opens, awaiting her first words to me in the fifteen months since her death. I look my mother in the eye and then—

She smiles.

Oh.

And then I close my eyes and smile to myself.

———

The text from Andy simply reads:

> Happy birthday, sis.

And then a second message comes through right below it:

Remember when Mom made us those
ridiculous matching outfits for our 8th birthday?

Downstairs, the boys have prepared chocolate chip waffles, covered with sickly sweet syrup. I eat every last one, and then ask for seconds.

———

Daisy picks me up in her oversized SUV and treats me to coffee at Foxtail. It's not lost on me that the last time we were here together was shortly after my mother's funeral. Even after all this time, Daisy's words that day are still fresh in my mind. *You've been so wrapped up in Jack and Max that you've forgotten about you.*

Daisy orders for us, her usual confidence guiding the interaction.

"I can't believe how much has changed since we were last here," I say, once we sit down.

Daisy nods, a knowing smile on her face. "You do seem... different. Happier, maybe?"

"I think I am. It took a long time but I feel like I'm finally beginning to feel comfortable in my own skin."

"I'm sure Matt had a little to do with that." She grins sheepishly.

I bob my head from side to side. "It didn't hurt," I admit. Matt helped me to see a different side of myself, namely one who thoroughly enjoys sex and shouldn't be afraid to be honest and exactly who I am.

"Getting older does that to you," Daisy says. Her fortieth birthday is only five weeks away. "You start to care less about what others think and more about what makes you happy."

I smile, feeling a sense of camaraderie. "You're right. I used to be so focused on being the perfect wife and mother. Like you said, I lost myself in it. But now, I feel like I'm finding my way back."

Daisy reaches across the table and squeezes my hand. "I'm proud of you, Hazel. It's not easy to confront those things, but you've done it."

Her words fill me with warmth, and I realize just how far I've come.

We sit in comfortable silence for a moment, the bustling café around us a stark contrast to the calm I feel inside. It's good to be here, with my best friend, in this place that holds so many memories. And it's even better to know I'm finally starting to create new ones—ones that are all my own.

An hour later, I step through my front door and am met with a wave of clapping and cheering. Strings of twinkling lights hang from the doorways, casting a warm glow over the gathering. My heart swells at the sight of my friends and family, all here to celebrate this milestone birthday with me.

I knew all along that Daisy taking me out for coffee was to get me out of the house, but it doesn't at all detract from my elation at seeing everyone here.

My eyes scan the small group until I find Jack. He gives me a nod, a silent acknowledgment of everything we've been through, everything we've overcome.

Max comes bounding toward me. "Happy birthday, Mom!" Though he's much too heavy for it, I scoop him up, his arms wrapping around my neck, and for a moment, I forget about everyone else. It's just us, our little family, reunited and stronger than ever.

"Happy birthday, baby," Jack says, his voice low and full of emotion as he steps closer, placing a gentle kiss on my forehead. I close my eyes, savoring the moment, the warmth of his touch. "I told you I'd still love you when you're forty."

"Hazel." I hear Andy's voice and turn to see him making his way through the crowd. I pull him into a tight hug and hold him, my words eluding me.

Later, there is cake. Homemade and completely misshapen, with *HAPPY 40TH HAZEL & ANDY* written in wobbly blue icing.

The room erupts in applause and cheers as Andy and I step forward, side by side. I glance at him, and he's smiling broadly, his eyes shining with the same emotion I feel.

"Happy birthday, twin sister," he says softly, leaning in closer. "And might I add, you wear forty remarkably well for someone who spent the first half of life copying my every move."

I roll my eyes, nudging his shoulder. "Please. I was the original. You're just the slightly less charming sequel."

"Slightly?" He arches a brow, feigning offense.

"Well, I didn't want to hurt your feelings *too* much on our birthday," I say with a smirk.

"Big of you," he says, crossing his arms. "Though I do recall being the one who got you through eighth grade math. That alone should secure my 'charming' status."

"And I seem to recall being the one who bailed you out of the Great Prom Disaster of '03," I shoot back. "Face it, Andy, you owe me for life."

He lets out a laugh, shaking his head. "Okay, truce. But only because I'm feeling magnanimous today."

I grin, holding out my hand. "Deal. Twin solidarity, right?"

He shakes my hand, then leans in conspiratorially. "Twin solidarity, sure. But if this cake tastes like cardboard, I'm blaming you."

Per my request, there are only two candles—one for each of us. Though I've nearly overcome my silly fear of turning forty, I don't need the reminder staring up at me from my birthday cake.

I laugh as we step toward the cake together, the candles flickering. "Just try to make a wish that doesn't involve besting me, okay?"

"I'll do my best," he replies, smirking.

"Make a wish!" someone calls out, and I bark out a laugh, thinking about the wish I made a year ago. The wish that eventually led to all of this, to this moment of clarity and truth.

I look around at the faces of those I love—my family, Daisy, Amelia, Lucy, Jenny, and even Quinn—the people who've helped me beyond words this past year, and my heart feels full.

I close my eyes and make a new wish.

This time, it's not about change or fixing things. This time, I wish for the strength to continue being honest with myself, to keep growing, and to embrace whatever comes next with an open heart.

Andy and I blow out the candles together, the cheers and applause ringing in my ears. I open my eyes to see the smiling faces, the joy and love that surrounds me.

Jack wraps his arm around my waist, pulling me close. "Here's to the next chapter."

I smile up at him, my heart full. "Here's to us," I reply. No more lies, no more pretending. Just us, as we are, ready to face whatever comes next.

And as the night continues, filled with laughter, stories, and the warmth of those I hold dear, I know I will be okay. I am finished with one chapter, ready to start the next, and for the first time in a long time, I truly believe in my happy ending.

I am more than fine.

ACKNOWLEDGMENTS

Thank you to my friends, support network, and early readers: Jordan Hansen, Suzy Krause, and Dela Ballard.

To all the readers, bloggers, and friends who read, reviewed, and shared my first book, your support means the world to me.

Many of the words in this book were written during WFWA writing sessions. To all the amazing women I wrote alongside, thank you for your camaraderie and inspiration. You've been such an important part of this process.

Thank you to my editor, Amy Briggs for all of your hard work, and to Ellie Folden for giving my stories a home with Love N. Books Press.

Lastly, to my husband and son—you are my happy ending.

A LOOK AT

ANOTHER KIND OF GREEN

The grass isn't always greener on the other side...

Colette Dawson feels like she's barely holding it together. Her starter home is too cramped, her work is thankless, and her marriage is running on fumes.When her husband, Nick, agrees to tour the home of her dreams, Colette thinks she might finally get some relief...until Nick hires a contractor to renovate their home. "Make a list," he says, convinced they can make do with what they already have.

When Colette's best friend, Zoey, reveals her picture-perfect family is being torn apart by infidelity, Colette realizes that settling for what she and Nick have is not the answer. Desperate to avoid a similar fate, she caves and comes up with a list of home improvements. Then she makes another one: everything he'd have to change for their marriage to survive.

What seemed like a smart idea soon spirals out of control and, caught in a web of emotions, Colette and Nick quickly discover that sometimes the most profound renovations take place within ourselves.

AVAILABLE NOW

DISCUSSION QUESTIONS

1. The book explores the tension between staying the same and adapting to new roles (e.g., as a spouse, parent, or individual). How do the characters navigate this tension, and how does it affect their relationships?
2. Hazel frequently reflects on aging and the passage of time. How do her perceptions of aging impact her actions and her relationships?
3. How does Hazel's perspective on love, family, and herself evolve throughout the novel? What pivotal moments drive her transformation?
4. The relationship between Hazel and Jack is central to the story. How does their dynamic shift over time? What do you think ultimately drives the distance between them?
5. How do Hazel's relationships with her mother and brother Andy shape her outlook on life and love? How do these familial connections compare to her bond with Jack's family?
6. Daisy and Hazel have a long-standing friendship. How does Daisy's role in Hazel's life differ from Jack's? What does this say about the importance of chosen versus given family?

7. What does the novel say about the nature of commitment? Are Hazel and Jack's struggles representative of a broader commentary on marriage?

8. Both Hazel and Jack confront regrets in their marriage. How does the novel explore the idea of second chances, and do you believe the characters find redemption?

9. The novel begins, essentially, at the beginning of Jack and Hazel's relationship and moves forward. How does this structure enhance or detract from the storytelling? Were there any moments where this approach added depth to your understanding of the characters?

10. The story is told from Hazel's perspective. How does her narration influence your view of the other characters? Are there moments where her perspective seems unreliable or biased?

11. Were there moments in Hazel's story that resonated with your own experiences? If so, how did these moments shape your reading of the book?

ABOUT THE AUTHOR

Rachel Del Grosso was born in Ontario, Canada. She began writing at a very young age, but has since learned to write in complete sentences. She writes fiction about imperfect marriages, messy friendships, and complicated families. She lives in Las Vegas with her husband and son. She is the author of Eleanor & Sam, and Fine, But Not Finished.

Find her on Instagram *@authorracheldelgrosso* and TikTok *@authorracheldelgrosso* and sign up for her newsletter at *racheldelgrosso.substack.com* or www.racheldelgrosso.com.